CROWN OF FATE

DARK MAGIC SHIFTERS 3

EVERLY FROST

DISCOVER THE EVER REALMS

Seven series. One world.

Suggested Reading Order:

Bright Wicked
Storm Princess
Assassin's Magic
Soul Bitten Shifter
Supernatural Legacy
Dark Magic Shifters
Kingdom of Betrayal

Don't get too comfortable, Darkness,
because the monster you thought you were hunting...

...is not the one you'll find.

CHAPTER ONE

The keeper is my enemy.

The shock of this discovery is breaking my heart into tiny pieces—each one fracturing and falling away.

More than anything, I don't want it to be true. I don't want to believe that the keeper betrayed me.

But there's no denying the look in his eyes. The truth he has confirmed.

He accepted the name I gave him: Emil. *Enemy.*

Tears of rage stream down my cheeks as my lips clash against his.

With every stab of pain in my chest, fresh blood spills from the cuts across his face and torso.

I gave him the power in my heart—it's how I freed him from his realm—and now he feels all of my heart's pain as if it were his own.

As my heart breaks, his too is breaking.

We're kneeling side by side on the cold, stone floor of a catacomb buried deep beneath a church in New York City.

I came here to steal *The Book of Dark Magic* from my father, who believes that I will start a war among dark creatures that will fill the streets with blood.

Instead, I was forced to read the book, which showed me how my mother really died ten years ago.

The images leaped up from the pages and surrounded me as if I'd been part of them.

I watched as the keeper—my keeper, the man who had walked beside me ever since I'd escaped my cage—tore out my mother's mechanical heart.

Her heart was unique, its delicate, interlocking, metallic parts moving in perfect harmony to a *thud-thud* that had slowed and finally stopped.

In the vision, he told her that he would take everything from her. And then he took her life.

Now, black dragon scales cover Emil's skin while inky-dark, leathery wings rest at his sides. Those same wings that once cradled me and kept me safe from harm are torn up and hanging low.

To destroy him, all I have to do is let my heart crack apart completely.

Let it shatter.

But I can't allow his end to be that simple.

Oh, no.

The mess of betrayal and fury and sadness within me demands that he suffer.

He must pay.

His words, spoken only seconds ago, spiral around and around within my mind. It's the question that has taken root at the center of my existence and driven my actions ever since I escaped the prison where I spent the first twenty-three years of my life.

My Veda. My beautiful, dark love. Will you have your revenge?

I grit my teeth against his mouth, tasting the warmth of his blood on my lips and sensing it beneath my hands, where I press them to his injured chest.

"Oh, Emil," I whisper, pulling back to speak. "I promise you: I will fight for my vengeance with every dark fiber of my being."

Against him.

And against my father, who looms over us both.

He is a dark angel named Taiven Nostra, head of the Nostra Empire, to which thousands of dark creatures owe their allegiance. He is the power behind other dark powers, controlling other families, clans, and packs—even influencing humans—from the shadows.

His skin is luminescent, his irises are golden like mine, and his feathery, black wings are tucked regally to his sides. Every angle of his face is so flawlessly smooth that he could be made of light, not darkness.

Currently, he stands not more than five paces away from us, positioned slightly behind Emil.

"Poor Daughter," Taiven croons, his melodic voice a grating hum in the echoey chamber. "To discover that your true enemy was right beside you all along, holding your hand, giving you false comfort and feigned protection."

His gaze flickers to *The Book of Dark Magic*, which now lies on the floor to my left.

I thought I could take the book in an act that was intended to strike at the heart of my father's power, leaving him anchorless and directionless without its guidance.

He was the one who had my mother imprisoned when she was six months pregnant with me.

All because of his belief that I am an evil being that should never have existed. He was the reason I spent so many years in a dark cell with no fresh air and no natural light.

I came here to this crypt to walk a path that would shatter my father's power.

Now, I'm trapped with two of the most dangerous men in existence, both of whom are my enemies.

While my father speaks, Emil's focus is entirely on me. One of his big hands is wrapped around the back of my neck, and his fiery eyes compel me not to look away from him.

He's strong enough to snap my neck if he wants to.

He is the keeper of dark magic. For thousands of years, he was confined within his realm—his only purpose was to gather up the magic of dark creatures when they died. He tethered the remnant power of witches, warlocks, dark shifters, demons, and deadly mythological creatures.

All of that magic was siphoned into his metal crown, which he now wears in the form of a ring around the forefinger of his left hand.

With it, he can harness the power of every dark creature whose magic he bound to it. He can create illusions, use compulsion to get what he wants, harness the power of nature, and drain life to feed his dark magic. He can take the form of any dark creature: a devil, a blue-skinned draugr, a demon of smoke and ash, a fiery dragon, a dark wolf, a wicked warlock.

His power is immense and endless.

But his deal with me binds him to me. In exchange for the power in my heart that freed him to walk this Earth, he has promised me vengeance, and he made it clear that *how* I achieve that vengeance is up to me.

I'm certain that it's only because of our deal that he has remained kneeling where he is.

He has the power to translocate himself out of here in the blink of an eye—and yet he remains.

Even as his body breaks with every growing crack within my heart.

My father circles around behind him, angling to position himself between me and the only way out of this chamber—a single, wooden door that's curved in an arch at the top and opens outward from this room. It's a solid forty paces away from me. Far enough that my father could easily strike me down before I could reach it.

Where he stands now, both he and Emil are facing me.

My father clicks his tongue and shakes his head at me, his smile growing. "Poor, *poor* Daughter. How can you possibly hope to survive now?"

His confidence isn't false.

He controls the keeper of light magic. Somehow, he must have freed her from her realm, just as I freed Emil.

Because I'm a creature of the dark, her light magic can strip the flesh from my body and burn me to my very bones.

Right now, she slumps against the stone wall to my far right, at least thirty paces away. Her form appears insubstantial, fading in and out of view, disappearing completely for long seconds before it becomes clear again.

Her eyes are empty, golden orbs and her arms hang at her sides. Her labored breathing causes her to sway from side to side against the rock at her back. She's wearing golden armor while a curved blade rests in a harness that's visible at her left shoulder, the weapon's edge rasping against the wall with every shuddering breath she takes.

As for the rest of the room, it's circular and stretches at least seventy paces in each direction.

Despite the room's size, the ceiling is low, not high enough to fly around inside.

Not that flying would help me, anyway, because the wings I kept hidden until recently are still not much use to me.

In the exact center of the room, not ten paces away from me, are four stone statues. They stand in a tight circle, each one facing outward so that their backs are to each other.

Each one is a different color: one white, the next golden, then black, and finally crimson.

They are depictions of the four keepers of magic.

Their arms are bent at the elbows, their palms turned up.

Until minutes ago, the black statue held *The Book of Dark Magic*.

Once again, my own father has given rise to a deep despair and powerlessness within me.

"Your keeper is weak now, Daughter," he says, continuing to croon at me. "Which means you have two choices."

I could tell him to take his choices and shove them somewhere dark, but instead, without taking my focus off Emil, I demand to know, "What are they?"

Taiven steps closer to us, his focus flickering again to *The Book of Dark Magic*.

No doubt, he is desperate to retrieve it now that it has done its work and hurt my heart.

"You can't defeat me," my father continues. "The light magic I control can flay the flesh from your bones within mere seconds. You must surrender to your death." He nods to himself as if it's a foregone conclusion. "But before you die, I will give you the chance to decide your keeper's fate. Because I am merciful like that."

As he speaks, bright light glimmers around his palms, casting up across his triumphant features and sizzling in the air across our heads.

Each time he draws on the light keeper's magic, she shudders harder against the wall.

I feel the heat of her energy burning through the air around me. Its destructive force.

Tearing my gaze away from Emil, who has remained unnervingly silent, I ask my father, "What are my choices?"

Taiven relaxes a little, white light continuing to spill around his fingertips as he lowers his hands. "You can kill your keeper yourself by stabbing your claws through the heart in his chest."

He pauses for a moment, as if he thinks I'll immediately choose that option.

As if I would.

I have no idea what will happen to me if the keeper's heart is destroyed. My own physical heart still beats in my chest, but my heart's power connects him and me in ways I don't completely understand.

He feels my pain, my heartache. He even sensed when I had nightmares while I slept. I kept him awake many nights because of it.

I can't be certain that if Emil's physical heart is torn out, my own physical heart will keep beating—or if it will destroy me, too.

Of course, my father wants us both dead, so it makes no difference to him.

In fact, I imagine it would be quite an efficient way to get rid of me. Especially if he thinks my current pain and anger will cloud my judgment.

Taiven's eyebrows rise when I grind my speech through my clenched teeth. "Or?"

"Simply move aside." He shrugs. "Let me flay open your keeper's chest with my light magic. I will tear out his heart for you."

I latch on to his last words. *"For* me?"

"A final gift," my father says with a smile. "Before I kill you."

No, thank you.

Although, the fact that my father thinks he will have to kill me separately indicates his belief that tearing out Emil's heart won't end me.

Whatever he believes is only that: a belief. I can't assume he's right.

My fate was already balanced on a knife's edge, and it is more so now.

I blow out a soft exhale, putting on a show of considering each of my father's proposals. "Well," I murmur. "What a difficult choice."

What a terrible game I must now play.

I'm counting on my father underestimating my desire to survive.

He doesn't know what I went through while I was living in prison, the mental fortitude it took to retain my sense of self, my determination, and my belief in a future where I would be free.

He has no fucking idea what I'll do to survive.

I make a very deliberate show of returning my attention to Emil, who hasn't taken his eyes off me.

"Which will I choose?" I ask him. "To kill you myself or let my father end you for me?"

CHAPTER TWO

I allow my claws to extend as I reach for Emil's face, resting them lightly against his jaw. "You betrayed me, Emil. How can I possibly decide which choice will bring you the pain you deserve?"

His hand tightens around the back of my neck, multiple sharp pricks of pain telling me that his own fingernails are sharpening—maybe into the claws of a wolf or the talons of a hawk.

When he speaks, his voice is broken. Disturbingly so.

"Betrayal is in my blood," he says. "It's a curse I can't escape."

"You lied to me," I snap back at him, fighting a new dread that's growing within me.

It's the growing fear that he will give up. That he won't fight for his life like I will fight for mine.

Because, for better or worse, his fate is entwined with mine.

"It's in my nature to lie." He nods. "The rules of my creation dictate that I cannot choose any other way."

No. He doesn't get to justify his actions because of what he is.

I fight the very real anger and pain rising within me. Fight to stay in control of these next few moments—moments that will determine my survival.

"You took the only precious thing I had." My voice chokes up at that declaration—a truth that's torn out of me—but I force myself to continue speaking. "You took away the only person who loved me. Then you made me believe she didn't love me after all."

A month ago, when I asked Emil if he'd tethered my mother's magic, he told me he hadn't. He allowed me to believe that the woman who had raised me had not been Galeia, my biological mother. He let me believe that Galeia had chosen to abandon me.

"No!" he snarls back at me.

His denial takes me by surprise, as does the sudden fury in his eyes.

"You leaped to that conclusion all on your own," he says.

My eyes widen, a new anger threatening to swamp me, but this time, I let it grow because it's cold and it will dampen my other, more vulnerable, emotions.

"You swore to me that you didn't tether my mother's magic." My voice is deep with rage. "You made me believe that Galeia left me to rot in darkness for twenty-three fucking years!"

"I didn't *make* you believe anything," Emil snaps. "Your own pain and fear led you to that belief."

"You *let* me believe it!" My hand tightens around his jaw, the tips of my claws dragging at his skin.

These black claws are practically indestructible.

They can cut through anything.

Dragon scales. Stone. Steel.

His flesh is no challenge.

His pupils dilate, but it can't be with fear. Emil has rarely shown fear.

At the appearance of my claws, my father starts to cackle. He probably thinks I'll lose control of my anger and drive my claws into Emil's chest after all.

He has remained looming a step behind Emil but is now standing farther to my left. It's a location that keeps him positioned steadfastly between me and the only way out. It also puts him closer to *The Book of Dark Magic*.

He smiles with apparent delight at our conflict.

I'm sure he's reveling in my pain, but while I keep him within my sights, my focus on Emil doesn't waver.

To Emil, I repeat my accusation, daring him to contradict me. "You *allowed me* to believe my mother had betrayed me."

Emil is like stone opposite me.

And then, instead of drawing away from me like I expect him to, he leans into my clawed hand as if I were cradling his face instead of threatening to rip him to shreds.

Pinpricks of blood form across his skin where the tips of my claws cut his cheek and jaw.

His eyes close and the breath *whooshes* audibly from his chest, an exhale that appears to sap everything from him.

"I did," he says quietly. "I let you believe it."

His shoulders slump even farther forward, his weight becoming so heavy against my hand that I'm forced to retract my claws before they tear down his cheek.

It's the only movement I can manage right now because his admission has frozen me to the spot and the speech has died in my throat.

I never expected him to agree with me, let alone without anger.

As I try to catch my breath, his shape changes again.

His dragon wings retract and his black scales peel away. His jaw becomes chiseled and his shoulders become impossibly broad.

His clothing transforms into a white tunic and pants, the sleeveless shirt revealing all the defined muscles of his biceps and forearms. The style of this clothing is similar to the training clothes we wore back on the island, but the weave of the material is much finer, shinier even, the kind that might be worn by a king.

A white belt rests around his waist with a silver buckle and a small sheath attached to it that could be intended to hold a weapon—except that it's empty.

At the same time, his hair slowly bleaches of color until its strands are like silver metal. They catch the rays of light magic glimmering around my father's hands, fracturing the magic in the same way that my heart is cracking, splintering it into rainbows around us.

Where Emil's face rests against my hand, his skin is unnaturally cold, an icy temperature that makes me want to withdraw.

He opens his eyes, and they are the color of the palest-green leaves.

Now, my breathing has stopped altogether because his face…

This unearthly, beautiful face…

It scares the fuck out of me.

"I chose to hurt you," he says in a soft murmur that feels as if it wraps around my chest. "That is the truth."

He was wearing this face when he warned me that *The Book of Dark Magic* would destroy me.

I asked him to stay with me. To stand with me. I promised him I wouldn't break. When he didn't believe me, I told him that nothing was impossible.

And now, he whispers the same question that he asked me before, his voice hollow. "Will you have your revenge, my Veda?"

Even now, he calls me *his*.

His Veda.

His *conqueror*.

I inhale what could be one of my last breaths, preparing to leap into the unknown, an abyss where the tiniest sliver of faith is all that could keep me alive.

It's a faith that doesn't belong to a dark creature like me. But still, I dare to reach for it.

I remain aware of my father, who has taken a small step farther to my left. His eyes narrow as he fixates on Emil's new form. There's a hint of wariness in my father's posture for the first time since he appeared in this room. The smallest indication of fear, as if something about Emil's face scares him, too.

I'm conscious of the keeper of light magic with her dazed eyes as she slumps against the far wall.

But most of all, I'm mindful of my left hand where it rests benignly on my lap, the claws on that hand completely retracted, the muscles of my left arm deceptively relaxed.

To Emil, I say, "My mother raised me to understand love. She taught me its value, even for a dark creature like me. I knew love for the first thirteen years of my life, but when she died, I lost it."

My jaw clenches and the claws of my right hand dig deeper into his skin.

I will him to hear the power in my words.

"And then I found it again," I say.

I found it in my new family. I found it in the loyalty and care of the shadow panthers who form my pack: Anarchy, Riot, Rumble, and Strife. They are dark elves, cursed to take the form of panthers for thousands of years until I freed them from their cage, after which the keeper broke their curse.

I found it in my half-brother, Lucian, who vowed to stand at my side, helped me start using my previously useless wings, and told me that I have what no other dark creature he has ever met has: an internal moral code all my own.

I especially found it in Emil.

In the way he brought Anarchy back from the dead when she had been badly injured. In the way he healed *me* after the last time I'd fought my father. And in the way he respected my body.

He slowly opens his eyes and now there's a slight crease in his forehead, a wary purse to his lips.

"You thought I would break when I read *The Book of Dark Magic*," I say, nodding softly to him. "And for a moment, I did. But this book gave me a gift. It restored the truth of my memories. And I am stronger for it."

As I speak, I reach for that tiny kernel of faith, of belief, that I am worthy of more than darkness and pain.

"I am not broken." I return Emil's gaze, daring to meet his pale green eyes, which are like coils of rope winding around my soul, binding me to him.

His weight against my hand eases, less heavy, more in control, a small sign of his returning strength as his gaze burns into me.

My father, on the other hand, is now poised nearby, his forehead deeply creased and an alarmed expression spreading quickly across his face.

His focus flicks urgently to the book lying close to my side, and I can see him calculating how fast he can get to it.

As much as he wants me dead, his first priority will be retrieving the book. It's everything to him.

I have only seconds to act.

I lean closer to Emil, certain now that his power has returned enough for him to fight back.

Pressing my forehead to his, I say, "My fate is in your hands now, Enemy."

And with that, I extend the claws of my left hand in a flash and drive them down.

CHAPTER THREE

y claws hit *The Book of Dark Magic.*

As seamlessly as cutting through water, they impale the book's cover and its thick pages, all the way to its back cover before hitting the stone floor and impaling it, too.

There's a moment of pure silence and a strangely dark peace.

Within that heartbeat, I sense an unexpected connection with the magic in the book, as if the dark soul of it actually welcomes my touch.

As destructive as it is.

Even stranger is that this dark peace—this sudden sense of *wholeness*—triggers a spark of deep rage within my body and mind.

Suddenly, there's a whisper within my mind. A burning impulse that's as clear as if the book had spoken to me.

Take control of the light and the dark.

Mold the living to match your will.

Fight the old and find the new...

Power, so pure and intense that I feel like I'm breathing for the first time in my life, floods through me and my back arches with the force of it.

Opposite me, Emil's eyes have flown wide, undeniable shock reflected in their green depths as his focus flashes from me to the book and my black claws rammed through it.

I'm certain he thought that I would choose to drive my claws through his heart.

And still, the powerful impulse flows through me.

Take control of the dark.

Mold them.

Make them yours.

I grit my teeth against it.

This book is the reason my father hates me. The vision he saw within its pages showed me slaughtering dark creatures without mercy. This book has wormed its way into his mind. If ever there was a truth that Emil has spoken, it was about this book.

This book wants bloodshed, and it serves only itself.

My father lurches desperately down toward the book, his arms outstretched, a shout of protest roaring from his lips. "Daughter, do *not* dare—!"

As if I would obey him.

With all the ferocity of my dark nature, I snarl, "Die, book. Fucking die."

With an outward sweep of my hand that feels as easy as pushing it through air, I rip my claws through the book's pages.

My claws shred it from the center and out across its spine, breaking the central parts that keep it bound, leaving it barely held together by the top and bottom of the spine.

Despite how easily I move, the tearing sound my claws make is like metal cutting through iron, shrieking and high-pitched, as if two metallic forces are grinding against each other.

For a second, I imagine that I can hear screams raging from the pages and it's impossible to sense if they're screams from battles long past or the souls of a thousand dark creatures crying out for mercy.

At the last moment, before my claws exit the book, a hard bolt of energy leaps up through my fingers, traveling across my palm, up my arm, and into my chest.

The power I sensed when my claws first impaled the book now strikes directly through my heart.

It's cold and full of malice, flooded with hatred and cruelty.

My dark heart inhales it like air, pulling it into me with purpose. I will take whatever anger the book has to give, as long as I hurt it as much as it has hurt me.

I breathe through the painful sensations, accepting the flood of dark magic.

At the same time, my left arm continues its upward arc even as my father leaps down toward me.

The trajectory of my claws takes them up, out of the book, up through the air, and directly into my father's face.

His downward momentum works horribly against him.

My claws slice through his outstretched right forearm and continue upward to cut neatly through the entire right side of his jaw.

With a scream, he tries to reverse his direction, his wings whipping outward as if he could flap them fast enough to get away from me.

The damage is already done.

His blood splatters across the floor and soaks into the cover of the now-ragged book.

Still screaming, he throws himself backward, scrambling away from me, trying to clutch his face with his uninjured left arm.

I have no illusions that he'll be out of action for long.

And he's still located between me and the only exit.

What's more, a flood of light magic is already building around him. I'm certain he's drawing on the light magic keeper's power as fast as he can and will let it loose the moment the worst of his pain subsides.

The book, meanwhile, lies completely still on the floor.

When I was forced to read it, the book itself had turned into vines and daggers, pinning me to the spot so that I couldn't look away.

Now, it looks like nothing more than black paper bound together. When I grab the side of it that's still intact and scoop it up against my side, pressing it close to my body, it's heavy and awkward, parts of it flapping like ribbons.

But I feel nothing of the power I sensed from it before.

As my father's screams continue, I finally look at Emil.

His hand hasn't wavered from its spot at the back of my neck, but it has tightened.

I find him frozen opposite me and I don't have a hope of interpreting the expression in his icy-green eyes.

"I've said what I needed to say, and I meant it." I force sound through my lips. "The truth is a gift, however dark it is. My fate is now up to you."

For a terrible moment, his eyes search mine.

I force myself to meet his gaze. To face the fear that his current form brings to me.

Only he has the power to get us out of here and, by taking control of my pain and mending the cracks in my heart, I've ensured he has enough strength to do it.

Without a word, he lifts his left arm, wrapping it around me and swiftly tugging me closer—all while avoiding contact with the book.

For some reason, I am one of the few beings who can touch this book without it destroying my mind. When I first showed Emil a page that had been ripped out of this book and left for me in secret by my mother, he turned away from the page, not even wishing to look at it.

Emil's cheek is cold against mine, a deathly iciness that defies his beauty.

In the next second, his transportation magic bursts to life, a tornado of mist rushing against my skin and enclosing us.

Not so much that I can't see my father's silhouette beyond it.

A flood of white light pours toward us, cutting through the farthest edge of the mist.

Dark light bursts around us a second before the light magic would reach us.

I can't see exactly where Emil's dark power is coming from —his hands most likely—but it forms a shield against which my father's light magic can only spread outward, never making it through.

My father's shouted threats are garbled but becoming clearer as his healing power seems to be repairing his jaw. "I'll tear you apart, Daughter! I'll rip the flesh from your—"

A second burst of dark light completely obscures my father's form, blocking him from view.

Within the dark shield, the transportation mist storms around me faster than before, spinning in dizzying ribbons within the cocoon, and pressing in on my chest, plastering me against Emil.

His head remains bent to mine and finally, his voice sounds in my ear. Not the growl of a dragon or a wolf or even the snarl of a warlock or a demon. He sounds almost human, and the sheer simplicity of the baritone of his voice chills me to my bones.

"You should have killed me," he whispers.

A violent shiver racks my body.

Emil's transportation magic has already taken hold of me, and now I'm at his mercy.

CHAPTER FOUR

Emil's magic is a savage tug, angry and uncontrolled, nothing like the smoothness of our more recent travels.

His energy compresses my chest so tightly that I can't breathe. My heart thuds in my chest, a powerful rush of blood pounding in my ears as I brace to find out where he has chosen to take me.

To my shock, the swirling mist parts to reveal the alley at the side of the church where I left my pack only a short time ago.

The moon is high in the night sky, but even without it, the streetlights filter across the space, making everything within it clearly visible.

Only five paces away, Anarchy and her three brothers are engaged in a savage battle with one of my father's most loyal soldiers: the vampire named Gad.

Gad is incredibly fast, moving from one place to another in mere blinks, but Anarchy and her brothers are keeping him constrained. For now.

My half-brother, Lucian, is poised farther behind them, his wings spread, guarding the open end of the alley in such a way that he must be the backstop in case Gad gets away. We don't want him calling for reinforcements.

Only a short distance behind the fight with Gad, the fire jotunn called Jonah, with whom I have a fragile truce, is fighting another of my father's soldiers—the berserker woman known as Valki.

She has multiple piercings and her tank top is stretched to near bursting now that her muscles are pumped up. Usually, she wears a solid metal wire wrapped around her arm. It looks like jewelry but doubles as a weapon that can wind around someone's head and rip it off.

It looks like she may have tried that approach on Jonah, but he must have burned the metal to ash, given the smudgy, black ring of dust currently decorating his neck.

The remainder of my father's guards lie unconscious at intervals along the alley. Many of them are propped up in sitting positions against the wall opposite the church.

Judging by their steady heartbeats, which sound in my sensitive hearing, they're all alive.

We didn't come here to kill my father's followers. Not even Gad or Valki. Given how neatly some of the guards have been placed with their legs tucked out of the way of being trampled, my family has taken my wishes seriously.

My father believes I will slaughter other creatures of the dark, and I'm hellbent on proving him wrong.

Of course, the fight would be much easier without that limitation.

Jonah has the ability to turn any living creature into ash within the space of seconds. Instead, he's continuing to go toe to toe with Valki in a fight that makes me wince.

Likewise, Anarchy and her brothers have stayed in their dark elf forms. Their bodies are strong and lithe, their pointed ears hidden beneath their gorgeous, lilac hair.

If they shifted into their shadow panther forms, they could

maul Gad to death within seconds. As it is, Gad appears to be giving as many bruises as he's receiving.

It's lucky we're in the alley because this kind of fight would draw a lot of attention from human passersby.

Emil and I have arrived in the same physical positions we were in when we left the catacomb—still kneeling on the ground. We're located at the back end of the alley and we're facing it side-on so I can see the entire alleyway, including the street in the distance.

Emil's decision to bring me here has surprised me.

Of all the places he could have taken me...

He chose to bring me to my pack—to these dark beings whom I now think of as my family.

My focus snaps back to him, my eyes wide. "Why did you—?"

While I speak, I'm instinctively tugging toward Anarchy, needing to join the fight, but Emil's hold on me only tightens.

His voice cuts through me like a dagger. "If you don't want your father to kill your pack, call them to you. *Now*. Before he follows us."

I draw a sharp breath with the realization that my father could very well have the same transportation powers that Emil has. After all, the light magic keeper controls all kinds of light magic, and there are many good witches who can translocate themselves using spells. It certainly isn't a skill that belongs only to dark creatures.

If my father knows that my pack is out here—which is highly likely—he could follow me here within seconds.

I don't waste another moment, raising my voice to cry out to them. "Anarchy! Lucian! Family! *Come to me! Now!*"

At my cry, every member of my pack breaks off from their fight and sprints toward me.

My heart leaps at how quickly they respond to me.

Even Jonah jumps away from Valki, leaving her lurching

across the alleyway mid-punch, her fist cracking the stone wall she hurtles into.

"Darkness!" Anarchy cries, her focus on me while her three brothers race along beside her. "You're alive!"

Before I went into the church, we'd all known my chances of survival had been slim. They still are.

Behind them, Lucian beats his wings, rises into the air, and dives over the top of both Valki and Gad, sweeping toward me so fast that he reaches me within a heartbeat.

Jonah skids toward me at the same time.

They're all aiming for the mist, still lingering for several feet around me and Emil.

They will know it's an indicator that the keeper is preparing to transport us out of here.

Back within the alley, Gad races toward Valki, assisting her to regain her balance before he turns to us. His fangs are drawn and I know he could reach me within a blink of my eye. Potentially get so close, he'll come with us wherever the keeper takes us.

He could do a whole lot of damage on the way.

"Vampire!" I shout, causing him to narrow his eyes at me and also, thankfully, to pause where he is. "If you value your life, you'll run—"

"We aren't afraid of you!" he spits back while Valki towers beside him.

In her berserker form, she's even larger in stature than Emil and Jonah, and right now, every muscle in her body is pumped and corded, her movements so twitchy, I could believe she'll move as fast as Gad.

"I'm not talking about me," I call, tension thrumming through me while the mist begins to thicken, another tornado of energy starting to build.

It doesn't feel fast enough. My only hope is to keep Gad on his back foot long enough that we have time to get out of here.

At the same moment that I speak, white light bursts to life within the church, splashing against the inside of the windows.

Cracks scatter across the stained glass, which makes a horrible shrieking sound as if it's about to explode outward.

Gad and Valki both shrink up against the stone wall opposite the church, as far back from the shrieking glass as they can get without leaping over the high wall.

I guess I don't need to explain to them that I'm not the worst threat to them right now.

Light magic is bad news for all dark creatures.

Based on what I've seen of my father, I suspect he'll be too angry to care if he hurts his followers in his efforts to catch me.

Satisfied that Gad and Valki will stay away from us for now, I reach out with my free hand to my nearest family members—Anarchy and Lucian—ensuring they've gathered close to me.

They all crowd in toward me and I'm hit by their familiar scents. The musky mix of panther and dark elf. The fiery ash of Jonah's presence. Even my half-brother's crisp, angel scent.

All of it is comforting. And sharply contradictory to the iciness of Emil's hand, which has remained around the back of my neck, and the ragged press of the broken book, which I've kept clutching against my left side.

"Veda?" Jonah's alarmed voice sounds. "What the fuck is that?"

"Light magic," Riot snarls, answering for me from where he crouches next to Anarchy.

Their faces are pale with the growing intensity of the light spilling beneath the nearby church door and the increasing pressure in the air.

It's been mere heartbeats since they all skidded to my side, each one of them now crouching as close to me as they can get.

Like me, they will feel the burn of the light magic across the distance. Sense the impending explosion. And know that we won't survive it.

My focus is now on Emil.

Once again, he has the power to save us or destroy us, but the mist still isn't thickening fast enough.

"Emil?"

His jaw is clenched and his cheeks are pale.

Maybe the cracks in my heart haven't healed enough for him to regain his full power. Maybe he can't transport us out of here after all.

Or maybe…

Suddenly, all I can hear in my ears is his warning that I should have killed him while I could.

My breath stops as I wonder if I've made a terrible mistake.

He surprised me by bringing me back to this alley, where I could rejoin my family. He told me to call them and bring them closer if I wanted to save them.

Like a fool, I trusted him.

Despite what I saw in the book…

I still. Fucking. Trust him.

He has all of us in his grasp now.

My father's light magic is spreading all the way across the alley, blocking the way out. Even Lucian won't be able to out-fly it.

If Emil wants to hurt me more than he already has, he could transport himself out of here, and me with him, concentrate his protective energy around only the two of us, and leave my family behind to be killed.

Torn apart before my eyes.

If he wants to destroy me, all he has to do now is rip away my hope that my pack will be safe.

With my heart in my throat and a terrible panic rising up within me, I ask, "What is our fate?"

He is like ice, frozen and cold, as the mist finally—*finally!*—thickens around us.

But then he replies, "I'm taking you to hell."

CHAPTER FIVE

*W*hat the—?

I've barely managed to gasp a breath before a storm of mist bursts around me, squeezing my chest so hard that I can't move, let alone voice a protest.

The ground beneath my feet falls away and suddenly, I'm spiraling, jolting away from Emil. I leave his grasp entirely until his hand closes around mine at the last moment.

The process of translocation has never been this unpleasant, not even the first time he tried it.

A sense of dizzying weightlessness fills me and then—

Smack!

My hand leaves Emil's and I land hard on my hands and knees on a cold surface.

I can't hold on to the book and it hits the ground beside me, sliding a few feet sideways. I'm too dizzy to reach for it, but I take comfort that its most ragged edge remains visible to me within the clearing mist.

Emil's icy scent fills my chest—or at least, I think it's his scent—until a rush of freezing air rages across me, coming from behind.

But worst of all, my family is no longer nearby and I can't make out any hint of them within the remaining mist.

"Anarchy! Lucian! Riot!" I scream for each of my pack members, my heart pounding hard with the fear that Emil left them behind after all.

Panic billows within me, only growing worse until the savage wind finally whisks the remaining mist away.

I make out the shape of a large cave around me—a long one that stretches far into the distance. The walls are black and appear to consist of some kind of rock that glistens with silver flecks.

Then I see my pack members, each of them tumbling away from me across the cave floor, as if the volatile transportation magic was even more unkind to them than it was to me, propelling them across the space.

They come to ragged stops on the sparkly, black stone ground, all of them facing away from me, having traveled a solid thirty feet.

Cries of alarm rise up into my throat as I scramble toward them, trying to hear their heartbeats to know if they're alive.

Nothing.

Then, their hearts all seem to kick into action at the same time, their heartbeats reaching me across the distance.

Thank the dark saints!

The dark elves, Anarchy, Riot, Rumble, and Strife, have landed to my left.

Lucian is closer to Jonah, both of whom are on my right.

Our immediate surroundings don't hold any other visible threats yet, so I take comfort in the possibility that we won't be immediately assailed by danger.

Lucian is nearest to me, and I reach him first. "Brother!"

His inky-black hair falls across the stone beneath his head, the dark strands nearly disappearing against the dark surface. His skin is fair and, like my father's countenance, Lucian's features remind me of the brightness of the stars in a night sky. His eyes, if they were open, are the same golden color as mine.

The edge of a tattoo is visible from beneath the short sleeve of his tunic. In all the time I've known him, I've never seen what the tattoo depicts.

I drop to the stone beside him, conscious that Jonah is also stirring, groaning as he slowly sits up.

Even though I can hear Lucian's heartbeat, he doesn't immediately respond, and I find myself seeking the pulse at his neck.

A moment later, he opens his eyes. "Veda?"

Lucian squints up at me for a moment before he startles upright, quickly scanning our surroundings, catching sight of Jonah first. "Jonah!"

Then Lucian twists in the other direction, his focus falling on the lilac-haired woman lying several paces to our left. "Anarchy!"

He scrambles toward her, calling her name again before he reaches her.

She stirs a moment before he pulls her into his arms and tilts his head to hers.

"Lucian?" Her voice is weak and barely audible above the raging wind that beats across the mouth of the cave behind us.

The freezing cold surface beneath my knees makes me shiver. Our pants and tunics are no match for the iciness of our surroundings.

Lucian's voice is too soft for me to hear what he says as he murmurs to Anarchy, pressing his forehead to hers while her palm cups his cheek.

They formed a bond during our stay on the island where we spent the last month, and it shines through now in their relief.

On their other side, Anarchy's brothers are also stirring, each one sitting up slowly, pressing their hands to their temples as if they're as dizzy as I was when I first landed here.

I sink down onto my heels, incredibly relieved that they all appear okay, even if their faces are a little green.

But…

Where is Emil?

I was sure I sensed his hand on mine while we traveled here, but his intense presence doesn't strike me instantly like it usually does.

I swing back to the mouth of the cave, finally locating him all the way back near its opening.

He, too, is kneeling on the black stone. He has remained in his silver-haired, green-eyed form, and his shoulders are slumped forward, his chest rising and falling slowly. I can't hear his breathing—not over the shrieking wind—but the rise and fall of his chest indicates that it's ragged.

What I see behind him makes me pause.

A storm of white particles rages across the cave mouth as thick as the mist that transported us here.

Because I spent the first twenty-three years of my life in a dark cell, there's a lot about the world I've never seen or experienced. It was only a month ago that I felt sand beneath my feet. Touched leaves and grass. Ate pizza and hamburgers. Saw a butterfly for the first time.

My mother once described snow to me. A white, powdery substance that she said would fall from the sky in winter and settle like a blanket over the ground. She said it was beautiful, reflective, *pretty*.

What I see now is nothing like that, which makes me doubt if what I'm looking at is, indeed, snow.

It would certainly explain why it's freezing cold here, but the white particles are raging with a fury that's nothing like the calm powder my mother described.

Emil said he was taking us to hell, but my assumption was that hell was a fiery place, so our surroundings are disconcerting to me.

While my family members find their feet, I take a moment to consider Emil, narrowing my eyes at the way his head remains bowed and the misty transportation magic still clings to his form. It looks like fingers plucking at his sides. The mist has never taken this long to clear from around him before, and I'm not sure what to make of it.

Perhaps he's preparing to leave us here—wherever *here* actually is.

Then the fingers of hazy energy disperse and I don't have time to consider him longer because the dark elves are racing toward me.

Strife is the first to reach me, leaping across the distance as surely as if he were in his panther form. Like his brothers, he has lilac-colored hair, pointed ears, and bright, blue eyes, but his chin is a little narrower. He is a little more elvish in his beauty. And his smile is far more mischievous than those of the other two.

Well, usually. Not right now.

I catch the fear in his eyes before he barrels into me, lifting me up, all the way from my knees into his arms.

The snarls on his lips are so savage that he really could be in his panther form. "Darkness!"

It's their name for me.

A powerful name.

They've never called me anything else.

Strife's arms are firm around me as he allows me to find my feet but doesn't let go of me. "We sensed the influx of light magic within the church. We thought we might have lost you."

His voice chokes up a little, and I recall the way Anarchy had exclaimed about the fact that I had still been alive right before Emil brought us here.

It's clear my pack was worried about me.

Before I can reply, Riot and Rumble knock into us, their arms somehow wrapping around me, too.

All three of them envelop me in a hug that feeds my wolfish soul with all the feelings of *pack* that I so desperately need right now.

Anarchy and Lucian soon join them, wrapping me up from behind.

"What happened?" Lucian asks, his voice muffled at my shoulder.

"Did you get the book?" Anarchy's question sounds right after Lucian's, but Riot speaks at the same moment, their questions overlapping.

"Where are we?" he asks.

None of them has any reason to doubt that the keeper is still our ally. When we parted outside the church, Emil was as much a part of my pack as they were. They won't know that they can't fully trust our surroundings like they could when he transported us places before.

He never endangered us before now, but to believe that he won't betray me would be foolish.

My voice sticks in my throat as I try to find a way to tell my pack what happened.

I'm honestly not sure if we should be standing around discussing it. I have no idea what dangers lie in this place or if we should be running for our lives already.

Before I can find the words, Anarchy asks softly, "Darkness… what's wrong with the keeper?"

Her eyes are wide as she tugs away from me. Wide with concern. Not fear. She has always made it clear she doesn't entirely trust him—which was smart, as it turns out—but the press of her lips and the soft light in her eyes tells me she's concerned about his welfare and not the possibility of betrayal.

Emil has remained exactly where he was before, uncharacteristically motionless and unusually quiet, his head still bowed and expression obscured.

I try to tell myself I can't be concerned about his welfare

right now. I don't know what his end game is, and his demeanor could be a ploy to soften my distrust.

"The keeper is no longer my ally," I say, hardening my voice. "He is not to be trusted. And so I have named him *Emil*."

Names have power.

The dark elves, Lucian, and even Jonah, know this. So the meaning of my declaration won't be lost on them.

Anarchy's lips part. "Enemy?"

She and her brothers and Lucian stiffen where their arms remain wrapped around me.

Jonah, on the other hand, speaks wryly from the other side of our group. "Well, it makes sense now why we're here. Because only an enemy would bring you to the mouth of the Underworld."

The Underworld.

I fight the urge to turn around to check Emil again.

He told me he was taking us to hell, but I didn't imagine he meant literally to the Underworld.

Anarchy's line of sight doesn't waver from Emil, but her voice is filled with new alarm. "We're in hell?"

Oh, in so many ways.

At that moment, the sound of footfalls reaches me from within the long tunnel. They're soft and prowling and can't be good news.

"It seems so," I say. "And now we've got company."

CHAPTER SIX

My pack instantly fans out around me.

The elves will be able to use their panther senses to detect the oncoming threat, and Lucian and Jonah quickly respond in kind.

Strife was directly in front of me and he steps to my left as the tangle of their arms unfolds.

Riot and Rumble move farther left of Strife while Anarchy and Lucian spread out on my right with Jonah beside Lucian. They all form a protective boundary around me while giving me a full view of our surroundings.

Ahead of me, within the cave, four men prowl toward us.

Well, *men* might not be an entirely accurate description.

Despite myself, I shrink back a little at the sight of them.

They're all at least seven feet tall, each one naked from the waist up, wearing only black pants. Long claws extend from their fingertips, not smooth like mine, but jagged. Their eyes are fiery red and full of what appears to be literal fire, and their chests are crisscrossed with streams of lava.

They're a little reminiscent of Jonah's full jotunn form,

except that these men have the teeth of beasts and the faces of hounds.

I once saw a picture of a statue of an ancient Egyptian god in one of the books my jailor had brought me while I was imprisoned. It had the body of a man and the head of a jackal.

These men look a hell of a lot like that.

Their eyes burn across me, their growls sounding beneath the shrieking wind as they come to a stop twenty paces away, each one with muscles coiled as if they're preparing to strike.

I brace for an attack, taking deep breaths and reminding myself that my pack and I have faced dragon shifters together. I'm certain that we can bring down these hounds if we need to.

Then, another figure rushes toward us from the darkness of the long tunnel.

The central two men step aside to let the newcomer through.

I recognize Hel, the Goddess of Death and the Underworld, hurrying toward us. Or, as she prefers to be called, *Halle Vanguard*. She is the sister of James Vanguard. Both of them used to be generals in my father's army.

That is, until my father betrayed my mother.

One half of Halle's face and body is blackened and charred, reminiscent of the black bones I exposed when I first fought her. Her eye on that side is gleaming red, a darker crimson than the eyes of the hellhounds.

Her clothing is split right down the middle, black leather on her charred side—or, as I like to think of it, her *dead* side. On her other side, she wears the overly sweet face of an auburn-haired pixie with bright-green eyes and fairy-like features topped off with freckles across that half of her petite nose.

Like Emil, she can change her appearance at will, and she does so now, shifting out of her half-dead-half-pixie form and becoming a regal sight in a pantsuit of deep red with impossibly high heels.

Flowing, brunette hair appears, piled on top of her head and cascading down her sides. Her skin takes on a light-brown hue while her cheekbones round out softly and her eyes become a deep, dark chocolate.

Trust me, her expression says.

"Veda!" she cries. "You survived!"

She looks almost happy to see me.

Before I went to the church to steal *The Book of Dark Magic*, I'd had an unpleasant encounter with Halle. She'd claimed to have been my mother's ally, but I'm still not entirely sure how much I believe of her story about the days before my pregnant mother was imprisoned.

She told me that if I survived stealing the book, I should come and find her because there is much we need to talk about.

I'm unsettled that Emil acted on Halle's invitation—especially given that I might not have.

Now, she's racing toward me, her arms outstretched as if I'm her long-lost daughter, an expression of pure joy on her regal face.

I have to remind myself that she isn't my friend.

I can probably trust her as far as I can trust Emil.

Before Halle can make it within ten paces of me, my hands fly up, my claws fully extended. "Stop!"

Halle pulls to an abrupt halt, eyeing my hands warily.

The first time she and I met, I broke her bones and very effectively cut up her face with these claws. Not that she didn't heal almost instantly. But I'm certain she remembers the damage I can do.

"Veda?" she asks. "Do we have a problem?"

"I'm not here by choice," I say.

She arches her eyebrows at me. "Well, of course you're not here by choice. Nobody visits hell because they want to. Most creatures do everything they can to avoid meeting me." She sniffs loudly. "But I did invite you to come find me. So naturally, I assumed you were here on that invitation."

Before I can respond, Emil speaks up from behind me, his voice clear and strong. "I brought her here," he says. "Without her permission."

Halle cranes her neck and narrows her eyes, her forehead creasing in a way that tells me she can't quite see him very well in the distance. Given the color of his silver hair and white clothing and the brightness of the icy storm behind him, I'm sure she's struggling to make him out. She doesn't have a wolf's perception like I do.

"*You* did, keeper?" she asks, her shoulders tense. "I can't help but wonder why?"

I have the same question. He was present when Halle told me to come and find her—but why he, as my enemy, would choose to bring me here is a concern.

I don't want to take my eyes off the four hellhounds, but I risk a quick glance back at Emil, hoping to discern his intentions from his expression.

He still hasn't raised his head.

"Take a look at her feet, Hel," he says, the baritone of his voice sounding like a warning now.

My feet? What the fuck is wrong with my feet?

I glance down, suddenly focusing a little to my left.

The Book of Dark Magic lies only a few paces behind my left heel.

Halle gives a soft exclamation. "What happened to the book?" she asks, her eyes wide as she appears to fixate on it.

Technically, *The Book of Dark Magic* belongs to her.

Because of her affinity with the underworld, she has the ability to resist its power. Like me, she is one of the few creatures who can read the book's pages and not lose her mind.

She'd protected it for millennia until her brother stole it from her and gave it to my father.

Now, I've stolen it back.

And for some reason… which I struggle to believe is related to my continued wellbeing… Emil has brought me *and* the book back to Halle.

Behind her, the hounds appear alarmed, all of them shuffling and glancing at each other.

Halle's question this time seems directed at me.

"What happened to the book?" I ask, opting for the simplest explanation. "I broke it."

"You… *broke*… it?" Halle asks.

"I clawed it apart."

It occurs to me now that none of my pack members have paid any attention to the book until this point. They all know how dangerous it is and would never willingly touch or read it.

Lucian, more than the others, understands how destructive the magic in the book can be. Our father forced Lucian to read the book to confirm what it showed about me. When I needed Lucian to recount what he saw in its pages, the memories caused him significant pain. He barely got through the retelling of them.

I suppose I expected them to immediately shrink away from it, especially now that it's been drawn to their attention.

Yet Lucian stares at the book as if he's more puzzled than anything else, his forehead puckered and lips pursed. He gives a small shake of his head. "Is that the same book? It doesn't hurt to look at it…"

Anarchy and the others wear similar expressions, even Jonah, all of them muttering quietly about the fact that it looks like an ordinary book.

"Where has its power gone?" Anarchy quietly asks, taking her eyes off Halle for a moment to bend and peer more intently at the book. When she rises, her head is tilted and her forehead is deeply creased.

My pack's reactions unsettle me even more than Halle's incredulous stare.

I'm now wondering why the book has remained in its torn-up condition. If it can alter its own form to create vines and daggers, then surely it could rearrange itself to bind itself back together—

"No." Halle seems to get a hold of herself before she firmly shakes her head at me. "No, dearest, you can't have broken it."

Again, Emil speaks up. "She did."

Halle shakes her head harder. "Not possible. Not even remotely likely." Her speech is rapid and sharp and far jumpier than I would expect from the Goddess of Death herself. "The four books of magic have an internal power source created from magic that doesn't exist anymore."

She holds up a finger as if she's giving him a talking-to. "They can react to their surroundings, even choose to become volatile and destructive. They can change their own form, but they are inherently untouchable. They *cannot* be physically altered by any power that exists today—"

"It was," Emil says. "Altered."

More than anything, I wish he'd look up because my need to understand his intentions has reached desperation levels.

Inwardly, I sigh because the reality is that even if I *could* see his expression, it could be a façade. A visual lie. I may never be able to correctly interpret his body language ever again.

"No!" Halle snaps at him, seeming to dig in her heels. "The only way Veda could alter that book is if she—"

Halle suddenly stops speaking and reconsiders me, her focus flashing from my claws, up to my face, and then back to my claws.

My shoulders tense at her increasingly wary expression, and my anxiety only worsens when Emil finally makes a move.

Where before I was hoping to understand his motivations, now I would prefer if he had stayed exactly where he was.

He rises from his kneeling position to his full height, his white clothing settling around his muscular form, making him appear even taller and more broad-shouldered. More imposing.

I'm half-turned toward him while attempting to keep the hounds in my sight. I'm conscious that my pack members are doing the same, each of them tense as they appear to brace for attack from both sides.

Emil lifts his head, his pale green eyes visible through the silvery strands of his hair. His focus strays to me for all of two seconds, and my body reacts in a way that I wasn't expecting.

Heat floods me. As if he reached out and ran his hand up the side of my neck and to my lips. A soft touch that contrasts sharply with the fear I should be feeling.

Emil approaches and stops a disconcertingly short three paces behind me.

Halle takes a quick step back, her face deathly pale, which is saying something for the Goddess of Death.

"That face..." Halle's voice is strained as she continues, "Keeper, why are you wearing that face?"

"Because it's mine," he says.

She swallows visibly. "But if you..." Her focus flashes to me. "And Veda..." Her focus flashes back to him. "And you..."

"Yes," he says.

I have no idea what he's confirming.

Every member of my pack appears even more confused about the conversation between Emil and Halle than they were about the book. Their tense postures tell me they aren't sure which threat to worry most about right now: the keeper, Halle, or the hounds.

I'm not sure I can, either.

The dark elves are thousands of years old. Jonah, too, is ancient. But it seems that Halle and Emil are speaking about matters that even the elves and Jonah aren't familiar with.

Halle's chest is rising and falling rapidly. She presses her hand to her heart. "Dark saints, save us all."

Her focus finally settles on me, and for a moment, her death-goddess appearance reasserts itself, her eyes turning red and her charred bones becoming visible beneath her skin.

Then, her hesitation seems to break.

"Well, then, I have no good choices." She clicks her fingers at the hounds. "Take Veda into custody. Quickly!"

"What?" The shocked exclamation leaves my lips before I chastise myself for it.

Of course, she would turn on me sooner or later, even if I don't understand exactly what has caused her to do so now.

The hounds surge forward, masses of molten muscle that remind me of how badly Jonah's power can burn me.

If these hounds are creatures of old magic—which is very possible—then their fire will hurt me as badly as light magic can.

My pack responds by taking battle stances around me. Lucian keeps his wings tucked tightly to his sides, but I take comfort from the glittering ends of each of his feathers. They're edged with stone and can be used like blades if he sweeps them through the air quickly enough.

Anarchy and her brothers all hiss like the panthers they appear to be on the verge of transforming into.

My hands fly up, claws still extended, preparing to slash at the first opportunity. If it were only me and the hounds, I'd have more room to move, but as it is, I'll need to be careful I don't hurt my allies.

At the same moment, I'm conscious of Emil crowding in behind me, as if he'll press me forward. But of course, he'll help the hounds capture me.

It's clear to me now that he brought me here to be caged.

I snarl back at Halle as her hounds close the gap far faster than I would like. "I won't go easily, Hel."

"Veda, I'm deeply sorry," she replies, the sight of tears in her eyes shocking me. "But your father was right about one thing: you should not exist."

CHAPTER SEVEN

Before the hounds can get anywhere near me, Jonah darts between them and me.

I'm surprised by the level of anger in his voice.

"Think carefully before you make another move," he says.

While the hounds slow their approach, Halle scoffs. "Jonah, dear, you know as well as I do that you can't burn me to ash."

Shortly before we went to the church, Jonah was Halle's prisoner. She captured him because she thought he would be able to tell her where her brother, James, was.

He probably can. But he didn't.

If I look carefully, I can still see the wound at the side of his face where Halle must have taken out her feelings on him earlier. She has the ability to leave scars where other supernaturals can't. And because her true form consists of ash, he can't burn her.

The expression on his face when he glances back at me tells me he's less-than-impressed to be facing Halle again. But he doesn't appear deterred.

Jonah has ice-blond hair and amber eyes that blaze with

determination. His skin is fair, his shoulders are broad, and his physique is muscular.

"I may not be able to burn you, Hel, but I can certainly hurt your hounds," he snarls back at Halle. "I hope you're not attached to them."

With that, the heat radiating from Jonah's body increases rapidly, becoming so hot that it suddenly feels like we're back on the beach and standing under a scorching sun.

The lava lines on the hounds' chests pale in comparison. They draw to an abrupt halt, faltering between Halle and Jonah, and glancing back at Halle—no doubt for instructions.

Her brow is deeply furrowed. "Do *not* threaten my hounds, Jonah."

"Don't threaten Veda," he snaps.

"Threaten?" Halle stiffens, drawing herself further upright. "*You're* the one putting her in danger! The longer we linger at the cusp of hell, the greater the risk."

It's Jonah's turn to falter.

Halle takes another look at him, and then at me. "Oh, dear," she says. "It seems we've had a misunderstanding."

"I don't think we have," I snarl. "You're trying to cage me and I won't go down without a fight."

She splutters. "Cage you? I would never!"

Jonah appears as confused as I am.

Did I not understand her correctly? Is my lack of experience with the world getting in my way again?

I don't think so, because my pack reacted with the same alarm that I did—and Jonah certainly got mad about it.

I narrow my eyes at her. "You said 'captivity.' I don't see how that can be misinterpreted."

"No," she says firmly. "I said *custody*. There's a difference."

I scowl at her. "If there is, I don't see it."

"Custody," she snaps. "Protective custody."

"Protective...?" I arch my eyebrows at her. "I'm supposed to believe that your intention in seizing me is to *protect* me?"

She presses her lips together. "Well, maybe I'm a little rusty on the whole godmothering thing, but yes."

I latch on to the most absurd part of what she said. "Godmother?"

She beams at me. Then her smile wobbles. "Well, I would have been. It's what your mother wanted."

I scowl at Halle, since I only have her word for it. I risk retracting my claws to rub my eyes. "Let me get this straight. You want to take me into protective custody... by escorting me forcibly into the bowels of hell?"

I peer past her into the darkness of the long tunnel that stretches ahead of us.

"Well... yes," she says with a bright smile, as if there's nothing wrong with that. "It's the safest place for you to be right now."

Each of the hounds nods with a sincerity that makes me blink at them.

I find myself wondering if they can talk. Not likely with those heads.

"So you claim," I say to Halle. "But I can't trust you."

She sniffs. "Well, you *should* trust me. Your mother did."

"Again, so you claim." A heavy exhale rests on my lips, defeat pushing its way through my thoughts.

I try to recall the way my mother spoke about Halle. What I do remember is the way my mother would smile softly and tell me that the gods make mysterious moves and that they are not for us to question.

I wonder now if she was telling me to take Halle's word at face value. To follow her mysterious—or in this case, fucking clumsy—moves and not question them.

The trouble is that I don't really have a choice.

I have no way of leaving this place without Emil's help and, once again, I'm faced with the reality that it was his decision to bring me here in the first place.

I'm not certain that I could convince him to take me somewhere else.

In fact… I have no idea how much control I actually have over him anymore.

It's a question that burns me and I vow to find out the answer, but for now, I need to tackle the dilemma directly in front of me: the Goddess of the Underworld and her backward attempts to 'protect' me.

Ahead of me, Halle bounces on the balls of her feet, her high heels clacking against the black stone. An impatient sound. "I really would prefer if you make up your mind quickly, Veda," she says. "It isn't safe to stay here much longer. The mouth of hell is its most vulnerable point."

Again, so she says.

Although this time, Jonah gives me a short nod, as if to indicate that Halle's telling the truth. As a jotunn, he is as old as Halle and would have spent his youth surrounded by old gods. It's possible he has more knowledge of this place than any other member of my pack—even the keeper.

But if this spot is hell's most vulnerable location, then that probably means it's also the only place from which I could launch a successful escape.

Right now, I might prefer to take my chances with the snowstorm raging outside—if, indeed, it is a snowstorm.

"Answer me this," I say to Halle, my voice harsh. "You said you were trying to get my mother to safety before she was imprisoned."

Halle nods. "I was. And your question is…?"

There's a growl in my voice. "How am I supposed to believe that you didn't deliberately take her into danger?"

Halle immediately stiffens and a flush crosses her light-brown cheeks. "Because Galela was a daughter to me!" she snaps. "Because she called me 'Mother'. And I called her 'Daughter'."

A powerful relationship.

"I would never betray her," Halle continues with such force that her voice echoes around us with a hint of the magic she controls.

I want to believe her. I really do.

But my father taught me the meaning of distrust and Emil has only deepened it.

"If you'd succeeded," I continue, quietly this time, "what would my mother's life have looked like?"

As I speak, my eyes burn with unexpected tears. I fight them, refusing to shed them because I can't allow myself to wallow in the *what-ifs* of how different my life could have been. Even if I need an answer to my question.

Some of the anger fades from Halle's expression. "I was taking Galeia west," she says. "If I could have trusted any warlock at the time, I would have paid to transport us there in an instant, but we couldn't trust anyone."

"Why west?" I ask.

"There's a place in Portland," she replies. "A supernatural shelter where women can be safe from those who mean them harm. Your father would never have been able to find Galeia there, let alone hurt her. That place is protected by the most powerful of old magic. Even I can't breach its walls."

Halle pauses to take a deep, shaky breath, her voice straining as she finishes. "You would have been born in a safe place, where you could have thrived."

"That sounds like rainbows and sunflowers," I say, wrinkling my nose. "Even if such a place existed, they never would have helped a dark creature like my mother."

"It was certainly a risk," Halle says, with an acknowledging nod. "But Galeia was adamant that they wouldn't turn her away. She wouldn't tell me why, but now I understand. In fact..."

She takes a step forward before she stops again, her eyes wide. "They couldn't have denied her even if they wanted to. Not while she was carrying you."

Her focus switches disconcertingly to the keeper, and there's a question in her eyes.

His voice sounds from close behind my left shoulder. "Veda's mother didn't tell her anything."

"I can see that," Halle snaps. "Or Veda never would have torn through the book." She rubs her eyes. "Oh, but Galeia didn't warn me, either… The secrets she kept… Darkest of saints."

I've had enough of their cryptic conversation. "Stop!" I snap. "Both of you."

I have no explanation for their conversation. I don't know why Halle was so alarmed to see the face Emil's wearing or why the state of the book has worried her so much.

As far as I'm concerned, it's a good thing the book seems as dead as a book like that could get.

"It's clear I need answers," I say. "But it's also clear I won't be able to trust the answers either of you give me."

"I might have a solution for that." Halle edges closer to me, now within striking distance of Jonah, who is only a few paces in front of me and to my right. "You don't trust me. I don't blame you. But I find myself recalling an accusation you leveled at me when we first fought each other."

"Oh, yeah?" I ask, a little thrown.

"I told you I would never betray your mother. And you said to me… Let me make sure I get this right…" She tips her head as if she's thinking hard. "You said, 'My mother died in that prison, gasping for breath. Nobody came for her, and for that…'" Halle pauses, her lips pressing together for a moment. "Well, you promised I would pay."

I nod. "Where are you going with this?"

And what does this have to do with a solution to our trust issue?

She gives me a grim smile. "Just last night, when we fought

for the second time, you led me to believe that you didn't know what happened to your mother. You claimed to have been separated from her during your imprisonment."

"Yeah." I can't stop my sigh. "After we fought the first time, I became convinced that the woman imprisoned with me was not my biological mother, after all. So it wasn't a lie. Not within the context of what I thought I knew at the time."

My forehead creases as I try to explain, but Halle's smile softens.

"I sense you have a story to tell, Veda," she says. "And you must have many questions for me. But, you see, we're at the edge of the Underworld, where all power and deceit are stripped away and everyone's lies are exposed. It is the nature of hell to make us vulnerable to our own darkness."

"What are you suggesting?"

"Please step into the Underworld with me," she says. "It's one of the few places your father will hesitate to follow you, and there are safe spaces within the rings of hell where he won't be able to reach you at all. I can protect you here. And, if you're willing, there is a place within the Underworld—one of the deepest places—where I, too, will be forced to speak only the truth. You can have your answers there."

It isn't lost on me that if such a place exists, and if it can force Halle—an old god—to tell the truth, then no doubt I will have to tell the truth, too.

What a dangerous thing.

To swap truths.

Halle considers me carefully. "I will pay the price you wish me to pay for failing Galeia," she says. "I will pay it by giving you all the truths you clearly need, even if it could hurt me."

She holds her hand out to me. "Will you come with me?"

CHAPTER EIGHT

I look at Anarchy and Lucian and my panther brothers.

They trust me to lead them, but this decision can't be mine alone.

Anarchy is closest to me, and the way she has edged in toward me ever since Emil stepped in behind me tells me she's ready to shift into her panther form and take him the fuck out.

She hisses at him, baring her teeth and revealing her two pointy canines. They aren't as long or as prominent as a vampire's fangs, but they secrete a substance that can knock people unconscious.

I find myself wondering if it would work on the keeper.

I file that possibility away in case I need it.

"I'd rather take my chances with the snowstorm," she hisses. "Fuck your enemies, Darkness. Let's get out of here."

Around me, my pack is nodding.

Jonah is the only one shaking his head, and it's with an intensity that alarms me.

"That isn't any ordinary snowstorm." He shudders as he points at it. "Hell is the coldest place on Earth and that is a shield of magic that forms its first line of defense from any living creature who tries to get inside."

"Who would *want* to come here?" I ask, truly baffled. After all, as Halle said, most creatures spend their lives trying to avoid this place.

"Well, nobody, of course," Jonah says, the fire across his chest fading and shadows forming in his eyes. "But there are those who have lost loved ones to the darkness and wish to save their souls."

Fuck me.

"Also, I should point out that many battles have already been fought here and lost." He gestures to the ground and the walls around us. "Black doesn't show the blood."

Behind him, the hounds give me broad grins.

Halle merely wears a prim expression, as if it's all part of her job.

"You've been here before," I say to Jonah.

"Not happily," he replies. "In case you haven't guessed, we're in the middle of Antarctica."

He visibly shudders again. But of course, any freezing-cold place would be torturous to a fire jotunn like Jonah.

He continues. "Even if you could get through the shield without a near-instant magical escort off this continent, you'll freeze to death in the snow."

Fuck. Fuck me.

Of all the members of my pack, Lucian is the quietest right now. Not that he has the ability to express himself in snarls and growls like the panther-elves can. He has remained on the other side of Anarchy and is closest to Jonah.

"You need answers, Veda," Lucian says, his focus falling to the book. "I couldn't look at that book without experiencing excruciating pain when I first saw it, and now... nothing. You need answers before you can move forward."

I meet his golden eyes.

It took a lot for me to trust him. I didn't at first. He didn't trust me, either.

Then he declared that the chances of dying at my side were way higher than anywhere else, so at my side was where he'd like to stay.

I took him at his word and he hasn't betrayed me since.

Riot chooses that moment to speak up from my other side. His voice is solemn, as is his way. "A path forward is impossible to discern without truth."

Where before Rumble and Strife were both indicating they wanted to leave, now they give me firm nods.

"We're here for you no matter what you decide," Rumble says.

"Besides," Strife adds, a little hint of mischievousness returning to his expression. "I'd like to see what hell has to offer."

He tips his chin at the hounds.

One of the hounds is eyeing Strife a little more intently than the others are, a curious gleam in his fiery eyes.

My eyebrows arch. "Oh?"

Strife shrugs. "Hell could be fun."

A little of the heaviness lifts from my shoulders when the others shrug and even Anarchy, who was most vocal against staying, seems to relax.

"We're headed here eventually, anyway," she says, one corner of her mouth twitching upward. "We may as well get a tour in advance."

I can practically read her mind: she will want to find out all of hell's vulnerabilities and weaknesses in case that comes in handy for future purposes.

"Okay, then," I whisper.

But at Halle's sudden, gleaming grin, I hold up a finger. "We're only staying until I have truthful answers. And only with one guarantee."

Her smile fades. "What guarantee?"

"We're free to leave whenever we want." I step away from the safety of my pack to advance on her, drawing level with Jonah. "No traps."

Halle folds her arms across her chest and tips up her chin. "Don't insult me."

It's my turn to smile and I let my canine teeth sharpen in the process. "Dearest Hel, be prepared to be insulted many times."

"Fine." She huffs. "No traps. No cages. No tricks. You're all free to leave whenever you like."

Her focus slides past me and farther to my left.

"Even the keeper." Her eyes narrow for a moment before she spins away from me, muttering to herself. "What a face for him to claim as his own."

I glance back again, surprised to find the keeper now leaning up against the tunnel wall on the left side. He has struck a seemingly nonchalant pose, but his non-threatening demeanor doesn't make a difference to my instinctive reaction.

What is it about that face that's so startling?

Another question for which I need an answer.

"Come. Quickly now." Halle waves us toward the depths of the tunnel ahead of us while the hounds step clear of the path.

It looks like they intend to bring up the rear when they head in twos to the side of the tunnel and wait there.

I hurry back to retrieve the book, scooping it into my arms while my pack rapidly fans out around me again.

Without speaking, they seem to know exactly where they want to be. Anarchy and Lucian stand in front of me while Rumble and Strife cover my back. Riot flanks my left side while Jonah resumes his position on my right.

"You, too, keeper," Halle calls back. "Don't fall behind."

Emil lifts himself off the wall, remaining like a shadow behind me while the hounds follow behind him.

The path has a very gentle decline that tells me we're heading slowly downward.

Halle mentioned something about 'rings', and I have the sense that the path curves slightly, such that we could be traveling down in some sort of extremely wide spiral.

Halle glides ahead of us, the outline of her crimson dress merging with a growing amber light that tinges the air as we descend into the Underworld.

It's surprisingly quiet, other than the soft, crackling sounds of firebrands that rest against the walls farther along the path.

I suppose I expected screaming. Certainly sounds of pain. The clank of metal. The crack of whips.

There is none of that.

What's more, the whole place smells oddly sweet and homey.

I lift my nose, inhaling deeply, aware that the dark elves are doing the same, their noses shifting momentarily into panther form.

Halle seems to have eyes in the back of her head, or maybe she simply heard our deep inhales because she drops back a little to walk on my left.

"It smells like home, yes?" she asks. "A final reminder to those who come here of what has been lost. Cruel, I know. But that is hell."

"Cruel?" I shrug. "Not to those who never had a home."

There were a few moments in time when I called the apartment in New York 'home', but that was an illusion. Before it, I only had my cell.

Halle flinches, but I ignore her reaction. It may have sounded harsh, but it's the truth.

"It smells like a treat," Anarchy says from in front of me, licking her lips as she throws a dangerous grin at Halle. "Dessert, perhaps."

I'm honestly not sure if Anarchy's referring to the scent in the air or to the likelihood that she'd like to sink her teeth into Halle.

The goddess looks a little thrown.

Regardless, I can see how the environment around us is designed to create an illusion of safety. Warm light. Nice smells. Peaceful.

If someone likes that sort of thing.

I find myself squinting every time we pass one of the firebrands on the wall.

My eyes are better able to handle bright lights these days, but the years I spent living in darkness took a serious toll on my ability to handle both sunlight and loud noises.

I suppose from that point of view, I can't resent the quiet.

As we progress farther along the tunnel, doorways appear within the walls. The doors within are all closed, and each is made of what looks like the same black stone as the rest of the tunnel. They're so shrouded in darkness that I might have missed them if not for my sensitive eyesight.

Along the way, Emil is also quiet. I find myself missing his presence at my side—and then chastising myself for feeling that way.

Damn him.

Finally, Halle stops at a large door on our left.

It looks like every other door we passed.

"Veda, you will need to place your palm on the groove in the center of this door," Halle says, gesturing at it.

I eye the goddess with suspicion as I approach the door and my pack fans out once more—this time to position themselves between me and the hounds.

I expand my senses as I step nearer to the stone.

Still, all remains quiet. But my awareness of deception increases. It doesn't feel as if the space around me is an illusion, but it certainly feels manipulative, as if the sensory input is deliberately calibrated to elicit a desired response.

In my case, a sense of calm.

I hesitate, my palm hovering over the door's surface, as I make out the indentation in it.

Weirdly, exactly the size of my hand with my claws extended.

Halle must catch me eyeing the claw extension on the indentation because she says, "Claws, too, please."

Her politeness sets me on edge.

But once again, I have few choices.

I extend my claws and press my palm to the door. My hand fits perfectly within the grooves.

My eyes narrow when nothing happens. "Is that it?"

Halle's forehead puckers. "Well… normally, it opens right away, so I don't understand—"

"Wrong hand." Emil's baritone breaks the expectant silence behind me. "Veda needs to use her left."

"Her left?" Halle stiffens again.

"That's the hand that ripped the book to shreds."

Halle's forehead creases. "Oh."

I don't wait for her to ask.

I quickly switch hands, raising my left. The moment I extend it toward the door, the indentation changes shape.

Once again, there are grooves for my claws, but the thumb is now on the other side.

I slap my left hand to the stone, at which the door immediately opens.

CHAPTER NINE

I step inside a place that can only be from my dreams.

Or, perhaps, from my nightmares.

A dark night sky stretches high above me for as far as I can see. A round moon rests within it, casting soft enough moonlight over the scene below so that it doesn't hurt my eyes.

On my right is an orchard of trees, all fruit-bearing. I recognize the shapes of apples hanging from the branches, their bright-red skins easily visible.

Directly in front of me is a sculpted garden filled with rose bushes. They're black roses. Their branches are so heavy with flowers that they droop to the ground. In the center of them is a bubbling fountain.

Behind the sculpted garden is a dark forest that extends far into the distance. The trees within the forest are set close enough together that cold shadows rest beneath them, but far enough apart that the thought of running through that forest is tantalizing.

What's more, if I listen carefully, I can make out the soft scuffling of what could be creatures of prey.

I sense the reactions of the elves as they step inside the

room, the buzz in the air and their increased heart rates telling me they're already picturing themselves hunting in that forest.

On our left is a cottage with a thatched roof, two stories, and small windows. Gauzy, black curtains waft at the open windows on both levels, the soft material lifting in a gentle breeze that brushes my skin.

At first glance, this place has everything I could need for a safe stay: space to run, a water source, food to be hunted, and a place to sleep.

But there are too many aspects of it that are far too personal.

Nearly every night since my mother died, I've dreamed of her.

In my dreams, I can't reach her. Her silhouette always passes across the edge of my vision and her form disappears before I can get to her.

Always, within my dreams, she moves through a room with inky-blue walls into a garden with black roses. A dark forest looms in the background.

Now, as I inhale the scent of the roses, I can nearly hear her humming.

I can imagine her bending to one of the rosebushes, snipping at the stem of her chosen flower while deftly avoiding its thorns.

I close my eyes, shivering.

Without stepping inside the cottage that sits to my left, I'm certain that the walls will be the same inky blue as the walls of the home in my dreams, right down to the swirling, silver filigree that decorates them.

Emil's voice sounds softly at my shoulder. "I warned you to guard your dreams, my Veda."

I startle at his sudden nearness. Ever since he started wearing this face, his presence has become harder to detect, his movements almost impossible to follow. And that's saying something, given how finely tuned my senses are.

I had no warning of his proximity now, although I'm aware of the way my pack members are all edging toward me, as if they'll leap to my defense if needed.

I raise my hand to tell them to stay put.

I can manage this.

As for what Emil said, he did warn me.

The first night I spent outside my cage after I fell asleep on a warm beach under a beautiful night sky, I woke to find him guarding me. His hand was pressed to his chest, as if it hurt.

He told me he couldn't sleep that night because my dreams had kept him awake.

They've kept him awake many times since.

Now, somehow, the magic in the Underworld has recreated the home I dreamed about.

Whereas sweet scents and soft lighting had no effect on me, the environment in front of me is truly cruel.

Because my mother is not in it.

She remains out of my reach.

And it's because of Emil.

"And I warned *you* that I would have my revenge," I snarl softly.

He responds with a dark smile that belies his silvery-bright hair. "As you like."

Halle has ventured farther inside the space than I have, her hounds staying close to her heels now.

"Well, this is certainly interesting," the goddess announces.

She stops right beside a rosebush, where her stiletto heels sink into the grass, one of them impaling a rose that has dropped to the ground.

For some reason, she fixates on the keeper as she breaks into a broad smile. "Would you look at those apple trees? So delightful!"

As she speaks, the last of the sunlight fades, and the trunks of the trees within the orchard light up from their bases to the tips of their branches, glittering, sparkling light gleaming from within them. The brightness mutes the color of their fruit, leaving it looking as black as the roses instead of red like it appeared only moments before.

It's a sharp contrast with the cold shadows beneath the trees that form the forest up ahead.

Beside me, Emil is as silent as stone, his expression hardening in the face of Halle's exuberance.

"That orchard is very intriguing," she persists, and, even though I'm not sure why she's so focused on the apple trees, it's clear to me that she's poking hard at the keeper. "Wouldn't you agree, keeper?"

"*Emil*," he snaps back. "Remember what I am: your enemy."

She doesn't appear at all perturbed, her bright smile remaining plastered on her face. "Such a clever evasion of my point. Please do continue to hide your true feelings, *Emil*."

Without missing a beat, she turns to me. "As you've probably guessed, this part of the Underworld adjusts itself to the needs of the person whose blood was taken at the door."

I rub my left palm, remembering the sharp prick even if I can't see a wound.

"I'm pleased to see, Veda, that you've given your pack and yourself everything you could possibly need," Halle continues as she gestures to our surroundings. "A forest in which you can hunt. A cottage to accommodate various sleeping arrangements. Black roses to remember your mother by." Her eyes glitter at me as she continues. "And an apple orchard to torment the keeper."

I return her gaze without flinching, as if the apple orchard had been a deliberate choice on my part, but for the life of me, it's the only thing that *isn't* the same as my dreams.

"Well," she continues, her bright smile never wavering. "I'll leave you to rest for tonight. But I'll be back in the morning. And then, if you're ready, Veda, we can take a journey to the truth." She glides toward the door but pauses beside Jonah. "I don't suppose you've decided to tell me where my brother is?"

The fire jotunn scowls back at her.

"Very well." She shrugs. "Maybe Veda will wrangle it out of you."

James Vanguard's whereabouts are the least of my concerns right now, although I haven't forgotten my vow to bring him to account for his part in my father's crimes.

Halle pauses when she reaches the outer door. "Oh. I should have said: to exit this place, all you have to do is walk through this main door and you'll find yourself in the external tunnel once more. From there, you're free to leave."

She holds up a finger. "But please be aware: transportation magic does not work within *this* space. You must step outside into the tunnel and, better yet, proceed to the mouth of the Underworld again." She gestures to our surroundings with a firm nod. "I mention it just in case you were to try to translocate yourselves from here and you find it doesn't work. I don't want to be accused of trapping or tricking you."

I acknowledge her with a nod. "Understood."

"Good." With that, she opens the door and sails on through it.

The hounds silently follow her out, but as they pass me by, one of them shifts into full humanoid form. He's the one who was eyeing Strife.

The hellhound loses some of his height but is still a solid six feet tall. His skin becomes a reddish-brown color while his eyes are now brown with darker rings around his irises. Dark-brown hair sits in waves around his face and his jaw is shadowed with growth.

He casts a silent glance back at Strife, who has paused near one of the rosebushes and appears suddenly transfixed.

As the door closes behind Halle and all of the hounds, Strife gives himself a shake.

"Damn," he whispers, but his face has fallen with not even a hint of his mischievous smile remaining, and I'm not sure why he's suddenly so subdued.

Riot is immediately at his side, a hand gripping Strife's shoulder, to which Strife returns his brother's solemn gaze.

"Yeah, I know," Strife says. "Fun is easy. Getting attached is not. That hound has my heartbreak written all over him."

"I'm sorry, brother," Riot says. "Save yourself the pain."

Heartbreak is a pain that Riot knows only too well.

Back on the island off the coast of Japan, Riot had bonded with one of the female dragon shifters, Miku. She's the sister of the dragon master who controls the island. All dragon shifters are creatures of light magic.

For the duration of our stay, Riot was still cursed to exist in his shadow panther form, but on the last day, the keeper broke the curse. In his dark elf form, Riot was finally able to speak with Miku.

When she came to say goodbye, he asked her to come with us.

She refused.

As much as I hated what she said to him, I couldn't deny the truth of it. She said that they were creatures of opposite magics. They would never be safe to be with each other. They would be hunted by both sides because of their bond. She told him she wouldn't risk his life like that.

I'll never forget what Anarchy said to Riot as he watched Miku fly away.

She told him to accept the pain because we are dark creatures and we will never be anything but broken.

My shoulders slump.

As much as I'm seeking the truth, right now, I hate it.

I turn to find Anarchy and Rumble studying the cottage, which sits right at the edge of the rose garden on my left.

Anarchy's head is tilted and her right hand is outstretched

toward the cottage's open door. "There's an aura around this structure. Do you sense it, Rumble?"

"I've felt this magic before," he says, his forehead puckered. "But where do I know it from?"

Anarchy's expression suddenly clears. "Our former queen had a room that felt like this."

Rumble's eyebrows rise. "Do you think it's a soul catcher?"

"What's a soul catcher?" I ask, interrupting them.

"Dark magic, naturally," Anarchy replies. "Our queen used to entrap bright creatures this way, but it works on anyone with a soul."

I try to detect what the elves are sensing, but even standing this close to the cottage, I come up empty. The breeze is gentle, the black curtains swaying harmlessly, and the fountain bubbles quietly behind me.

I guess I'm tired. It's been a long night.

"So much for no tricks," I mutter. "Halle said this place is a product of my needs, but I guess she must have interfered somehow."

Emil's voice sounds at my shoulder. "She didn't."

Once again, he has crept up on me.

"This place is your creation, Veda," he says. "Even an old goddess could not interfere with what you want."

I turn on him. "Why would I want to trap my friends?"

"Not your friends," he says. "Your enemy."

His eyes glitter at me as he steps toward the cottage's open door. "Your heart yearns for a cage to place me in. A cage as dark as the one you survived. The trouble is, my Veda, I don't have a soul."

With that, he steps inside the cottage, his imposing figure filling the opening for a moment before the shadows within the cottage's lower level engulf him.

He disappears so completely that I'm suddenly alarmed.

I tell myself he must have simply stepped to the left or the right and out of view, but even Anarchy is craning her neck, looking as intently for him as I am.

Before I know it, I've taken a step closer to the cottage.

Anarchy's hand wraps around my arm before I can get too close to the building. "Even if what Emil says is true—that the soul catcher is of your own making—you can't risk going inside."

I understand her warning, but I can't fight my sudden panic.

For the first time since I gave the keeper my heart's power... I can't feel it. Even when we were separated after my first fight with Halle, I didn't have such an empty feeling within my chest.

"Emil!" I shout, unable to keep the panic from my voice.

My only answer is silence, and my blood rushes loudly in my ears.

I latch on to the only challenge I can think of that might compel him to obey me. "If you don't have a soul, come out and prove it!"

Emil appears in the doorway again, but this time, his footsteps are slower.

"As you like," he says, and I'm confused to hear a sigh in his voice. It doesn't sound like an exasperated sigh, more of a tired one, his voice low and surprisingly bleak.

He steps right up to the outer edge of the doorway, his front foot meeting it, and then—

He stops.

A furrow appears in his brow as he raises his hand toward the space within the doorway. His palm appears to hit an invisible barrier right at the outer edge of the doorway.

"What?" His soft exclamation sounds bewildered. "This can't be."

He presses both of his palms flat against the air in front of him, the tension in his muscles telling me how hard he's pushing against it.

My eyes are wide. He said he doesn't have a soul, and I absolutely believe him and yet...

With a roar, he turns his shoulder and rams himself against the invisible barrier.

The *thud* his body makes as he hits the barrier is so loud that I instinctively take a step back.

"*I don't have a soul!*" he roars, his shout directed at me.

The corners of his mouth turn down and his chest heaves as his green-eyed gaze burns me more deeply than his fiery dragon eyes ever could.

Then I'm struck by the dark rings beneath his eyes and the flash of pain across his face before he backs away into the shadows.

His voice fades as his form disappears into the dark. "I don't have a soul."

CHAPTER TEN

can't move or speak.

My feet have taken root on the grass outside this cottage of my own making where the keeper is now trapped.

"I don't understand," I say. "I honestly don't fucking understand anything right now."

A deep sadness wells up within me, and I can't fight it off.

I saw the truth of my mother's death and it was like reliving that loss again.

Since seeing it, I haven't had a moment to process it.

I haven't had time to begin to understand why the keeper would do everything that he's done—so many contradictory things: keeping me alive, healing me, helping me, all after he took my mother's life and only to confirm that yes, he is my enemy.

I'm aware of my pack gathering around me.

Even Jonah has stepped close, his amber eyes dull.

"Darkness." Anarchy nudges me gently. "None of us can go in after him and Halle was right about one thing: we need to rest. And eat. And talk. You need to tell us what happened so we can understand and try to help."

I appreciate that ever since I told them that Emil is now my enemy, they haven't questioned me about it. They didn't demand an explanation or need to be convinced before they believed and followed me.

They're here for me. And I need to tell them everything.

I give Anarchy a nod and my pack quickly rallies around me.

A few minutes later, I'm settling down at the edge of the forest where the grass is soft and dry and the night sky remains visible above me.

Jonah and Lucian quickly set about building a cozy campfire —an easy task when Jonah can light up the wood they gather with a single touch—and Rumble and Strife head off to hunt, shifting into their panther forms before they disappear into the woods.

I place the broken book on the grass in front of me before I pull my knees to my chest.

Anarchy and Riot take positions like sentries on either side of me.

Within minutes, Rumble and Strife return, this time in their elven forms and with their arms full of food. They've both taken off their shirts and are using them to carry multiple items, which, when they crouch and let them tumble to the ground, turn out to be a variety of vegetables.

Anarchy arches an eyebrow at them. "Vegetables?"

Her brothers shuffle a little as they rise back to their feet.

"The rabbits were too cute," Strife mumbles beneath his breath.

Anarchy narrows her eyes at him. "'The rabbits were too cute'?"

"Yep."

Rumble, too, shrugs.

"I'm a carnivore," Anarchy grumbles, lurching to her feet. "We'll see about *too cute*."

Rumble and Strife watch her disappear into the trees.

66

"I was a rabbit once," Rumble declares. "Rabbits are off the menu."

Before the keeper successfully broke Anarchy's curse, allowing her to return to her dark elf form, he'd inadvertently turned her into a fluffy, little rabbit. When he tried to recreate the curse-breaking spell, he tried using the same sequence of magic. Rumble ended up with big rabbit ears, a tail that resembled a ball of fluff, and a rabbit's mouth and teeth. All while the rest of his body remained that of a panther. The spell took hours to wear off, and he was not impressed.

All of one minute later, Anarchy reappears.

Her hands are empty.

She plonks herself down beside me with a huff and a scowl. "They're too cute."

At that moment, one of the little critters scampers in from the trees.

It's small enough that I could easily snuggle it in my arms. It has floppy ears, a button tail, and rich, brown fur that's fluffier than anything I've ever seen—even fluffier than the little puppies the keeper turned the panthers into once.

If I dared to reach out and pet it, I wonder if I'd have a new 'soft as' comparison.

Soft as towels. Soft as sheets. Soft as kisses. Soft as... rabbit fur?

Then it raises its head and I can only gasp.

"I know I've never seen a natural rabbit in person before," I say, pointing carefully, "but that isn't quite right, is it?"

The little rabbit has a nose that looks like it belongs to a piglet.

It snuffles at the air, its eyes bright, before its ears flop back over its features and it bounds away again.

From across the way, Lucian is also staring. "No, that isn't right."

"Still too cute," Anarchy grumbles.

Her brothers sweep up the vegetables from the ground.

"Don't worry. I can make a mean vegetable stew with these," Rumble announces.

Strife side-eyes him. "You've never made vegetable stew in your life."

"And I'm sure I'll be great at it."

They continue their verbal jabs as they carry the vegetables to the fountain to wash them.

An hour later, we've prepared, cooked, and eaten what was a decent meal, after all, and my stomach doesn't feel quite so hollow as it did before.

Focusing on meal preparation and consumption has taken me away from my darker thoughts, but as silence settles around the campfire once more, there are things I need to face.

"Darkness?" Anarchy finally prompts me.

I pull my knees to my chest again. I'm still wearing my tunic and long pants and it isn't cold here, but I feel as chilled as if I were standing at hell's mouth.

"I read *The Book of Dark Magic*," I say. And then I quickly correct myself. "Or, rather, the book forced me to read its pages. As soon as I touched it, its spine unraveled into vines and pinned me down."

Anarchy reaches for me; her forehead puckered with apparent concern. She and Riot have maintained their sentry positions on either side of me, while the others are spread out around the campfire, where I can easily see them and their equally worried reactions.

"But, Darkness," Anarchy says. "That book..."

Anarchy once described the book to me as insidious and bloodthirsty.

Even among dark creatures, it's considered a dangerous, unreliable object.

"I know," I say. "It lies. It twists the truth. It serves only itself. I know this. But Emil didn't dispute what I saw. Of all the things he could have deceived me about—" My voice chokes up. "He could have told me that what I saw wasn't true, and I would have believed him. But… he didn't."

My pack is quiet for a long moment. I know they won't entirely understand what I said without context.

Lucian breaks the silence with a quiet question. "Can you tell us what you saw in the book?"

He knows, more than anyone else around this campfire, how easily the book can destroy a supernatural's heart and mind.

With a nod, I begin.

CHAPTER ELEVEN

I recount what the book showed me and how it started with moments of my life that I had already lived and knew to be the truth: my mother dying in my arms, after which her lifeless body was taken away by our jailer.

Then, how the vision had followed her. How our jailer had disposed of her body into the keeper's realm, which was somehow connected to the veil prison.

I tell my pack how the keeper had kneeled at my mother's side and she'd suddenly woken up.

My voice chokes again as I recount the way she'd spoken with Emil, the strange way she'd greeted him, and how their conversation was muted for a full minute, at the end of which he had torn out her heart—a heart that had been unique.

I'm aware of the increasing widening of their eyes as I speak, especially when I talk of the way my mother had woken up and her muffled conversation with the keeper.

But I make myself continue because it's important that they know what happened after the book released me from its grip.

I describe the way Emil had confirmed what the book showed me.

I tell them about the way his power had started breaking when my heart was breaking. And how my father harnessed the light magic keeper's power.

And then I finish by telling them how I ripped through the book.

But I leave one thing out: the dark impulses that flooded through me when I broke the book, those commands that roared within my mind and only stopped when I tore the book apart.

When I finish, the others are very quiet.

Jonah's expression is the most far away and I realize that hearing how my mother died must have a more significant impact on him, since he was once her friend.

As for Lucian and the dark elves, they're all contemplating me solemnly.

Anarchy speaks first with her forehead gently creased. "So… Galeia didn't appear frightened when she opened her eyes to find the keeper of dark magic looming over her?"

It isn't what I thought she would ask first, but it's certainly right up there among the things I don't understand.

"Well…" My own forehead creases. "No."

"And she didn't try to get away from him?"

"No."

"And you didn't hear what was said between them for a full minute?"

"I didn't." My head hurts and I rub my temples before I acknowledge what Anarchy must be trying to say. "I need to know what I missed."

"You do." She nods emphatically. "The book must have hidden that conversation from you for a reason. Most probably because it doesn't align with what the book wants. In fact…" She glances at Lucian, who gives her a firm nod before she continues. "I would even venture to say that *that* conversation could be more important than anything else the book showed you."

I draw away a little. "Even my mother's death?"

She shakes her head rapidly. "No, of course not. Darkness, you know I would never hurt you by minimizing your pain."

She wouldn't.

It was Anarchy who first reacted with rage when Lucian had even hinted that the woman who'd raised me might not have been my biological mother.

But now she persists. "The book lies. It *lies*, Darkness. But most importantly, so does Emil."

She searches my eyes, reaching for me again, her lilac hair catching in the firelight. "Darkness, you can't trust that Emil's confirmation of events wasn't a lie, too."

Fuck... me...

I squeeze my eyes closed and rub my forehead harder, but I don't shake off the hand she wraps around my forearm.

I need my pack right now.

I need their help.

But it also feels like nobody can really help me because nobody else was there when my mother died.

They don't know what really happened to her and I don't, either.

Lucian speaks up from Anarchy's other side. "Veda, I've read that book. Other than you, I'm the only one here who has read it." He inclines his head toward where I placed the tome in front of me. "All I know for certain right now is that it may as well be dead."

He glances at Anarchy before his focus returns to me. "I'd like to test it by picking it up."

Anarchy immediately gives a cry of alarm. "Don't."

But Lucian reaches for her. "I couldn't look at that book without experiencing physical pain before, but now it has no effect on me. Trust me, *Anna-ve-shaleia*, I'm not being reckless. I believe we need to know the status of the book now."

The use of Anarchy's original dark elf name seems to settle her nerves.

"Okay," she whispers. "But I'm ready to tear it to shreds myself if it hurts you."

He leans across the space between them and brushes a kiss to her lips. "I know you will."

Then he turns to me. "May I?"

I give the book another moment's consideration before I nod.

At which he leans forward and reaches for it, scooping it up with both of his hands—an awkward task, given how shredded its pages are and how precariously they're held together at the spine.

I hold my breath, but…

Nothing happens.

Lucian glances around at the rest of us before returning his attention to the book and, moving more slowly this time, he opens the front cover.

The pages inside are as black as they were before I tore through them, although they're also now slightly charred-looking and curled at the edge of each shredded portion.

They're also completely blank.

Not a single image leaps up from them.

Lucian carefully flips through the pages to a central point, where he pauses. "This is where I saw the vision of the future that our father made me watch."

In that vision, Lucian saw bodies, countless bodies of dark magic creatures: shifters, witches, mages, vampires, and others. Claw marks had been gouged deep into the walls of every place where they lay.

And then he saw me.

I was the one killing them.

Lucian places the book back on the ground.

"It's dead," he says, looking up at me. "But I don't understand how."

I chew my lip, suddenly replaying the moment when I'd swept my claws through its pages.

"Die, book," I whisper, repeating what I'd snarled at the time. "I told the book to fucking die."

I meet the startled eyes of my pack.

"You told it to die, and it did?" Riot asks, his blue eyes wide.

Opposite me across the fire, Rumble and Strife are both shaking their heads.

Rumble murmurs, "The power it would take to kill one of the books of magic…"

"No wonder Halle was so alarmed," Anarchy says.

Only Lucian is grinning. A dark smile. "Our father would not have been pleased to watch you do it."

"He was not," I reply.

"Damn, Veda," Lucian continues. "You really fucked up his prized possession."

"I did." A little of the weight inside me lifts because, at least in this one thing, I succeeded at what I'd set out to do: deprive Taiven Nostra of *The Book of Dark Magic*.

My smile fades. "But what are the consequences?" I stare at the book. "What does this mean?"

Jonah speaks up from the other side of the campfire. "It means you're impossibly dangerous, Veda."

I meet his piercing gaze, my own unwavering. "Jonah?"

"I was fully grown when the books were created," he says. "I never met their creator, and I was grateful for that because her power was terrifying."

"Her?" I ask.

"A woman who wielded the same arcane magic that was used to create your mother's heart." Jonah nods in slow motion. "She used that power to create these books."

He gives me a hard stare. "Even more dangerous is the power that could destroy them."

I'm tense where I sit, fully aware of the friction rising around me and the way my pack is leaning protectively toward me.

"Are we going to have a problem, Jonah?" I ask him.

"Fuck, no," he says, his declaration bringing the tension down a notch. "You're Galeia's daughter. You're family."

But then the tension rises again when he continues. "But until you understand how you did what you did, you're a danger to everyone around you."

CHAPTER TWELVE

*J*onah rises slowly to his feet.

There's a part of me that wants to stand and face him, to downplay what I did to the book and all its unknown consequences.

But I can't.

If I believe that my father once loved my mother, then he imprisoned the love of his life because of the danger she carried: *me*.

He asked me if I had ever seen true darkness, and he implied that true darkness was me.

Even Halle said I shouldn't exist.

And Emil brought me here... for what? Protection? Imprisonment? Or perhaps for some other purpose that has yet to reveal itself.

So I stay exactly where I am, my knees drawn to my chest, a storm of uncertainty within me as Jonah slowly circles the campfire and steps toward me.

I know Anarchy and Riot well enough to believe that at the first hint of danger to me, they'll spring into action. Rumble and Strife will attack Jonah from behind, and Lucian—well, I'm certain he will be conflicted because Jonah was the only person who looked out for him while he was growing up.

But I also know that Jonah could turn them all to ash in a blink.

"Don't," I whisper to them. "Don't react. If there's a fight, then it's mine."

"There will not be a fight." Jonah lowers himself into a kneeling position in front of me, somehow managing to squeeze between me and the campfire. But of course, he's a fire jotunn, so the flames won't worry him.

His voice is quiet as he says, "I want to tell you about the first time I met your mother."

I'm cautious. "Okay?"

"My people, the jotnar, fought and died in the final battle against the primordial deity, Typhon. I was only a child at the time—too young to fight—which is why I survived."

I rapidly recall what my mother told me about the old gods and the jotnar. Many perished in the old wars against the Titans. She mentioned Typhon several times and there was a warning in her voice because even in death, his bones were considered dangerous.

"I was raised in the north by the Valkyrie," Jonah continues. "They chose to take me in, even though I was not one of them," Jonah says. "When I was old enough, I repaid them for their kindness by protecting them and watching over their followers: the humans called 'Einherjar'."

It isn't a total surprise to me that Jonah was raised by the Valkyrie. Lucian mentioned it to me when we were talking about learning to fly. It was Jonah who helped Lucian understand how to use his wings, teaching Lucian in the same way Jonah had observed the Valkyrie teaching their young.

"When the Valkyrie Queen was forced into a deadly war, I fought beside her," Jonah says. "But the devastation to her race was horrific. I lost my family for a second time and after that, my purpose was gone."

He falls silent, and I give him the space to remain quiet for as long as he wants, the fire crackling softly nearby and my pack unmoving around us.

Jonah finally clears his throat. "About five hundred years ago, I was wandering across the forests and mountains of what is now known as the Cascade Range east of Portland. I found myself within a ring of mountains to which I had never been before. I stumbled through a wilderness of overgrown foliage that appeared to have claimed what might once have been a great city. It was all crumbling stone by then. In the middle of that wilderness was a single intact building: a cottage very much like that one."

He inclines his head at the structure that now sits on my right before he turns in the other direction toward the orchard on my left. "Right beside the cottage was an apple orchard, much like that one."

I clamp my arms closer to my legs, unnerved by the existence of these structures outside of my dreams.

"Galeia stood in the open doorway of the cottage holding a broom, of all things," Jonah says. "She took one look at me, held out the broom, and told me to sweep."

A smile plays around his mouth. "I asked her where I should sweep and she told me—" He stops, swallows visibly, and I'm shocked when his eyes fill with tears. "She told me to sweep wherever the pain needed cleaning out."

He takes a deep, shaking breath. "She had a way of knowing what to say."

Suddenly, I'm hanging on to Jonah's every word, afraid of asking him to tell me more about what she was like, what her dreams were, and who she was.

Somehow, he seems to know that's what I need. Maybe it's

the way I'm leaning forward or the desperation that I can't keep from my face.

"She had an infectious smile," he says. "And a wicked sense of humor. And she could take down an opponent in less time than I could transform into my full jotunn form. And then, somehow, she'd make friends with them."

He gives a laugh. "Fuck, I could never figure out how she did that. She gathered people around her. Sometimes, I thought that Halle and James followed *her* and not the other way around. She was her name, Veda. Galeia means *new life*. Did you know that?"

I nod. When we were on the island, Ryuji, the dragon master, told me the meaning of my mother's name. As he said, it's a confusing name for a dark creature.

"Wherever she went, a sparkling darkness seemed to follow her." Jonah shakes his head. "By the dark saints, she was loved."

My mother's long-ago voice echoes in my memories, a constant reminder of the message she gave me.

We were loved.

"Why are you telling me this now?" I ask, my voice strained as I fight the burn of tears in my eyes.

Fuck, I yearn for my anger and rage to surge again. I hate how much my sadness is overwhelming me right now.

"Because you need to know how badly she wanted you to live." Jonah's eyes are even duller now. "In the first few months of her pregnancy, she collapsed. Twice. Her heart stopped entirely. We couldn't revive her. We thought we'd lost her until her heart started beating again all on its own. After the second time, we searched for answers."

His focus shifts to the book and my shoulders slump as I mentally follow what must have been the path of their reasoning at the time.

"You thought the book could help her," I say.

"Halle was adamant that it couldn't. But even though she was its custodian, she had never dared to read it, so she couldn't say for sure.

"She refused to open it. She and James argued like they'd never argued before. He, and your father, were convinced that because Galeia's heart had been created from dark metal, the book would tell us how to save her. When Halle wouldn't hand it over, James stole it."

I consider my clasped hands where they rest in my lap and the tips of the dark metal that will protrude further from my fingertips if I call on it.

If I'd been in the same position as them, I wonder if I would have stolen the book, too.

When I look up, Jonah says, "James has never regretted anything more than the moment he handed the book to your father."

I give a single nod, the only acknowledgment I'm capable of giving.

When I first met James, I needed his help so I could get close to my father—or, rather, to get close to the usurper I thought had killed my father. While working toward that goal, I'd helped get James's son, Elijah, away from my father.

Elijah had been my father's leverage over James.

By helping his son, I gave James his freedom.

Since then, I found out that James was the reason my father came into possession of the book. And now, it seems the context of that choice is far more complicated than I first believed.

"Where is James now?" I ask the very question that Halle envisaged I might ask.

Without hesitation, Jonah replies, "He's with Elijah's mother."

His reply doesn't tell me anything since I don't know who Elijah's mother is or where she could be.

My forehead creases as I consider my next question. "And is Elijah's mother with Elijah?"

I have an idea where Elijah might be, so the answer could give me a clue.

Jonah shakes his head. "To keep their son safe, they've given him over to the care of a group of extremely powerful supernaturals." Jonah grimaces. "The kind of supernaturals who have no hesitation tearing dark creatures like your father apart. Elijah is safe with them."

It isn't lost on me that if those supernaturals would tear my father apart, then they may not feel very kind toward me, either.

I didn't see what happened to Elijah after the fight on the train. I manipulated events so that the keeper would take him to safety while I continued on to finally meet my father.

But I do remember one thing.

"St. Michael Cemetery," I murmur, recalling the place where Jonah told the keeper to take Elijah to safety.

Jonah gives me a grim smile. "No dark creature will set foot near there."

I file this information away in case I need it.

Focusing on Elijah for a few moments has helped to pull me out of the dark pit I was descending into.

Freeing that boy from my father's clutches has been one of my few successes since I escaped my cage.

I don't push Jonah for more information about James's whereabouts, instead asking him the more pressing question. "What about you, Jonah? It looks like you're stuck here with me, at least in the short term, so I need to know: where do you stand?"

Assuming he will tell me the truth.

CHAPTER THIRTEEN

The fire jotunn meets my eyes. "I trusted Galeia," he says. "In fact, I trusted her as fully as I trusted the Valkyrie queen who raised me. Galeia wanted you to live. Therefore, I will do everything in my power to keep you alive."

My eyes widen at the intensity of the resolve in his voice.

How did my mother engender such trust?

"That is where I stand," he says.

Rising to his feet, he takes a careful step back, no doubt in case I don't believe him.

He's not standing right at the edge of the fire, but if anything, he seems happier near the flames.

He turns to acknowledge my pack. "Thank you for the meal," he says to them. Then to me, he adds, "I would like to venture into this forest now and find a quiet place to meditate. It's how I conserve my energy. I don't want you to think I'm slinking off into the shadows. You're welcome to come and find me at any time."

"Okay," I say.

He lumbers around the group, giving the elves a wide berth,

but he pauses at the edge of the trees. "Veda, if I may give you some advice?"

"Yes?"

"When you drag the truth from Halle tomorrow, ask her about Galeia's parents—your grandparents. Galeia never spoke about them, but I believe Halle knows who... or *what*... they were."

He gives me a pointed stare before he prowls away into the trees and disappears into the shadows.

I track his footfalls with my sensitive hearing for the next ten paces before they disappear.

Damn jotunn is as quiet as Emil has become.

"Darkness?" Anarchy's voice breaks through my thoughts. "Did your mother ever speak of her parents?"

I shake my head. "Not once." I can't help sighing. "The focus was always on my father and the Nostra Empire."

"It's highly likely that your maternal grandparents were alive at the time of the keeper's creation," Lucian points out.

"Without a doubt," I whisper, a heavy weight settling over my shoulders again.

There are so many things my mother kept secret from me. Her mechanical heart. The fact that she'd lived for so long.

Who she really was.

Suddenly, I'm fixating on Emil's earlier declaration to Halle: *Veda's mother didn't tell her anything.*

"I need to speak with Emil," I say.

Every member of my pack suddenly lurches upward where they sit, as if they would physically stop me, but they all stop themselves.

Riot speaks first, his objection far more measured than I was expecting. "That seems unwise."

"You could get trapped in there with him," Rumble points out.

"Possibly," I say, releasing my legs to hold out my hands in a calming gesture. "But in a cottage of my own making?"

I don't fancy the idea of having a conversation with Emil at the door and it's unlikely he'll stand there for me, anyway. The easiest way for him to avoid answering my questions is to simply stay where I can't see him.

"I need to know what he knows," I say. "I need to know why my mother wasn't afraid of him. Why she didn't try to get away from him before he ended her. I need to know how I destroyed the book. And most importantly, I need more information about my mother's family."

I'm already rising to my feet as I speak.

"Then we'll come with you," Lucian says, jumping up to join me.

"No." I shake my head firmly at him and the others. "You really could get caught in that cottage."

"Because I have a soul?" Lucian asks.

I nod. "Because you clearly have a heart."

"Careful," he says with a gentle smile. "You're talking to a dark angel. I could take offense."

I return his smile before I consider my pack. All of their fierce, trusting faces.

"You all have hearts." I try to find the words to say what I need them to know. "If at any stage I really am a danger to you... well... I don't plan on letting it get to that. But if it does, I expect you to protect each other. No matter what."

Bending to scoop up the tattered book, I step quickly around the campfire and toward the cottage.

More than anything, I want to drop back to the ground beside my pack, curl into a worried ball, and let them comfort me.

I only make it ten paces before the sound of quick footfalls behind me makes me pause.

I half-turn back to find Lucian coming after me.

He quickly draws level with me, reaching for my hands, even though they hold my deadliest weapons: my claws. "Sister?"

I struggle to keep my voice clear of the sadness that's welling inside me. "Yeah?"

"I need you to know what frightens me the most about what I saw in the book."

I try to smile. "All the dead bodies? Murderous me cutting through them without mercy?"

He shakes his head, his expression deadly serious. "It was watching you die at the end."

A shiver runs through me before I can suppress it.

When Lucian first recounted the vision to us, he said that when I'd finished slaughtering all of the dark magic creatures, a new being had come to fight me.

He couldn't see that being's face. He doesn't know who they are. He said they'd had wings, and their wings might have been red, but he couldn't be sure.

That being kills me.

They lift me to a great height, and, while I'm still alive, they drop me.

I break against the ground because I don't spread my wings.

Fucking useless wings.

Lucian did everything he could over the last month to teach me how to use my wings, but I still can't fly.

Now he's tense where he stands opposite me, his shoulders hunched and his expression drawn. "Can I show you something?" he asks.

"Of course."

He rolls up the short sleeve of his black tunic, enabling me to finally see his tattoo.

It depicts rocky mountains, inked in gray, but surrounded by a golden circle. Through the circle is a flow of amber lava that cascades from one of the mountain peaks.

"I don't know a lot about my mother's people—the gargoyles

—but every gargoyle clan had an emblem. A mark they would give their brethren," Lucian says. "Her clan, the stone gargoyles, apparently dwelled in the mountains—inhospitable ones. The kind with volcanos in them."

It isn't lost on me then that Jonah—who acted like a father figure to my brother—is a jotunn who has an affinity for fiery volcanos.

"When I was fifteen," Lucian continues, "Dad gave permission for me to get my mark. Actually, he didn't object at all, and I think it was because he hated me so much. Far better that I was marked as a gargoyle than as his son."

My chest constricts. I was the firstborn. I have the black blood and the ability to heal quickly. As the second-born, Lucian was a punching bag.

Lucian clears his throat. "It was the one time I was allowed to connect with my mother's old clan."

"The clan who betrayed her," I say.

"Fucking monsters, the lot of them." Lucian nods. "It was dangerous for Mom to go back there, but without my mark, I would be clan-less. Their culture demanded that they couldn't deny me my mark. Of course, the ink they used was deliberately infused with toxins and I was sick for days. But I survived."

My blood boils, my anger nearly as strong as my sadness. That gargoyle clan is on my list of targets when... *if...* I ever claim the Nostra Empire.

"My point is that I never had a home until now," Lucian says, reaching for my hands again. "This pack—*your* pack—it's my home. It doesn't matter where we are. As long as we're together, that's where I belong. You're part of my home, too, Veda."

Tears appear in his eyes, but his mouth is down-turned, telling me they're angry tears.

"Don't fucking die on me," he says.

"I won't," I whisper, even though it's a promise that could become a lie.

CHAPTER FOURTEEN

The cottage is silent as I approach.

The windows are dark, the black curtains wafting quietly.

On impulse, I scoop up a fallen rose, holding it to the surface of the book, which is cradled against my side. I keep my right hand free, and I'm fully prepared to drop the book if I need to defend myself.

I step through the dark doorway, finding the shadowed hallway just as I imagined it would be.

The walls are inky blue and decorated with swirling, silver filigree. The furniture is ornate and carved, but sparse, each wooden piece in just the right place.

This is the home of a dark creature.

Before I obey the urge to move farther inside, I take a step back, testing whether or not the cottage will trap me.

I'm relieved when it doesn't.

As I move easily back into the garden, I'm aware of my pack watching from a distance.

Even from afar, I can hear their relieved sighs.

Either I have no soul, or the cottage is simply obeying my wishes as its creator.

I remove my boots and place them at the door so I can walk more quietly along the hallway.

So far, there's no sign of Emil, and like before, I can't sense his presence.

He may as well be a ghost.

Multiple rooms lead off from the hallway. Farther ahead on my right, I make out the shape of what could be a kitchen, but I can't bring myself to go that far.

Too loud in my imagination is the sound of my mother humming within that room.

I swerve instead toward the second room on my left: a sort of living area but without large chairs. An ornate table rests against the far-right wall, a black rug covers most of the floor, and a fireplace burns softly within the opposite wall.

There's no other furniture in the room.

The fire has completely died down and the soft glow of the coals isn't too bright for my eyes, nor too dim for me to see clearly. Not that I can't see in the dark.

Given how comfortably warm the air is outside, I would have expected a fire to make this room overly hot, but it doesn't.

Once again, this environment is perfectly adjusted to my needs.

On impulse, I step toward the table and place the damaged book onto its surface, positioning the black rose beside it.

It feels like an offering, but I'm not sure to whom I'm offering it.

Or maybe it's a declaration of war.

"You shouldn't keep that book so close."

I'm not surprised that Emil crept up on me.

Without turning, I close my eyes, sensing his location.

Behind me... and maybe a little to my right...

"The pages may be dead," he continues, "but the book's malice lives on."

The memory of the book's impulses thrums through me, at which my claws suddenly itch to be released.

"Take control of the light and the dark," I say, repeating the clear instinct that raged through me when I tore through the book's center.

There's a pause behind me, and even if I listen hard and try to scent the air, it's as if Emil has vanished again.

"That was the command of one of the darkest beings who ever walked this Earth," Emil says with a soft snarl. "He was the one who wielded the arcane magic that turned soil to ash and rain to blood. His command has echoed through time, enduring despite the sacrifices that were made to defeat it."

The nearness of Emil's voice tells me he's close to my right shoulder now.

I could simply turn around, but I'm not ready yet. Not when he's giving me information I desperately need.

My fingers haven't left the black rose and one of its thorns pricks my skin. Black blood seeps from the wound and drips, very slowly, onto the table.

"Take control," Emil whispers at my shoulder. "Of the light *and* the dark."

I stiffen as I suddenly realize…

That's what my father has done.

I can't stop my surprised whisper. "My father was obsessed with this book and now he controls both light and dark."

"A feat that only a creature born of both light magic and dark magic could ever truly achieve."

While Emil speaks, my fingertips leave the rose and brush the book's torn edge.

Then, my focus flickers to the fireplace on my left. "I could burn what remains of this book."

He's so near to me that I sense the way he shakes his head. "External forces—"

"Can't affect it," I say. "But I'm not talking about external forces."

Again, I sense his reaction, reading the small silence to mean I've given him pause.

Taking a guess as to his exact location behind me, I step directly into him, satisfied when my back connects perfectly with his front.

"I'm talking about a fire of my own making," I whisper, holding my breath as I take everything I can from the physical closeness between us and the illusion that I can sense my heart again. "This place is of my creation. Surely, I can create a fire hot enough to burn these broken pages. Turn them to dust—"

I catch my breath as his arms wrap around me from behind, one at my waist, and the other across my shoulders above my breasts. He draws me close enough that every hard plane of his chest and thighs presses against me.

"You told me we were bonded in fire and betrayal," I say, raising my arms to press them over the tops of his, as if I were the one holding him and not the other way around.

"What do you want from me, my Veda?" he asks, his voice more broken than I was expecting. "Why did you come inside this place when you could have remained free of me?"

What do I want from him?

I want to drag my claws across his chest and make him feel my heartache.

I want to sink my teeth into his neck and taste his blood.

I want to scream at him that I will have every vengeance that is owed to me.

But more than all of that, I want to forget all the ways in which he shielded me, protected me, healed me, soothed me, helped me, fought for me, bled for me…

And now I want to forget what Anarchy so aptly warned me about: *he lies.*

"I want you to tell me the truth," I whisper. "I want you to tell me what my mother said to you before she died. I need to know why she looked at you as if…"

In the vision, she was lying on the cold, marble floor of his realm while he kneeled beside her, gripping her shoulders.

She had reached up to gently press her palm to his cheek, a gesture that was far too compassionate to be shared with an enemy.

I continue speaking past the lump in my throat. "As if seeing you brought her deep sadness."

He's quiet, but now that I'm pressed up against him, holding on to his arms, he is *real* to me. He can't slink back into the shadows as if he has ceased to exist.

His response is wooden, and it's like an echo from the past, a repeat of what he said to me when things were far simpler between us. "I am a dark creature, and I have the power to choose."

It isn't an answer.

Unless it's an answer within an answer to a question I haven't asked yet.

I remember when he first said that same thing to me. It was in the context of him explaining when he would drain life to feed his dark magic. He made it clear to me that *he* would choose when to take life.

But very soon after, when we spoke about his choice to become the keeper of dark magic, he made it clear that…

"Choice is an illusion," I say.

So, then... which is true? Does he really have the power to choose or is his belief in choice an illusion?

My head spins as I try to focus on why I stepped into this cottage in the first place. "I need to know how I destroyed the book. I need to know about my mother's family. You have the answers, I know you do—"

He cuts me off with a sudden snarl. "Lie or truth, you cannot trust my answers. Even less than you can trust what anyone else tells you."

Beyond frustrated now, I can't stop myself from spinning in his arms, my claws snapping out to press into his chest. "I will give you a truth and here it is: I want you to hurt as much as I'm hurting."

Despite his snarl only moments ago, his response is quiet. "Your heart's pain is already mine."

His arms drop away from around me to hang at his sides. When I last saw him, he was wearing a white tunic and matching ivory pants, but now he's bare-chested.

Only the long pants remain, along with the belt with a harness that's empty of whatever weapon might be intended to rest within it.

"Whatever pain you're feeling," I say, shaking my head at him, my claws extending further, dangerously close to cutting his skin. "It isn't enough."

CHAPTER FIFTEEN

Emil barely reacts to the threat of my claws, even when pinpricks of bright red blood form across his chest and little droplets slide down his skin.

His green eyes search mine as I try to rein in my anger, desperate to keep my rage in check so that I can persist in seeking answers. *Somehow.* I can't give up yet.

With his right hand, he brushes the wayward strands of my hair from my face—the gray ones that sit closest to my cheek and turn blonde at the ends.

His voice is barely above a murmur. "Why did you come inside this place when it hurts you to be here?" Then his expression hardens. "Is it because you know I feel your heart's pain and you wanted to hurt me more?"

I grit my teeth against the ache in my heart, even though his accusation isn't true. "Will you answer me one thing truthfully? Does our deal still stand?"

"Our deal?" He narrows his eyes at me and a cold smile touches his lips. "Be honest, my Veda, it isn't our deal that's at the heart of your question."

It's my turn to narrow my eyes because I'm not sure what he's getting at.

He shakes his head at me, a slow, side-to-side motion, while his other hand rises to press against my lower back, drawing me closer, inch by inch, even though my claws press more deeply into his chest.

"Ask what you really want to ask, my Veda."

Take control of the light and the dark.

That insidious whisper suddenly echoes around in my mind again, but it isn't the book's darkness I'm thinking of now.

How many times did my mother tell me that control was everything?

As many damn times as she told me I was loved.

And with that thought, I understand what Emil means.

I ask the question that lies at the heart of my relationship with him. "Do I still have power over you?"

The corners of his mouth rise. A soft smile. His fingers play against my cheek while he makes a humming sound in the back of his throat. "I can say *yes* or *no,* and you'll have to decide if you believe me."

I try to read his expression, his pale eyes, the dark rings under them, the press of his lips.

"Which is it, Emil: yes or no?"

"*Yes,*" he says. "As long as your heart's power keeps me alive, you have power over me. Vengeance is yours to take. And I am a slave to your desires."

He doesn't look away from me, but, even though I continue searching the depths of his eyes, I have no fucking idea if he's telling the truth or not.

He leans closer to me. "Do you believe me?"

I can't.

I can't believe a word he says anymore. I shouldn't have even fucking asked.

I should have stayed outside, just like he said.

But I'm here now and I may as well put his claim to the test while I have the chance.

I lift my left hand from his chest and wrap my fingers around the back of the hand he's resting against my cheek, my fingertips brushing the back of his wrist.

He watches my hand more carefully than I was expecting him to, especially when I allow the tips of my claws to extend a little further.

I narrow my eyes at how tense he is, this dark creature who can use his crown to wield the magic of every dark being who has ever died.

Even if I don't have power over him, he is clearly wary of me now.

"Do I believe you?" I ask before I issue a challenge. "Prove that I still have power over you."

His focus flickers to my eyes and then quickly back to the fingers I've wrapped around his right wrist.

He doesn't try to pull away, but I'm suddenly aware of a dark light growing behind me.

His crown rests in the form of a ring on his left hand. The palm of which currently rests against the small of my back.

"Prove it how?" he asks, his voice rough.

"Bind yourself," I snarl at him.

Some of the tension eases from his shoulders and the dark light fades from the edges of my vision so fast, I could have imagined it.

His left hand slips away from my spine as he takes a step back, although he extends his right arm so that he doesn't tug his hand out of my hold.

"Like this?" he asks.

Sapphire light bursts from the crown-shaped ring, at which rusty, metal shackles appear around his ankles and wrists, short chains extending between them and clanking as he adjusts his position a little.

The color of the sapphire light that glowed before he created the chains tells me that they're pure illusion. They may look and even feel real, but they don't exist.

I purse my lips at them, but before I can speak, he continues.

"Or like this?" he asks.

His power flashes again, but this time, it's a black light that makes me freeze.

Black light means he's using dark magic to create something very real. But to use dark magic, he has to drain life from a living thing.

He has destroyed whole trees this way.

Now, my left hand clamps around his wrist, as if I could stop him. My claws dig into his flesh so hard that blood drips from between our clasped hands.

I could tear off his right hand in a blink.

This time, he doesn't seem to care.

"Don't worry, my Veda," he says. "There are plenty of rosebushes outside this cottage from which I can drain life. I haven't harmed your pack."

There are no windows in this room for me to check the truth of what he said, but despite my distrust, I don't hear any screams or shouts from outside. On the contrary, if I listen hard enough, I can hear my pack talking quietly among themselves.

They're worried about me. They don't like that I've been gone so long already.

Emil shrugs. "You're free to check on them."

I nearly pull away from him, nearly give in to the fear that, even though every member of my pack sounds perfectly fine, something might have happened to them.

But then I narrow my eyes at him, mentally replaying the eagerness of his suggestion. "You *want* me to leave."

The corners of his mouth turn down. "The longer you remain in my presence, the more painful it is."

Which would be why he used his dark magic just now. To fucking scare me away.

I can't stop my smile. It's cruel. I'm fully aware. "Then I'll stay."

"As you like."

The dark light swirling around his left hand spreads rapidly outward, moving across his body to reach the shackles he's wearing.

The metal transforms from rusty iron to a gleaming bronze, each shackle thinning out.

I expect the bindings to disappear entirely, but, while the chains retract so that only bronze anklets and bracelets remain, the excess metal becomes liquid. It quickly ascends his legs and chest, traveling outside his clothing, while the liquid at his left wrist rushes up his arm and also across his torso, all of it meeting in the middle and solidifying for a few moments like plates of armor.

It's beautiful armor, etched with what looks like runes, before it, too, re-liquifies and continues on its path.

Now gathered together, the metal streams toward his right hand, which is clasped in mine.

I edge backward, eyeing the bronze liquid warily as it slows, forming another plate around his forearm before a thread of bronze very slowly glides forward around his wrist and then onto mine.

It forms a new shackle binding me to him.

I take a sharp breath. "Stop."

At my command, the liquid stops extending along my arm, but it doesn't cease moving, flowing around and around my wrist.

Emil tilts his head. "Are you sure?" He edges closer to me

again, the backs of his fingers feathering the inside of my wrist. "We're already bound, my Veda. Even without these chains."

"I can cut through any chains you make," I whisper. "All I have to do is extend my claws."

"True," he says.

My heart beats harder when he asks, "But is that what you want?"

CHAPTER SIXTEEN

I lean in closer to Emil, aware once more of how cold his skin feels now. It's a strange sensation. As if he himself isn't generating the iciness.

As if the cold is coming from his surroundings, which is odd, because the air around me is warm.

I dare to draw our connected hands to my side, pressing his palm to my waist.

The way the metal remains wrapped around us forces my arm to bend at the elbow, as if I'm putting my hand on my hip, but it isn't too uncomfortable.

My chest is now a mere inch away from his and I don't miss the way he sways toward me.

Meanwhile, the metal gliding around and around my wrist slows a little.

I tip my head back and rise up on my tiptoes, edging forward until my lips are dangerously close to his.

"Stop wearing this face," I whisper, brushing my lips ever so briefly to the corner of his mouth. "Show me Diavolo. Be him again."

During the time when I called the keeper *Diavolo*, he

predominantly alternated between two faces. One was his most in control. In that form, he had the darkest-brown eyes, light-brown skin, high cheekbones, and lips shaped like a god's. It was his tallest, most muscular persona.

The other form was the one I associated with his anger. His hair was as inky-black as the panther's fur, his eyes were dark blue like a churning sea at night, and his body was leaner, sleek and deadly. In that form, he called me a 'beautiful darkness'.

He said he couldn't wait for me to unleash my rage on the world.

Such a contradiction to what my father wants: to stop the destruction he believes I will bring to all dark creatures.

And now, I would give anything to go back to the moments when I trusted Emil, even if that trust was misplaced.

"Show me your darkness," I whisper to him. "Put away this beautiful façade… these eyes and this silver hair… and show me your darkness."

"I can't," he grinds out.

I narrow my eyes at him, because there's a difference between can't and won't.

"You *won't*." It's a soft accusation. "Which means you lied. I don't have power over you."

A snarl leaves his lips and his hand tightens against my waist. "My Veda, you have more power over me now than you ever did."

His other arm sweeps up my back and into my hair, cupping the back of my head.

He bends his head to mine and the breath catches in my chest a moment before his lips clash with mine.

My chest collides with his and heat bursts through my body, an intoxicating, needy heat because he has never kissed me like this before.

Not even on the island. Not even under the moonlight on a deserted beach.

Always, he held something back, focusing on my body and every pleasure point on it, but never so fully focused on my lips.

Now, his tongue demands entry to my mouth, his lips coaxing mine apart, and he groans when I open to him.

My head swims with the taste of him, and all of the protective layers I placed around my thoughts and feelings before I entered this cottage peel away, leaving only a burning need.

How can I want this connection so badly that I'm willing to risk my life for it?

I gasp for breath as he breaks the kiss and pulls away from me just the slightest and, for a moment, I think he's going to step away from me, but then he sways inward again, claiming my mouth once more.

I want the use of both of my hands, want to run my hands up his back and trace his muscles, but it's impossible while the chain is binding our wrists together.

"Off," I snarl against his lips, tugging at the metal that joins our hands.

"As you like," he rasps, at which the metal rapidly retracts, its molten form warmer than before as it slides away from my wrist—and his wrist—and away across his chest.

I catch the briefest glimpse of it returning to his black ring before he cups my cheek with his left hand and his kiss deepens again.

There's a very clear part of my mind that tells me I'm being reckless.

Horribly reckless.

I need to keep him at a distance. I can't let him get close to me. Not physically—not closer than this—and not emotionally.

And then there is another part of my mind that is purely calculating.

He kissed *me*.

He told me I have more power over him than I ever did before.

He refuses to tell me the truth or give me the information I need, but this kiss...

Dark saints, it's pure, desperate abandonment.

He's pulling me so close, cupping my head so urgently that I could believe he needs this kiss so that he can keep breathing.

My head swims with the memory of the moments when my body was broken, and he healed me in the forest of Portland.

Beautiful dark magic poured from his crown-shaped ring and streamed toward me in ribbons that wound around my legs, torso, arms, neck, and head, raising me off the ground.

His power descended far beneath the surface of my skin, coursing through my body in a loop of pleasure and pain, and for the first time, I was aware that it was costing him.

Healing me came with a price, although I could never quantify it.

That was the first time I saw the face he wears now. The first time his eyes became the color of pale leaves and his hair like strands of fine, silver metal.

The shadows of this cottage engulf me in the same way now, and it feels like we could be back in his realm, the darkness forming a cage around us.

Around him.

Because within me, there is only a sense of quiet.

A tiny spark of control.

Unbidden, I hear my mother's voice, reminding me that sex is about power and control, not pleasure.

So I let go.

CHAPTER SEVENTEEN

It's far easier than I thought it would be.

All I have to do is rake my claws down the side of my clothing, ripping the material so that it falls from my body the moment I pull slightly away from him.

He draws me right back to him, seeming unaware of what I've done until my bare skin collides with his.

He barely pauses, a groan of need rumbling through his chest as his hands tangle in my hair and then press against my back as he pulls me even closer.

"Off," I snarl again against his lips, this time tearing through the waistband of the pants he's wearing, shredding the material that's holding them up.

Again, it takes only the barest separation of our bodies for the material to slither to the floor.

And still, he kisses me as he wrenches me upward, drawing my legs around his hips and turning to place me on the edge of the table.

My knees are on either side of his hips, and his hard length presses against my core.

I push against him, registering the pleasure it gives me, moaning against his mouth, even though it's a calculated sound.

Our bodies are closer than they've ever been before, and it would take very little effort to draw him inside me.

All the while, his mouth claims me. One arm supports my back while his head lowers to my neck, trailing kisses to my breasts, where he draws more moans to my lips.

I know my body well enough to be certain that I'm ready. Beyond ready.

I take hold of his length between us, tipping my hips enough that it will be easy to take him inside me as soon as his mouth returns to mine.

With my hand wrapped around him, I whisper, "Tell me what I want to know."

He groans against my mouth. "You are a beautiful darkness."

No. That isn't what I want to know.

But of course, my question was wrong.

"Tell me what I need to know," I say, drawing his lips to mine and kissing him as desperately as he's kissing me.

"You are a beautiful darkness, my Veda," he murmurs against my mouth. "A true darkness."

No. *Dammit.*

His hands clamp around my hips, and I'm certain he's going to pull me toward him, a thrust I want and need because I'm certain I can stay in control.

But instead, he pushes himself away from me.

His breathing is ragged and his eyes are flooded with desire, but his voice is harsh. "No full-on cock and vagina sex, remember?"

Suddenly, it's as if he can see into the heart of me.

I struggle to reply as the control I thought I had slips away from me. In those moments of my silence, his expression becomes blank, so devoid of emotion that it makes me shiver and then I can't find words at all.

"Now that you know I'm your enemy, you're in no danger of losing control to your feelings." He wrenches away from me, his hands finally leaving my hips before he turns away. "Control is everything to you. Fucking me is one way to take back the control over me that you think you've lost."

I can't stop the truth. "Yes."

Because he has never kissed me like that. Vulnerable, needy kisses.

I slide from the table, landing lightly on the rug before I raise myself up, completely naked, my shoulders squared.

I don't understand why my chest hurts so much at this moment.

The heart whose power I no longer control aches badly.

I can't stop the words tumbling from my mouth, the questions to which I need answers. "Why wasn't my mother afraid of you? Why didn't she fight you?"

He's only half-turned away from me, but there are too many shadows in his expression for me to decipher his thoughts.

"Only she knows that," he says.

I try again. "Did she know you?" I take a step toward him. "She greeted you as if she knew you."

He winces. "Nobody knew me, my Veda."

My brow furrows because that makes no sense.

"Did you hate her? Is that why you killed her?"

He's silent.

I wait for his answer, but now he may as well be made of stone.

"Did you hate her?" I ask again, my voice rising. "You ripped out her heart as if you hated her."

Suddenly, I'm crossing the distance between us and I can't stop myself from crashing into him. "Why did you kill her?"

My palms collide with his side, a half-punch, half-push that sends him back a step.

"Why?" I cry, the pain in my chest unbearable, so bad that I could believe I still have my heart. "*Why?*"

"Because I want *my* vengeance!" he roars, spinning and catching my fists, stopping me in my tracks. "Because I am *owed.*"

His eyes blaze at me, a light in them that makes them cycle, impossibly, through blue and gray and shadowy green and finally silver like his hair.

He drags in ragged, seething breaths and his lips move as if he will say more, but instead, he releases my hands and steps away from me, backing farther and farther away toward the darkest corner of the room, farthest from the fire.

"You should get away from me, Darkness," he says, calling me by the name the panthers use for me. "I can't give you what you need."

I struggle to breathe against the weight of my options now. Or, rather, the absence of options.

All I achieved from confronting him was more pain.

I reach for my clothing, sweeping it up off the floor, only to find that the material is too shredded for me to put back on.

Closing my fist around the torn pieces, I turn my back on the keeper, pausing now to consider the book on the table. When Emil hoisted me onto the table's surface, I must have bumped into the book because it now lies at an angle.

With a scream, I extend my claws and ram them down through the untorn parts of the book's spine.

There is no burst of energy this time.

The book was already dead.

But it breaks fully, tearing into separate chunks, the pages strewing apart.

Claw marks remain in the table's surface as I stride from the room.

I half-expect Emil to react to my sudden violence, but he doesn't, so I move onward, deeper into the cottage.

I need clothing and surely, this little house of my creation will provide for me...

A few rooms down the hallway is a bedroom with a large bed and an equally large closet, both made of gleaming wood and elegantly carved.

I pull open the closet to find only a single dress hanging within it, its gauzy layers shimmering.

One dress, huh?

It looks like it's designed to wrap around the body with a wide sash hooked through loops to keep it in place. It has an opaque inner layer that's strapless and extends down to my knees so it will cover my chest and thighs, but the rest is gauzy and transparent, with several layers that form the elbow-length sleeves and a flowing skirt.

I can barely see past my anger as I pull the dress around my body and tie it in place.

Trying to release some of my rage, I attempt to take deep breaths.

I'm angry at myself. For so many reasons. Trying to force answers from the keeper is one. Giving in to my impulse to try to control him is another. Nearly using my own body to do it, well—I'm not sorry he stopped me.

But even so, not all of it was pretend.

I'm forced to acknowledge that my physical need is real. It's pent up within me and I have no easy release for it.

The first time the keeper left me wanting, I did something about it myself, a move that brought him right back to me.

But this time...

There's a part of me that knows it's *him* I want and nothing else will be enough.

I want my enemy.

But I can't have him.

CHAPTER EIGHTEEN

I glide from the bedroom into the hallway and, once more, it's as if the cottage could be empty.

I pause at the entrance to the room with the table and the fireplace, but Emil isn't there any longer.

With a strike of sudden unease, I'm reminded of the moments back on the island when he and I immersed ourselves in the ocean to wash sand off our bodies.

Within the water, Emil's form had been like a dark shadow, so much more like the wraith he'd been when I'd first met him.

The moonlight had streamed through his entire form, halting only when it had reached the ring on his finger.

In that moment, it had seemed as if he hadn't existed at all.

Now, he's like that all the time.

I don't understand what's changed or when, exactly, it happened.

Was it during his fight with my father within the catacombs or after my heart started breaking?

Or even when I broke the book?

Only a little of my anger has gone and none of my physical need, but now worry joins it.

I may have tried to wrest back control, but the reality is that I have none.

With a shiver, I hurry from the cottage into the rose garden, pausing when the apple orchard catches my eye.

The way it sparkles, it's pretty, but not in a nice way. More in a pretty-thing-that-will-bite-you way. I haven't gone near it yet, and I'm not sure if I should.

Turning away from it, I hurry back to my pack, the gauzy, black dress swishing around my legs along the way.

They're all curled up around the campfire except for Riot, who's standing watch.

He greets me softly, but there's an urgency in his gaze as he looks me over—probably checking me for injuries. "Darkness, are you okay?"

"He didn't tell me anything."

Riot doesn't look surprised. "At least you tried."

"Yeah." I pause where I stand, not wanting to wake the others, but also uncertain if I'll be able to sleep.

When I glance at Riot, he's wearing a sad smile.

"It doesn't take a genius to know that you've got a lot on your mind," he says. "You could try running it off. This forest is deep, and if you head in that direction, you'll avoid Jonah." He points toward the west. "That is, assuming you want to be alone? If you'd like company, I'm happy to come with you."

The corners of his mouth rise. "Panther versus wolf could be interesting."

I've never run with the panthers in my wolf form. But there's a reason for that.

I grimace. "Unfortunately, I can't take my wolf form without my wings appearing."

Riot tips his head, his lilac hair slipping to the side. "And that's a problem because…?"

"They aren't exactly streamlined." My grimace grows and now I struggle to explain. "I mean, it's not as if I've ever really tried running with them. Not even back on the island. But I think they'll make it embarrassingly cumbersome."

Riot arches an eyebrow at me. "There's only one way to find out."

I clear my throat. "Maybe I'll try it on my own first."

"I can respect that."

"Thank you. But your suggestion is a good one. Running, that is."

Before I can turn away, he catches my arm. "Darkness." His expression is solemn again. "We care about you. You aren't alone in this."

"Thank you," I whisper, and, on impulse, I step into his arms, taking the hug he offers.

As his arms close around me, he murmurs, "Don't think for a second that we fear the darkness you could bring. *You* decide your future. *You*. Not a book. Not the keeper. Not the goddess of death. Not your father. Not some shit that happened thousands of years ago. Not even us—your pack. *You*."

He hugs me more tightly before he lets me go. "Don't forget that."

I try to find the words I need when all I can manage is, "I won't forget."

Stepping back from him, I turn to the forest and hurry into its shadows, taking comfort from the movement.

Riot was right.

As soon as I start running, even though it isn't in wolf form, I feel better.

Little, brown rabbits scatter ahead of me, all of them peeling off in different directions.

I pass the patches of wild vegetables where Rumble and Strife must have gathered our dinner. And then I veer wide of the location where my senses tell me Jonah is sitting, his breathing quiet and even.

Meditation could be another option for me, but not unless running doesn't cut it.

I pause only to hitch the dress up around my thighs, tying it at my hip to keep it away from my legs, and then I continue into the shadows.

The farther I run, the colder it becomes until my heaving breaths are frosting in the air.

Still, I push myself, on and on for hours until I find myself heading toward a bright spot in the darkness.

Something sparkles through the trees, but I'm not sure what it is.

I push myself faster, trying to make out the glittering light until I burst from the shadows and into—

No, wait. This isn't right.

I'm at the back of the apple orchard.

But I was headed far to the west of the forest—exactly the opposite direction to the orchard. There's no way I should have come all the way around to the back of it because that would have required running in a near circle.

Even so, if I peer hard enough, I can make out the shape of the cottage through the sparkling trees in the distance and the rose garden that sits in front of it.

I shake myself and step backward, turning and pointing myself in the opposite direction, deliberately heading *toward* Jonah this time, since he's a fixed point in the other direction.

Half an hour later, I burst into the orchard again.

My exclamation is breathless. "What the fuck?"

I was certain I was headed toward Jonah, and yet I'm right back here.

I'm suddenly horribly uneasy.

This place is supposed to respond to what I need, but I didn't think it would shift around on me like this.

And I sure as anything don't need to be coming up on the butt of this orchard again.

My unease grows as I wonder…
Am I stuck?

CHAPTER NINETEEN

*S*tuck in so many ways.

In this forest. In my uncertainty. Even stuck in moments of time, events I can't change.

I fight my panic as I wonder if I'll loop around every time I try to get back to my pack.

Pressing my palm to my heart, I try to stop its hammering.

I've faced my father, fought the goddess of death, and even tussled with the keeper, but yet a bunch of sparkling trees are scaring the shit out of me.

Instead of backing away again, I take a step forward, eyeing my surroundings as I go.

Each of the trees is large, but not near the circumference of the ancient trees in the forest of Portland. These ones are slender but sturdy, their branches stretching overhead and weighed with apples.

With each step I take, I assess my surroundings, noting that I seem to be moving forward normally.

Maybe I simply need to walk straight through.

Like moving through the bad to get to the other side.

When I reach the orchard's central point, the energy

radiating from the trunks of the nearby trees is the most intense.

It buzzes at the edges of my senses, sort of like the artificial lights in the apartment where we stayed in New York.

It was easy to ignore that electrical energy.

Not so easy to ignore the power in these trees.

It sends a prickling sensation down my spine, awfully similar to the feeling that overwhelms me when I release my wings.

It's painful. A tearing sensation even before the tearing has begun.

Fighting the impulse to spread my wings, I hurry onward until I reach the far edge of the trees and only a few steps will take me beyond it and into the rose garden.

The light outside the orchard is growing, indicating that dawn is only an hour away. I haven't slept and maybe that's a bad thing, but I'm not sure I could easily lay my head down and close my eyes in this place now.

I pause at the final tree, where an apple hangs right in my line of sight.

I could veer around it, but I reach up instead.

Extending the foreclaw of my right hand, I use it to cut through the apple's stem, catching the fruit with my left hand so it doesn't fall to the ground.

The claws of my left hand sink into the apple's flesh as easily as they tore through *The Book of Dark Magic*.

Suddenly, the same impulses flood through me again.

Dark, cruel, and malicious.

Take control of the light and the dark.

That insidious command slithers around and around within my mind. An unwanted directive.

Emil said it has echoed through time despite the sacrifices that were made to defeat it.

Take control. Make them yours. Seize the power. Take control—

But all I can feel at this moment is anger.

"Control is a fucking illusion!" I snap, as if I can tell the impulses to fuck off already. "There is no control! Only heartache."

At my declaration, the insidious commands stop.

They're so instantly gone that I'm a little surprised.

Even when I drag my claws through the apple's flesh, the commands don't come back.

My shoulders slump and my voice quiets. "There is only heartache and pain for dark creatures. And that is all there ever will be."

As if to punctuate my point, my stomach growls at that moment and I reconsider the now-mutilated apple.

Stabbing a piece with the foreclaw of my other hand, I pop it into my mouth.

I've never eaten a fresh apple straight from the tree before, only old bits of apples my jailer brought me, but this one is nowhere near as sweet as I thought it might be.

How fucking disappointing.

"Hamburgers and pizza are still my favorite," I mutter before I toss the partially eaten fruit over my shoulder and step away from the trees.

I pull up sharply when I make out Emil's form at the window of the cottage opposite me across the garden.

His eyes are wide and his lips are parted.

I can only stare back.

I'm not sure what I could have done to surprise him.

I'm certain apples are for eating, so it can't be because I've committed some sort of culinary crime, and, other than popping a chunk in my mouth, I've done nothing much more than mutter to myself like I'm losing my mind.

As soon as he catches me looking at him, his expression changes. His lips soften and so do his eyes. There's a little crease in his forehead and a slight tilt to his head. And then, mysteriously, a hint of a smile that makes me want to close the distance between us and ask him what he's thinking.

Not that he would tell me.

But. *Damn.* My body had finally cooled down and now that aching physical need burns within me again.

All it took was a look.

Damn him.

I grind my teeth together, sensing my sharp, black teeth descend.

"Control is an illusion," I say again, forcing myself to break his gaze and turn away from him, putting one foot in front of the other in the direction of my pack.

I am determined to find a spot next to Anarchy and force myself to fall asleep this time, but I've only taken a few steps when a flash of sudden movement from the cottage catches my attention again.

Emil now stands in the doorway, fully visible.

He must have conjured fresh clothing because he's dressed in undamaged white pants once more, although he's still shirtless.

I pause, this time standing well within the garden, my hand brushing the edge of a rosebush, the petals soft beneath my fingertips.

There's an intensity in his expression that I can't decipher.

He's... angry, maybe.

Very different from the surprised look he gave me only moments ago.

Oh, but it's so hard to tell...

He takes a pointed glance at the sparkling trees behind me before returning his focus to me.

What do you want from me?

It's the question *he* asked *me.*

Without taking his eyes off me, he takes a single step away

from the doorway, slightly farther inside the hallway, still fully visible, and then—

His right fist darts out and crashes through the wall at his side.

I jolt.

I can only stare as he throws himself through the wall with a roar that reaches me where I stand.

Wood splinters in all directions, some of the debris shooting through the doorway and more through the window, while I'm certain even more debris is spiraling within the cottage itself.

Emil himself has disappeared behind the outer wall, and now I can only hear him.

There's another crash, more sounds of breaking wood, followed by smashing glass.

What the fuck?

I don't understand what he's doing, but dark saints, the crashing and cracking sounds that are coming from inside the cottage tell me he's tearing the place up like there's no tomorrow.

My eyes are wide as I pause on my front foot, uncertainty raging through me.

I'm also aware of Riot running toward me and that my pack is stirring in the distance. But of course, the commotion is hard to ignore.

"Darkness!" Riot calls my name before he reaches me in a flash, veering toward the cottage, as if he'll run into it.

I catch his arm. "No, Riot. Stay out here." Then I spin to the rest of my pack, holding my hand up for them to stop. *Don't come over.*

"What the hell is the keeper doing in there?" Riot asks.

I can only shake my head. "Breaking things up, but I have no idea why."

At that, there's a sudden silence from within the cottage.

Riot and I both freeze, waiting and watching, and I'm ready for anything.

CHAPTER TWENTY

$\mathcal{A}$ few moments later, Emil reappears in the doorway, looming there like a quiet, angry beast.

He's covered in scratches, his chest is heaving, and he's holding the broken leg of what could be the table he hoisted me onto.

He draws back his arm and, with a roar of effort, he pitches the table leg through the open doorway and across the air.

It shoots like a spear all the way across the garden and impales the nearest apple tree with a *thud*.

His chest heaves, but then, unnervingly, he gives me that same heated smile that he gave me through the window.

I blink at him.

And then, slowly, I half-turn to consider the orchard and the apple tree he impaled.

Suddenly, a new impulse fills me and now…

I'm pretty sure I've finally lost it.

"Riot," I say quietly to the dark elf, who has remained protectively at my side. "Can you go back to the campfire and make sure nobody comes over here?" I glance at my pack. "Especially Jonah."

The fire jotunn has reappeared at the edge of the forest and looks as if he's two seconds away from rushing over to me.

I guess meditation time is over.

"Are you sure?" Riot asks me, his arms rising as if he'll whisk me away from the cottage.

"No, actually." I can't help the ridiculous laugh that bubbles up into my throat. "I'm not certain of anything. But I want you to stay away from this cottage. No matter how noisy it gets."

Riot arches an eyebrow at me before he throws a glance at the keeper. "Noisy in a good way or a bad way?"

Again with that crazy laugh. "I have no fucking idea."

A little of the tension in Riot's expression eases. "Maybe we'll disappear for a bit. But we're only a shout away, okay?"

I nod. "Thank you."

Riot waits another moment before he hurries back to the pack.

True to his word, he gathers them up and ushers all of them, including Jonah, into the forest.

Anarchy argues with him the whole way, taking a final glance at me. Her soft voice reaches my sensitive ears. "I hope you know what you're doing, Darkness."

"So do I," I whisper.

Then they disappear into the forest.

I take careful steps toward the keeper, stopping only a short distance away from him.

"You hate that orchard," I say, taking guesses from his actions. "You want to smash it apart."

"Yes," he says.

I wait a moment in case he wants to say more, but it seems that's all. But, hell, that's more honesty than I've had from him for hours. So, I persist.

"I'll destroy it for you," I say. "*If* you tell me why you hate it so much."

Instead of responding to my offer, he asks, eyes narrowed, "Why did you throw the apple away?"

"Because it was disappointingly sour."

He arches his eyebrows at me, repeating what I said, as if he doesn't believe me. "It was sour."

"*Disappointingly.*"

He gives a soft exhalation, a bewildered sound. "I thought you would—"

Frustratingly, he seems to pull himself up and doesn't finish his sentence.

"You thought I would what?" I press. When he remains silent, I can't stop my own sigh. "Do you want me to destroy the orchard or not?"

The furrow in his brow deepens and a new snarl leaves his lips. In his voice, I detect the smallest hint of a dragon's growl for the first time since the fight with my father.

"That orchard should fucking burn," he says.

"I can make that happen if you tell me why you hate it so much."

"I hate it," he says, "because the orchard it represents is where all the pain started."

My eyes widen. It isn't an elaborate answer, but it isn't an evasion either, and I'm surprised by it. Even more so when he continues.

"I hate it because of the malice that thrived because of it. I hate it because it tore my family apart. And I hate it because its history will continue to tear families apart."

His family.

He has never spoken of his family before. In fact, he led me to believe that he didn't remember anything about his life before he became the keeper. But then, as has become painfully clear to me, he lies.

He could be lying now, too.

I take another look at the orchard, recalling what Jonah told me about how he met my mother. He said he came upon a cottage that was situated beside an apple orchard, just like that one. She was sweeping out the pain.

Even my mother and Jonah associated the original orchard with pain, just as Emil does.

Which makes me believe there is truth in what Emil said.

I find myself scouring my memory for any instance where my mother described the cottage or the orchard to me. She must have at least mentioned the cottage, or I wouldn't have dreamed about it in so much detail. Maybe she spoke of it when I was very little so that the images live in my subconscious and only come out when I sleep.

"I need to sweep out the pain," I say, a quiet declaration.

"Sweeping is not enough." Emil backs away from the doorway, and I'm certain he's about to retreat into the shadows again.

I can't allow him to do that. Not when he's finally giving me answers.

"No."

I'm not sure exactly what I'm saying *no* to, but my left hand is raised.

As if I could stop him by the force of my will alone.

When he pauses, partially concealed in shadow, I lower my voice. "I know better than most that there are some wounds that never heal."

He is not so deep within the darkness of the cottage that I miss the way he flinches.

He will understand my meaning.

He can't atone for taking my mother's life. Assuming any part of what the book showed me is true.

"But I made you a promise," I say. "So stay and watch. Or don't. That's your choice."

I turn on my heel and stride back toward the orchard, intent on violence.

As I approach it, the energy within the trees strikes me hard.

All of its sparkling prettiness. All of the impulses that buzz at me. And then, once again, and horribly unbidden, those cold commands that rush through my mind.

Take control of the—

"Fuck you," I snarl.

With all of my strength, I swing my left fist, claws fully extended, punching through the nearest tree's trunk.

The wood shatters and shards fly in all directions, a sequence of satisfying *crack-crack-cracks* splitting the air. The shards cut up my hand, biting back like a living thing, but with a single punch, my indestructible claws have achieved my intended purpose.

I've created a massive gash all the way through the right side of the tree.

Without hesitation, I strike again, widening the gash even as I sense the energy within the tree fighting back.

Such a strangely familiar energy.

It reminds me of my mother, but also not. Once again, I'm certain that even in some brief exchange, she must have told me about an orchard like this. Or maybe apples like these.

But what did she say?

Suddenly, it comes to me. That moment in time. Her golden eyes were downcast. Her left hand clutched around the leftover core of a red apple our jailer had brought to us.

"Even a sour apple is delicious if you're starving."

She was right. We shared that core, seeds, and all, and it was the sweetest thing I'd ever tasted.

Not these apples.

The tree creaks and groans and I jump clear before it topples and crashes into the next tree's trunk.

Crack! Branches snap and apples fall.

I'm already leaping toward the next tree.

As I move, there's a tearing pain in my back, my wings

extend on instinct, and I gain enough air to raise myself higher, punching and tearing through the tree's trunk, felling it with a scream of effort.

My wings clip a nearby branch, and, to my amazement, the edges of my feathers cut right through the wood.

They've never done something like that before, but then… I've never tried to use them that way.

I've watched Lucian use the edges of his feathers in a fight, and, even though mine aren't tipped with stone, they're metallic like my claws, so I guess it stands to reason that they could cut through things.

Well, damn. I guess my wings are useful for something, after all.

I ram my heel down onto the nearest apple, squishing it to a satisfying pulp, before I launch myself at the next tree in a near frenzy.

I tear and shatter and punch, cutting down the trees with my claws and my wings, breaking branches and shattering trunks.

Destroying this sparkling beauty, ripping it to shreds.

Until I'm screaming, but not from elation.

From pain.

Because no matter how many trees I cut down, and no matter how many apples I render to a pulp, I can't bring my mother back. I can't eat that awful apple core with her again.

I can't get back the years I spent in darkness.

I can't heal these wounds.

And, just as painful, I can't get back the trust I gave the keeper.

The man I thought he was—the one who stood at my side— is gone.

I've lost him, too.

I stop in the middle of the carnage, surrounded by torn-up tree stumps, trying to balance on piled-up wood, black blood dripping down my face and chest and arms and legs.

Wood splinters are caught in all parts of my body, little splinters and big ones, but I don't fucking care about that pain.

I turn to the cottage and then I spread my wings, lifting myself just enough to aid my progression across the rubble until I hit the grassy ground again.

Then I'm running.

Running toward the keeper, who stands back from the doorway of his cage, where he's shrouded in the shadows.

I don't slow down, crashing through the opening and right into his chest.

"Fight me," I scream at him.

He tries to grab my wrists, but I slash at him with my claws.

"Fight me!"

CHAPTER TWENTY-ONE

Emil's voice is as angry as mine. "No!"

Wrenching back from him, I strike, not with my fists but with my feet.

My right foot connects with his chest, a hard hit that propels him back along the hallway.

I rage after him with a scream, my fists landing on his chest and then his face in a combination Anarchy taught me that would have taken off any other creature's head.

He ducks and angles his body to absorb the impact, veering left until he hits the wall with a *thud*.

I'm suddenly aware that it's the only wall in the immediate vicinity that isn't broken.

The other side of the hallway is pure carnage. Wood and glass and metal are strewn everywhere on that side.

Having registered the mess, I don't pay it any further attention, my focus back on him.

"Fight back!" I roar. "Show me that you really are my enemy. Prove to me you're the monster who killed my mother. Show me what a liar you are. *Show me!*"

Throwing myself forward and leaping to gain air, I fully extend my claws and drive them at his face.

He jolts to the side, and my claws crash through the wall. The surface rips apart beneath the force of my strike. Shards of broken wood fly across the floor, away from Emil's position since I was wrenching my hand in that direction.

I swing back to him, throwing my fist at his face again, but he ducks, and my claws catch the wooden support that's still intact on that side of the hallway.

Another batch of wood shards flies through the air, this time not entirely away from Emil, who leaps even farther to his right to avoid them.

"If you're my enemy, then *be* my enemy," I shout at him, retracting my claws and going after him with my fists instead.

"No," he roars back at me, but his refusal only makes me angrier.

My fists fly, each attempted hit harder than the last, and my strikes grow faster, more aggressive until my arms are a blur and Emil is breathing hard.

He manages to evade every blow, but his agility is decreasing, and his movements become more sluggish.

I don't know why and, dark saints, I don't stop to wonder, even though I probably should.

My next hit lands squarely on his chest.

I must have split my knuckles at some point because my black blood splatters across his torso and up across his chin.

Which I aim for next, an uppercut that hits his jaw.

Smack!

The force of the blow knocks him back into the doorway between the hallway and the kitchen—the one room I didn't want to go.

As his back hits the doorframe, his eyes fly wide, and then their shape and colors change.

There's a flash of amber in his eyes and his irises become more wolfish than they've ever been, even in his many personas.

At the same time, his hands come up.

Dark light flickers around his left hand where he wears his crown, and he moves with a burst of speed that defies me.

He catches my hands and spins me around, gripping me from behind.

His arms feel like iron wrapped around my torso as he propels me forward—not along the hallway but into the kitchen where the curtains flutter and the room smells like *home* and I can hear my mother humming to herself.

"No." A broken gasp is all I can manage before my remaining rational thoughts desert me.

I shove myself back against him, desperately trying to push him through the doorway and out of this room.

But he was already moving at an angle, and I only succeed in shoving him against the wall next to the door.

We've remained inside the room and now I'm facing it.

"No!" I cry, struggling against him.

"I won't fight you!" His dark light streams around me, coiling like chains that propel me around to face him again.

If the light were solid, I could cut through it, but it's energy —dark energy—and I have no defense against it.

"Stop, my Veda." His arms rise around me, and now I can't tell if he's using his dark magic or his arms to pull me closer.

"I can't stop," I say, fighting the tears flooding my eyes. "I won't stop until I understand why you did what you did."

He shakes his head, the strands of his hair falling across his eyes, clinging to his forehead and cheeks, where sweat has gathered.

"You aren't what I thought you would be," he says. "I thought you would grasp the power that has been given to you and instead, you rip it up and throw it away."

"Power? What power?" My voice is suddenly bleak. "Do you

know why I reach for control as hard as I can, Keeper? It's because I've never had any. My life was dictated to me. Captivity was my constant. And you—"

I try to breathe. Try to speak.

"You walked out of the darkness with me. *You* did that. Out of the darkness. *With* me. And now…"

He considers me quietly. The ropes of dark light disappear from around me, freeing me, even though all I want is for him to rage at me.

Rage like he did when he tore through the cottage only minutes ago. Tear me apart like an enemy would.

Instead, he's silent.

It makes me realize that it's his silence that I hate the most.

When I first escaped my cage, it felt like we didn't stop talking.

We were both discovering the world around us. He gave me the night sky and the beach and hamburgers and a too-soft bed and hot showers and he made me believe my wings were beautiful and he convinced me there were such things as shark shifters.

But now, he gives me silence.

And for the life of me… it feels like it means something.

This horrible silence around him.

Just like his presence no longer feels real and that must mean something, too.

"I've lost you," I say, tears welling in my eyes. "You were my enemy all along, and I didn't know it and now, the person I thought you were… I've lost him."

All of the fight drains out of me as I realize…

I am not okay.

It's an insight I probably should have had before I tore through an unassuming apple orchard and tried to pick a fight with the keeper of dark magic.

I am not okay.

But of all the situations where I could safely break down, this is not it.

He leans toward me, inching closer with every heartbeat, and I know I should probably step away.

"If I could change the past, I would," he says.

He lowers his head to mine and his lips brush my cheek, pressing where my hot tears have had the audacity to trickle down my face.

His touch is gentle. Soothing.

He moves to my other cheek, pressing kisses to the multiple tear tracks there, too.

His head is bowed, one cheek against mine. "I did not want this pain for you."

I prepare to push him away, because he has no right to comfort me right now, but before I can make a move, there's a sharp pain in my shoulder.

I lurch away from him, my claws snapping out again.

CHAPTER TWENTY-TWO

Emil's hands fly up, and I register that he's holding a small, sharp-looking object for me to see.

It's a sliver of wood.

A glance at my shoulder tells me it was one of the splinters that got stuck in me during my orchard-destroying frenzy.

I glare at him. "*Ow.*"

He points to his chin where I smacked him and pointedly says, "*Ow.*"

My glare deepens. And then eases. *Damn him.*

He reaches toward me again, eyeing me carefully. "There's another splinter in your arm. It's pinning the material to your skin. Let me just—"

I wrench backward, registering the way the final tendrils of his dark light recede, leaving me free to move around.

"I can get it out myself." I quickly pluck at the narrow splinter, then at the splinters in my thighs and calves. The way I'd hitched the dress up and tied it into a knot has left my legs very exposed to flying shards.

At least the dress won't be torn when I let it down again.

Each splinter stings when I remove it, but I heal quickly.

I can't, no matter how hard I try, reach the final splinter that's lodged beneath my left shoulder blade. I nearly turn in circles, trying to grab it before I stop myself.

"Here," he says. "Let me."

"No."

His forehead creases. "You can't leave that wood in your body. I don't know what kind of magic these replicas are made out of, but the original trees were old magic. You don't want to mess with them."

My glare deepens. "*Now* you warn me."

A hint of a smile flickers around his mouth. "I really didn't think you'd tear it up."

"I offered you a deal. You answered my question, so I ripped up the orchard." I glare harder. "I honor my deals."

He stops reaching for me. "As do I."

"Clearly not."

His shoulders slump and then he's silent again. But not for long. "Will you let me...?"

Very slowly, he reaches for my shoulder, persisting beyond belief, but I'm forced to acknowledge that I can't get the damn shard out on my own. If what he said is true—and indeed, the energy I felt within the trees tells me that even the replicas could be dangerous—then I can't let my pride dictate my choices right now.

I angle my shoulder forward and turn slightly to give him better access. "Okay."

He focuses intently on my shoulder, his fingers brushing my skin as he carefully parts the ripped material. The gauzy dress was certainly insufficient armor against flying debris.

I close my eyes as he takes his time inspecting the shard, his touch gentle and soothing, before he quickly yanks it out.

I wince. Damn thing must have been embedded deeper than I thought.

Only a moment of pain shoots across my back before he swoops in, pressing his lips to the wound, feathering my skin.

I choose to stay where I am.

I choose to defy reality and pretend, for a moment, that he isn't my enemy.

My voice is a whisper in the quiet. "If I keep my eyes closed, you will be my keeper again."

His response is low and soft. "I will be your keeper until the moment of my death, my Veda. I will not be anything else."

His hands slip around my waist, pulling my back to his front before his mouth nudges the side of my neck. His right hand rests low across my stomach, a tantalizing inch above the top of my pelvis.

His thumb brushes across the gauzy material, and pleasure spikes between my legs, a heat that I literally tried to run away from.

It returns with a force I wasn't expecting, a deep, aching need.

"Say the word," he murmurs at my ear, his lips brushing my earlobe. "And I'll ease the ache you feel."

How often I forget that my heart tells him everything, even my desires.

"I think you already know my answer," I say.

With a groan, he dips his hand between my legs, finding my clit beneath my dress.

Heat and need swirl within my core as he strokes me, pleasure flooding my limbs, intensifying when his other hand cups my breast and strokes through the material.

I arch into his hands, both of them, needing and wanting more even though I know this is as close as we'll get.

I want his vulnerable, needy kisses. I want his naked body between my legs. I want every moment when I could have lost control but chose not to.

The climax comes quickly, a rush of heat, a shuddering

release that crashes through me with a force I wasn't expecting. A release that's complete enough to wipe away all the need within me, and yet it does nothing more than skim the surface of what I want from him.

I take what I can from it.

Physical release. An easing of my desire. The ability to focus beyond the pleasure he can give me.

It isn't enough. It wasn't enough.

I want to tell him so, even though I'm sure he senses it, but he speaks first.

"You should hate me again now," he whispers.

Then his arms fall away from me.

I open my eyes and now I'm forced to face the room, the brightening light through the window, and the reality that comes with it.

The kitchen is quiet. Emil is quiet. I can no longer hear the echo of my mother's humming.

"My home was never here," I say, completely out of context, but I need to say it out loud. "This whole place is a nightmare dressed up to look like the home I never had. But I can't find my home in the past."

Emil takes a step back from me, his presence becoming distant once more.

Oh, this fading distance. I hate it as much as I hate the silence that falls once again between us.

Before I can turn to him, a voice calls from outside the cottage. "Veda, dearest? Are you there?"

"It's Halle," I murmur.

She promised she would be back this morning.

My senses tell me that she isn't alone. There are two others with her, one with a burning hellhound scent and the other whose magic is more familiar. It can only be Orlan, the warlock who is loyal to Halle. I first met him on the train when I helped Elijah.

I step away from Emil but half-turn back to him. "Come with me or don't. It's up to you."

His forehead creases behind the curtain of his silver hair, a hint of confusion, but I sweep from the room before he can speak.

I'm satisfied when he follows me into the hallway, even though he keeps his distance.

Ahead of me outside the cottage, Halle stands within my direct line of sight.

As I sensed, the warlock Orlan is with her. He's dressed in a suit but wears it casually, with the shirt unbuttoned at the top and the jacket undone. He has neatly cut hair, bright eyes, and a strong jaw, and my guess is that he's only a few years older than me. He also wears tattooed runes on his palms, which he uses when he accesses his magic.

One of the hellhounds from yesterday stands with Orlan, and I recognize him as the one who took humanoid form. His skin is reddish-brown and his wavy, dark-brown hair is pulled up into a warrior's bun at the back.

As for Halle, she's in black jeans and a black T-shirt, although she has reverted to her sweet, fairy-dust persona with auburn hair, bright-green eyes, and freckles across her nose.

No doubt she chose it to disarm me.

Maybe she thinks I'll go easy on her this morning.

She doesn't wait for me to exit the building before she gestures to the cottage and then to the orchard behind her. "Dark saints, Veda. What happened here?"

My pack has gathered behind her and I'm struck with guilt at the worry in their eyes. They're all giving me a visual check over. Even Jonah is leaning forward, daring to stand near Halle and only stepping back once it must be obvious that I'm fine.

"I had feelings," I say to Halle as I pause at the door and still a step within the cottage.

She eyes the distance between us. No doubt because I

haven't exited the cottage yet. Maybe she thinks I'm trapped here, too. If she does, she doesn't say anything about it.

"Feelings?" she asks.

"Unhappy ones."

"But..." Once again, she glances at the rubble that remains of the orchard and then at the debris that has spilled through cottage door and windows. "Hmm."

I'm not sure what her humming sound means.

She considers me with a deep crease in her brow, and I suddenly feel like a specimen. Or perhaps a spectacle.

I guess I'm about to make myself more of one.

A reckless and possibly immensely stupid spectacle.

I scoop up my boots from beside the door where I left them earlier and shove them onto my feet.

Emil is now located only two steps behind me, and I exhale my doubts as I reach for him.

He stiffens when my hand wraps around his arm.

"Come with me or don't," I say again, tugging him firmly toward the door.

CHAPTER TWENTY-THREE

Emil's eyes are wide, but he doesn't fight me.

Why would he?

We step into the fresh morning air and his murmur sounds at my shoulder. "As you like, my Veda."

"Stop calling me 'your Veda.'"

He tips his head slightly. "Then choose a different name."

I nearly miss a step.

Choosing a name is easier said than done.

I chose *Veda*—Conqueror—based on a deep-seated rage when my vengeance seemed simple. I would cut off the head of the man who murdered my father, imprisoned my mother, and stole my birthright.

But now?

I am no fucking conqueror. I've failed at every turn. Even destroying the book feels like it's caused me more pain, more uncertainty, than it was worth.

My father is still alive. The Nostra Empire is still out of my reach. And my enemy stands at my right hand.

The air *whooshes* out of my chest. "I *will* choose a new name when I'm ready. In the meantime, call me your *enemy*." I tip my head back to look Emil in the eye. "At least there can be some honesty between us."

His expression is shadowed, but he responds with a soft, "As you like."

Then, my pack surges forward. We've made it three steps from the cottage and the wary looks they cast Emil aren't lost on me.

My brother reaches me first. "Veda, *why?*"

I've been asking myself the same thing.

That I'm acting on instinct doesn't seem like a good enough reason, but I try to explain. "Because nobody should stay here when I step through that door."

I gesture to the exit, then at our surroundings. "This environment is deceptive and volatile. I can't trust that Emil will remain caged when I leave. Better to keep him where we can see him."

Lucian makes unhappy noises, and so do the dark elves, but Jonah is quiet in the back. He's a creature of old magic and this place... this garden and forest and roses and apple trees... he may understand its nature far better than I can.

He gives me a small nod, an affirming gesture, and I hope it means he thinks I'm doing the right thing.

Halle's wry voice breaks across the air. "You certainly made short work of the orchard." She cranes her neck at the cottage. "And the furniture, by the look of things."

I give her a hard stare. "I'll make short work of any environment that threatens me or my pack."

Her lips pinch. "Still with the distrust."

"I've learned hard lessons," I snap back.

Her lips pinch before she shakes herself, clears her throat, and her voice becomes cheerful again. "Well, then, dearest, I'm certain that you're going to love Veritas."

I narrow my eyes. "Veritas?"

"It's what we call the place where truth can be sought," she says with a bright smile. "Distrustful creatures always love it."

From the tone of her voice, I'd think we were about to eat candy and ride unicorns across green meadows.

Oh, what fun.

"Lead the way," I say.

We follow Halle to the exit. Orlan and the hellhound proceed ahead of her and it's the hellhound who opens the door.

I don't tell Emil what to do, but he stays close to my left side while Anarchy remains on my right and my pack brings up the rear.

Jonah is last, following more slowly.

A glance back at him tells me that something is definitely on his mind. He keeps taking glances at the orchard and then to me.

He was chatty enough last night so I tell myself to wait. I'm sure he will choose to speak soon enough.

In the meantime, I focus on keeping Emil in my sights.

When we all leave the room, the door shuts quietly behind us, and I try not to wonder if the environment is wiping itself clean, ready for its next occupants.

We've stepped back into the main tunnel, and once again, I have a sense that the path curves very slightly, as though we're walking downward in a very wide spiral.

It feels like many branches extend from it since we pass doors and rooms and more tunnels along the way, some of them stretching off into the distance on either side. They're all different colors and none of them are as black as the main tunnel, so it's easy enough to stay on the main path.

"Nearly there," Halle announces after we've walked for a solid fifteen minutes.

A short time later, she slows her steps and finally comes to a stop outside an opening on the left-hand side of the tunnel.

"Do not step inside yet," she says, although she gestures me to her side. "There are rules you must understand first."

The opening is wide enough that it's easy for everyone to gather around me and still see inside. Emil stays on my immediate left, standing nearer to the side of the entrance, while the others keep a little more distance. I'm certain they will take Halle's warning seriously.

Unlike every other room and tunnel we've passed so far, the one that now sits on my left is as black as the main tunnel. Black rock rises up on all sides and across the ceiling. The space inside the room doesn't appear much bigger than that of my prison cell.

It looks like it will be a darn sight more cramped within it than I was hoping it would be.

A single word is carved into the stone above the entrance, each letter emblazoned in gold that catches the soft light: *Veritas*.

"Truth," Halle says, pointing to the carved name. Then, her attention snaps to Emil. "Stand clear of the magic," she says, her eyebrows pinching together. "The moment you touch it, the room will pull you inside."

Emil has lifted his left hand, his palm out. "This is old magic."

"That's why its power is unbeatable," she replies. "All creatures are affected by old magic. Even old gods like me."

Spinning to me, she continues. "Veda, it's very important that you understand the rules."

"I'm listening."

"First rule: only two may enter and both must come out. Second, once two enter, the room will seal itself off—you cannot see out from within it and nobody out here can see inside. Third, death cannot occur within this room. It's a mechanism for protecting the truth, since hearing the truth can sometimes induce rage."

She gives me a cold smile. "Of course, what happens once we exit the room is an entirely different matter."

Before I can comment on that, she hurries on. "Finally, and most importantly, this room will extract a price. It's why I didn't use it to force the truth from Jonah when I was trying to convince him to tell me where my brother is."

She gives Jonah a hard stare across the distance between them. He appears unmoved by her indignation, having taken up a position leaning against the other side of the tunnel as far from her as he can get without leaving altogether.

I arch my eyebrows at her. "But you're willing to risk a price by entering the room with me now."

"Oh, no, I should have clarified," she says. "Only the truth-seeker pays the price."

My eyes narrow at her. "That's a slightly important detail you omitted yesterday."

She shrugs. "The price is different for everyone. Some pay in physical pain. Others pay in mental anguish. The truth is not always what we want to hear. You won't know until you ask your first question."

She peers at me expectantly, and I have no doubt it's because she thinks I'll back out now.

She probably hopes I will.

"To strip away the lies," I say, "I'm prepared to pay any price."

She gives me a solemn nod. "Very well. Then I should explain how the room works. You may ask as many questions as you want for as long as you want, and I must answer them. Only when you declare that you are satisfied with the truth will the room let us out again."

"How will I know if you've spoken the truth?"

"The room will echo my answer back to you. If I speak the truth, the echo will match exactly what I said. If I tell a lie, the room will speak the truth for me. No matter what it is or how much I don't want it spoken."

Some of the tension leaves my shoulders. After hearing that the room will exact a price from me, I was beginning to wonder if there would be other loopholes. "So the truth is inescapable."

She nods firmly. "It can't be concealed." She gives me a hard stare. "You understand, don't you, Veda, just how dangerous it is for a creature like me... A being who has walked this Earth for millennia... to step into a place like this?"

Oh, I certainly do.

Before I can say so, she moves right up to me. "Do you understand the trust it takes for me to believe that you won't ask me anything that could get me killed?"

I consider the intensity of her expression and the hint of fear behind it.

All the memories she must have.

All the deceit that could be stripped bare in that room.

All the information I could use against her...

"I do," I say, reaching for her arm. "Believe me, I do. Which is why..."

I try to calm the beating of my heart and the terrible, awful fears that are crowding my mind at the choice I'm about to make.

I take a deep breath and prepare to move fast. "Which is why I'm not taking you with me."

I shove Halle away from me as hard as I can, pushing her into the corridor and away from the room.

She gives a shout, but I'm already twisting, both palms shooting out to my left, connecting with Emil's chest.

I don't risk any hesitation.

I can't give him the chance to evade me.

Wrapping my arms around him, I throw myself forward, taking him into Veritas with me.

CHAPTER TWENTY-FOUR

Emil's roar sounds in my ears, angry and unintelligible, a shout of pure fury.

The magic takes hold even faster than Halle warned me it would, a sensation like iron bars wrapping around my chest and dragging me farther inside the room.

Whatever power has now taken hold of us, it doesn't stop Emil from pushing away from me, both of us tumbling to the floor and landing several feet apart.

Just as Halle described, the opening is now obscured. A thick curtain of darkness has descended over it, very similar to the black rock around us, while lamps have appeared on each wall, sending soft lighting around the room.

I don't hesitate to speak in case the magic that controls the room requires me to stake my claim. "I am the truth seeker."

Emil shakes his head at me, snarling like a caged animal as he lurches to his feet and strides to the entrance.

He rams his palms against it, roaring at it when it doesn't give way. "You don't want the truth from me."

I could ask him why not, but I'm certain the answer will be complex.

I need to test the room first.

Rising myself up into a kneeling position and trying to calm my rapid heartbeats, I listen carefully.

I assess the silence in the room first—a silence that's only broken by Emil's seething breaths and a final slap of his palms against the barrier before he begins to pace from one side of the room to the other.

The room is so small that it only takes him ten paces before he has to turn around again.

Watching him carefully from my kneeling position on the floor, I take a breath and ask him a question to which I already know the answer. "What were the first words you spoke to me?"

I remember those moments so clearly.

I'd found myself—inexplicably—in his Realm, a place of complete darkness.

Later, he explained that the angels had committed a crime that had thinned the boundaries between his Realm and the veil prison, which was how I'd stepped directly from the prison into his Realm.

At the time, he'd glided toward me across a black, marble floor, his tall, wraith-like figure swathed in a black cloak that had made an unsettling swishing sound as he'd moved. The air had blackened even further when he'd approached, as if he had brought the darkness with him.

I hadn't been afraid of him in those moments.

In fact, a thrill had passed down my spine, and it had only grown stronger when I'd seen his crown, its spokes rising up over his forehead and past the top of his head.

The immense power in the crown had called to me like water to my parched lips. I'd experienced an undeniable compulsion to connect with the crown and, despite the danger of the keeper's presence, I'd reached for it.

Now, Emil glares around the room, taking a few moments

longer to answer than I thought the magic would allow. "You greeted me by my title: the keeper of dark magic. I was surprised that you knew who I was. So I simply said: *You know who I am.*"

As he speaks, an echo builds within the room.

A male voice that sounds exactly like Emil's repeats every word he speaks, ending with: *"You know who I am."*

The echo repeats several times before it fades, an eerie declaration. *"You know who I am. You know who I am..."*

Fuck me. Those might have been the words he spoke, but I'm so far from knowing who he is that my heart hurts.

Still, the echo repeated his words, which means he spoke the truth just now. Which, of course, I already knew.

I pause for another moment, waiting this time for the price that Halle mentioned. She said it could be physical pain or mental anguish. I suppose I feel some mental anguish, but it's no worse than what I was already experiencing...

I push on, choosing now to ask him a question concerning which I already know he lied to me. "Did you tether my mother's magic?"

When I first asked him that question, he told me he hadn't tethered her magic. It was his certainty that sent me into a spiral, questioning who my mother was and what had happened to her.

Now he has the chance to tell the truth and have it confirmed.

He tethered her magic. He just has to be honest about it.

He stops pacing and his eyes meet mine. His lips press together before his shoulders slump and his hair falls over his face.

Then, he says, "I did not tether her magic."

Fury rushes through me that even now, he lies to me.

Even knowing that the room will call out his lie and proclaim the truth, still, he *fucking lies.*

I fight the urge to launch myself to my feet, forcing myself to remain kneeling as I wait for the room to confirm his untruth.

The echo says, *"I did not tether her magic."*

Wait... what?

The echo repeats, fading into a stony silence. *"I did not tether her magic. I did not tether her magic..."*

My eyes are wide. *Is the room broken?*

Or worse...

My heart sinks as I say, "You can beat the magic in this room, can't you?"

His shoulders remain slumped, but he shakes his head emphatically. "I can't."

"I can't," says the echo, and then, despite confirming his statement, it says more. *"I can't defy the truth."*

He drops to one knee with a groan, pressing his fingers to his temples.

Unable to remain kneeling any longer, I lurch upright.

I dart toward him, stopping at the last moment before I would touch him. Our positions are now reversed. I am standing while he is kneeling.

"You ripped out my mother's heart."

"I did," he says.

The echo whispers, *"I ripped out her heart, and it hurt. It hurt..."*

I take a step back, the corners of my mouth turning down, my teeth sharpening. "How dare it hurt you? She was my mother. She was all I had. And you killed her!"

"I did," he says, his shoulder slumping further.

But then the echo says, *"I did not."*

CHAPTER TWENTY-FIVE

He... didn't... kill her?

I'm certain I've misheard the echo, and for once, I actually wish it would repeat, but it doesn't.

My voice is a strangled whisper. "What did you say?"

"I killed her," Emil replies in a quiet declaration. "I ripped out her heart—"

The echo cuts him off with a roar so loud that I jump.

"I didn't kill her! I took her darkness so she could be free. I ripped out the malice so she could be at peace. I died so she could live. She lived while I died. It should have been her. Not me. Not me. Not me—"

"Stop!" Emil shouts, his head snapping up, his green eyes wide, and his face deathly pale behind his silver hair. *"Stop."*

"I cannot stop," says the echo. *"I am the truth."*

My chest is heaving, my exhalations overly loud in my own ears.

I stare from Emil to the room, wishing I could locate this bodiless voice whose truths I don't understand.

Emil, too, focuses on the room, following the words in the air with his eyes. "You lie."

"I am the truth."

"No!" he roars at the room. "I killed her."

"*I didn't kill her. She was already dying. I took her darkness. I took its burden so she could be free. I took the pain and the malice and the darkness so she could be at peace—*"

"*No!*" Emil roars, bellowing out the denial so loudly that it's like a knife in my sensitive hearing.

Yet, a single word comes back at us.

"*Yes.*"

"No," he whispers. "I am the darkness—"

"*I am the light.*"

His eyes widen.

So do mine.

I don't understand anything right now, and my stomach is churning, turning into knots of fear and confusion.

He was right. So fucking right.

I shouldn't have asked for his truths.

He snarls like a predator, "I am the darkness."

The echo also speaks in a snarl, but this time, its words feel like an accusation. "*I was born to the brightest light. My life was stolen. I paid the price for crimes that were not my own. What greater darkness could there be?*"

For the life of me, it feels like the echo is demanding a response from *me*.

My voice has strangled in my throat. I have no answer to that question. I can't speak. All I can do is back away.

Emil slumps to the floor, rocking forward, nearly doubled over, his hands pressing to his temples. "I was the dark one. I was the dark one. I was the dark one..."

The echo repeats, over and over, "*I was the light. I was stolen. I was the light. I was stolen...*"

And then, out of the blue, the echo says, "*Vengeance will be mine.*"

Emil gives a muffled laugh from beneath his hair that sounds like a growl. "There is no vengeance for me. My fury has no resolution. All those responsible for my cage are already dead."

"*But their magic lives on,*" says the echo. "*Their magic must be destroyed.*"

Emil takes a sharp breath. Then, "I can't do it," he says. "I can't end what I've come to love."

There's a pause, a brief silence, and then, for the first time in long minutes, the echo repeats exactly what Emil said. "*I can't end what I've come to love.*"

I am stricken with confusion and fear and an overwhelming and unexplainable grief.

My eyes fill with tears and I don't understand why.

None of this makes sense to me, and I know I'm missing something absolutely critical.

I'm missing the right answer.

But I don't know the question that will elicit it.

I approach Emil carefully and quietly, watching for a reaction—any reaction—but he remains where he is. Doubled over. Slumped to the floor. Driven down…

I lower myself into a new kneeling position, so close to him now that my knees are only inches away from the top of his bowed head.

I try to breathe out my anxiety, try to bring moisture to my lips as I ask, "Who *are* you?"

His voice is bleak. "I am nobody."

"*I am nobody,*" says the echo. It speaks only once and then falls silent.

Softly, I persist, "What was your name?"

"It was taken from me."

"*It was taken from me,*" says the echo, again only once.

And then, there's silence. It's the same terrible silence that feels like it means something.

I'm suddenly reminded of a heated conversation between

Emil and Anarchy. It was one morning back on the island outside the little hut where I slept.

I woke up to their voices.

Anarchy spoke about the other keepers. She had been a youngling when they'd been created. She said there were whispers about who they were *and* who they weren't. But as for the keeper of dark magic, there was only a terrible silence.

She asked Emil why there was such a hush around his name.

He didn't give her an answer.

Perhaps it was because he couldn't.

"Nobody named you," I whisper, although it's a guess this time.

"*You* did," he says, his voice still muffled. "Diavolo. Keeper. Enemy."

"*I am your enemy,*" says the echo.

I thought he was my enemy because he took my mother's heart, but now I'm not so sure.

"Why are you my enemy?" I ask.

"Because my entire purpose is to constrain your magic," he says. "From the moment of my transformation, this was my fate."

"*Because I have no choice,*" the echo says. "*The magic in your mother's heart should have died with her. Instead, she passed it on to you. It is a magic so terrible that wars were fought to defeat it. Hundreds died. The soil was turned to ash and the sky to blood. It cannot happen again.*"

"I accepted my cage," Emil says. "A cage of darkness and a black marble floor that once belonged in a throne room, and I accepted that I couldn't escape it, even as it stole my flesh and tore at my skin and left me with nothing but a crown for thousands of years. I accepted it because I knew that one day, I would finally seize the last of that cursed black metal and then..."

His heavy exhale sounds into the silence.

"Then it would be over. But it was not."

As he speaks, the echo whispers quietly, repeating every word he says, but now in a voice that's growing fainter.

And still, Emil speaks. "Because there you were. You and your shadow panthers, running through my cage. So free. As if that dark space was pure bliss to you."

He lifts his head, but only slightly. Only enough for me to see more clearly his clammy forehead and a streak of blood near his hairline.

As the echo repeats exactly what he said, I reach for him, intending to brush his hair away from his face so I can see him more clearly.

"You saw me," he says.

"*You saw me,*" says the echo.

My hand pauses, my fingertips so close to him.

"You gave me your heart's power and freed me," he says. "You filled my chest with air and gifted my mind with free will and you looked at the world with an awe and a thirst for knowledge that would surely swallow it all.

"I kept waiting for you to show your malice. I waited for you to harm without reason and to kill without thought. I maneuvered you into situations where you would face light magic creatures and old magic creatures and dark magic creatures—angels and vampires and wolves and dragons—and each time, you let them live. You made peace and walked away."

The echo is so quiet now that I can hardly hear it.

"I encouraged you to unleash your rage on the world, and I waited for you to do it because I needed a reason," Emil says. "A reason to cut the thread between us, end the magic you don't even know you control, and free myself once and for all."

Emil gives a harsh laugh. "I put you in front of *The Book of Dark Magic* and you tore it up. I gave you an orchard full of power and you drove your claws through it. You plucked its pieces from your body as if they offended you."

"Except one," I whisper.

"Yes." He's quiet for a moment. "But only because you couldn't reach it and you were unable to trust me—"

He coughs suddenly, a dry cough that seems to catch in the air, echoing back at us.

"I broke your heart," he rasps. "And still, you chose hope."

I was already tense but now I am stricken and still. My fingertips hover near his face and yet I can't seem to close the gap between us.

I still have questions. So many unanswered questions, but there's one that might help me finally determine whether or not he truly is my enemy.

"What did my mother say to you before you took her heart?"

He coughs again, another dry sound, and this time, the air around me chills so sharply that it makes me shiver.

"She told me not to break."

The echo says, "*She told me not to break.*"

He finally looks up, raising his head and then his torso.

His pale green eyes are threaded with blood, his lip is split and bleeding, and a crimson gash rests across his forehead above his left eye. His chest is crisscrossed with lashes that have cut deep into his flesh, one so deep, I can see his rib bone.

My hand flies to my mouth. *Oh!*

So many wounds… And he isn't healing…

He coughs blood as he says, "But… my Veda… my Enemy… I'm breaking."

CHAPTER TWENTY-SIX

My strangled whisper sounds in the cold silence. "How is this happening?" I cast a panicked glance at the room. "Is this my price?"

He gives a labored shake of his head. "When your heart broke, I broke," he says.

The echo is so quiet now that I can hardly hear it.

"But it's stopped." My throat constricts around my protest. "My heart stopped breaking."

He shakes his head and coughs. "Has it?"

It's the first time since we entered the room that *he* has asked *me* a question.

I'm not compelled to answer, but I know the truth.

My heart has broken more every time I've looked at him since. Not because I was reminded of my mother's death. It was because I lost the keeper as a result of it.

How cruel that my grief at losing the man I thought he was will be the reason I will lose him now?

I whisper, answering honestly, "My heart kept breaking."

As I speak, the façade the keeper wears peels away.

His green eyes, silver hair, and broken torso disappear to

reveal the beautiful face he used to wear. The one that spoke to my fury and my darkness and brought me comfort.

He has the darkest blue eyes, like the sea that once churned in front of me. Black as night hair that reminds me of the panther's fur, the mantle of a sleek beast. A lean and dangerous body and the voice of a predator.

This is the face he wore when he led me down to a beach for the first time and gave me the gift of the beautiful night sky. The face he wore when he burned the horizon with fierce lightning and told me *I* was a beautiful darkness.

But with the change in his appearance, his wounds only worsen.

This is my price.

Knowing the cost of my heartbreak.

Cuts appear across his arms while crimson blood seeps through the black material now covering his legs, soaking through so badly that it's impossible to ignore. Another gash appears on his face, this one across his jaw.

I remember when I asked him to take off his green-eyed form, and he told me he couldn't, and I thought he was making a willful and defiant choice.

"I'm dying," he says, and before I can process my shock, he lifts his left hand from his lap, his forefinger outstretched.

The black crown rests on it.

Oh, the number of times its power called to me and now he's holding it out to me.

Offering it to me.

"This crown must be claimed," he says. "Its power must be contained and controlled."

But even as he extends his hand, a new fury rises within me. "That crown is keeping you alive. I've sensed it."

I've also sensed the growing *nothingness* around him.

I've heard the awful silence, as if his heart had stopped beating and he had already ceased to exist.

"That crown is yours," I say. "And you will keep it."

His eyes are glassy, dull, and increasingly unfocused. "I can't." He pushes his hand toward me. "You must take it now."

"No."

In response to my denial, a new tone enters his voice that makes me shiver. "The power you control… you haven't even asked about it…"

He's mentioned it twice without explaining it, except to make it clear that it's dangerous and unwanted and connected to the metal in my mother's heart.

Maybe I should have asked.

Or maybe, like so many dark things about my life, I should not. Because power, of itself, is not important.

It is the choices of the wielder that matter.

Another protest rests on my lips, but that's when it dawns on me that the echo has stopped. But why would it stop unless…

Unless…

He is already dead.

"You can't die here," I snarl at him, my teeth sharpening, my fear making me angry. "That's a rule. No death."

How dare he? Doesn't he realize that if he dies, I can't take my vengeance against him? I can't punish him for hiding his wounds from me, or for keeping his true thoughts from me, or for trying to manipulate me into becoming something other than what I am?

Even as those furious thoughts rage through my mind, there is another that takes over.

I can't lose him.

I may not have the full picture of what happened between him and my mother, but his story is far more complex than I ever could have imagined.

"No," I say to him, a command. "You will not die. Not until I'm finished with you."

I slide forward, wrapping my arms around his bloody torso,

inhaling the dark scent of his skin, tasting the copper scent of blood in the air.

He doesn't fight me, leaning into my embrace, his head lowering to my shoulder.

His left hand presses to my chest, the crown-shaped ring cold against my skin.

So is he. *Freezing cold.*

His lips are turning blue and his breath is frosting in the air.

"Take the crown," he whispers. "Take it before it's too late."

Again, I prepare to rebuke him, but the room's echo bursts into life, such a sudden influx of noise that I flinch.

"Take the crown," it commands me. *"Make it yours. Mold the living to match your will. Fight the old and find the new. Take control of the light and the—"*

I scream back at the room. "Fuck you! I'll take the crown when I'm good and ready. Not when you want me to take it. *Fuck you, you fucking fucker!*"

Then I lower my head to Emil, whispering, "Fuck you, too, whoever you really are. Whatever your name really is. Fuck you for breaking my heart and keeping secrets from me and thinking you can die on me before I'm finished with you." I gasp for breath as tears threaten to choke me. *"Fuck you."*

He nods against my neck.

His skin is so cold where he touches me that I'm shivering and trying to produce enough body heat to stay warm.

"Temptation," he whispers, his voice trailing off. "What will you do now, Darkness?"

A growl leaves my lips. "I'll fuck with temptation, too."

My declaration falls into silence.

The room is quiet.

It takes me a moment to realize... Emil is quiet, too.

I try to see his face, suddenly aware of how heavy his head has become where it rests on my shoulder.

"Emil?" I press my hand to his cheek. "Keeper?"

My eyes widen when he slides slowly forward, and it takes all of my strength to hold on to him.

"Keeper!"

His head tips back. His eyes are closed and his breath no longer frosts the air.

No.

"No," I cry. "You can't be gone! You owe me revenge. *Keeper!*"

My scream tears the air around me, but he doesn't respond.

CHAPTER TWENTY-SEVEN

$\mathcal{F}$ury floods me, and with it, my claws sharpen and my voice becomes a growl.

My back aches with the painful, prickling sensation that precedes the appearance of my wings.

I grip the keeper, one hand tangled in his bloody hair, trying to keep his head from falling to the floor, my other arm holding his torso to my chest as hard as I can.

"Do you think you can simply slip away from me?" I snarl into the silence, my lips near his ear. "Do you think it's as easy as allowing yourself to fade into nothing?"

My voice rises. "You *owe* me, keeper. Do you think a broken heart changes that?"

The weight of his body only increases and the amount of blood seeping from his wounds makes his torso slippery.

"Do you hear me?" I scream at him. Hot tears slip down my cheeks. "I'm not done with you." My voice lowers to a whisper. "Not by a long shot."

I press my lips to his cold cheek and my claws into his side, and I snarl at him. "Now *breathe.*"

His gasp sounds at my ear. A rattled breath. But he doesn't

speak and his exhalation dies down, the softest sound in the silence.

For a moment, I think it was simply a final expulsion of air from his chest, but when I press my cheek to his, I feel the quiet movement of air.

Cold air.

He's still freezing.

And unconscious.

"I'm going to get you warm," I say, my voice strangled as I speak with him, as though he can hear me. "I'm going to keep you alive. Not because I care about you, or because I want you, but because I meant what I said: I'm not done with you."

My snarl fades as I hold him closer.

I'm not done with him.

Taking a shaky breath, I keep hold of his head and lower him carefully to the floor so I can adjust my position. Hooking my arms under his armpits and around his chest, I call on my strength and drag him toward the opaque opening.

A cry leaves my lips as I breach the energy that's keeping the room separated from the corridor outside. "Help!"

My pack is right where I left them all, although Halle and her hellhound are now standing farther away on my left.

Jonah lurches upright as soon as he sees me, hurrying across the distance.

As quick as the jotunn is, Riot and Lucian reach me first, taking the keeper from me while Rumble and Strife quickly step in beside Jonah to assist. I'm grateful that they don't ask questions, immediately working together to lift the keeper into the air.

Anarchy is at my side as I stumble backward. "Darkness! You were gone for hours."

"I... What?"

Her face is paler than normal. "We thought you might never come out. I was ready to rip out Halle's throat."

Anarchy might not be able to kill Halle, but she and her brothers once fought off James Vanguard with their panther claws and teeth. She could certainly do some significant damage.

"I'm okay. Really." I hurry to assure Anarchy. "But I need to get the keeper warm and figure out a way to help him."

I spin to Halle as I finish speaking. I want to take her to task for her claim that nobody could die in Veritas, but now is not the time to delay.

"I'm taking him back to that room. My place. With the forest and the cottage." I stumble a little because I have no idea what that place is called. "I need a warm environment, and it will respond to my needs."

Halle has already ventured forward to consider the keeper, her lips pursing as her gaze darts from his head—now dark-haired—to his bloody chest and finally to the ring-shaped crown on his finger.

I expect her to argue or have a different opinion, but she quickly nods. "Yes. Immediately."

She gestures to Orlan, who has also lurched away from the wall. "Orlan, if you will."

I step in front of the warlock. "If you plan on translocating him to that room, then I'm coming with you."

Orlan shakes his head. "Using translocation magic could cause him further injury. But I can use my power to carry him. It'll be quicker this way."

The warlock claps his hands together, the runes on his palms lighting up bright blue as he pulls his hands apart and stretches the light between them. Then, his fingers move rapidly through the air, weaving the light until it has formed a lattice that floats beneath the keeper's elevated body.

"You can let go now," Orlan says to my pack. "I will float him to your destination." He inclines his head at me. "Under your watchful eye, of course."

"Good. Keep him beside me." I step close to the keeper as my pack carefully releases their hold on him and he remains suspended in the air. "Let's go."

I hurry forward and Orlan keeps pace with me, half-jogging on the keeper's other side while my pack stays close.

Along the winding tunnel we go, moving silently until we reach the same door where the cottage and orchard are located. I lean forward and press my left palm against the door, waiting for the sharp prick when it takes my blood.

"Give me warmth," I whisper.

I'm surprised when it doesn't sting this time, but I guess it must know me already.

The door swings open.

A blast of cold air hits me, knocking the breath from my chest. "What? *No...*"

A snow-covered clearing lies ahead of me.

The brightness of the sunlight reflecting off the cold surface hurts my sensitive eyes, and I fling my arm across my face, squinting hard to see what lies within the snowy landscape.

Trees stretch out from both sides of the doorway, forming a line so thick that it feels like a barrier on this side of the clearing.

Directly opposite me, on the other side of the clearing, is a long, rectangular cabin. It's set against the side of a mountain that extends high into the sky.

There are no obvious openings into the cabin until I crane my neck to the left, identifying what looks like a door on the short end, and, if I peer hard at the cabin's roof on the long side, I can just make out concealed turrets in it.

On the left of the clearing are two smaller buildings, also hewn from wood. One is enclosed and looks like a little hut, but the other is open at the front and contains a solid-looking metal table, the shape of which looks a bit odd to me. It isn't like the kind of table I've eaten food at because it's narrow and tapered at one end.

It's a strange experience to see a door opening into a wild landscape like this while the trees on either side of the doorway give a sense that the area extends in every direction, including backward.

"What is this place?" I struggle to understand how it came to be when I asked for warmth. "This isn't what we need."

I lean through the opening while the keeper's unconscious form floats on my left.

Halle's voice sounds at my shoulder. "Are you sure? This room only opens in response to touch, and you—"

"*Oh.*" My gasp is strangled. "What if it wasn't me?"

I consider Emil as he floats beside me.

A chill settles at the base of my spine when I focus on the way the strands of his dark hair are floating outward and brushing up against the door.

My heart is in my throat as I whisper, "This place belongs to the keeper."

CHAPTER TWENTY-EIGHT

*N*ow I have a decision to make.

Do I take him inside? Or carry him away?

I shake my head in uncertainty. "How can this be what he needs?"

As I speak, my senses prickle.

The scent of a predator reaches me.

Distant growls waft across the air.

I take a defensive step back. "There's something else in here with us and it isn't a bunny rabbit."

My pack stiffens behind me. I hear their quick inhales and their shuffles. I don't want to take my eye off the environment in front of me, but I know they'll be taking up attack positions outside the door at my back.

Just then, a large, gray wolf burst from the trees that circle the clearing on the right, racing directly toward me.

Its fur is dark gray, its eyes are amber, and I'm struck with a startling clarity: it isn't a wolf shifter.

It's a natural wolf.

Which only makes it more dangerous. A shifter could at least be reasoned with.

I brace, ready to grab the keeper and push him behind me, my left hand reaching for the doorframe as I prepare to shove him back into the corridor and slam the door shut.

At the last moment, the wolf comes to a halt, leaps to the side, and turns in the other direction. Its hind legs bunch, as if it's about to pounce on something behind it, a confusing change of focus.

A heartbeat later, another wolf sprints into the clearing, this one pure white with bright, blue eyes.

It leaps at the gray wolf, but its claws aren't extended. It's a playful lunge, and they both tumble through the snow before tussling again.

Then they return to their feet, briefly nudging each other in an act the wolf in me recognizes as an expression of family bonds. At that, they pad away together toward the trees they first ran from.

Their heads are raised, their eyes bright and focused on the same point ahead of them. Focused on something I can't see, but they don't seem alarmed by it. They hurry eagerly toward it and then—

They're gone.

Vanished into thin air.

I can't stop my whisper. "What the fuck?"

I'm preparing to turn to Halle for an explanation when sudden movement makes me jolt back to the clearing.

The gray wolf races from the trees again, running forward before stopping in the middle of the clearing to turn around again.

Just like it did before.

My eyes widen when the white wolf darts from the trees to pounce on the gray wolf. They tussle, right themselves, nudge each other, and pad toward the trees and then—

They're gone again.

I spin to Halle. "What is this?"

Her face is pale. "Veda." She speaks cautiously. "When you created your cottage and your forest and all that… it was from your dreams, wasn't it?"

I nod. I'm not surprised she knows that because the keeper had leaned in and said as much to me at the time, reminding me that I should have guarded my dreams. She would have overheard him.

"And, just to confirm, it wasn't actually a place you had visited," she continues. "Was it?"

"Of course not," I say. Given what Jonah said about the original cottage and orchard, they no longer exist—they haven't existed at all in my lifetime."

Halle angles herself through the narrow gap between me and the door. Her feet sink into the snow and she gives a violent shiver. "This place, too, must be from the keeper's dreams. A place long ago destroyed."

She turns to me just as the wolves reappear behind her, playing in the snow without any awareness of our presence. Then they flicker and disappear again.

Halle gestures to them. "His dreams are breaking apart. Just like he is."

"I can't take him inside there," I say, still squinting at the brightness.

Goosebumps rise on my skin, and the breeze lifting off the snow chills me to the bone.

Jonah's voice sounds behind me. "You must take him inside," he says. "Look."

He points at the keeper's chest.

The blood has stopped flowing so freely from his wounds and his breathing is a little stronger. Just a little. But noticeably so.

Anarchy and her brothers are also nodding. "We are dark elves of the House of Dark Dreams. Sometimes, the most dangerous dream is the one that brings you clarity."

"Okay," I whisper. "But—" I can't stop my shudder. "It's fr-freezing."

Jonah squeezes past me, ignoring Halle's disgruntled glare.

"That's a longhouse," he says, gesturing at the building. "It's Einherjar architecture. Given its detail, I'm certain there will be coats and furs inside. I will bring them."

I remember that he mentioned protecting the Valkyries' followers—humans who called themselves 'Einherjar'—so I hope he's right.

Without waiting for permission, Jonah hurries across the snowy landscape and disappears inside the structure before coming back with his arms full of furs. He hands me a coat that's an eerily good fit before handing out the others.

Halle doesn't wait for hers, pushing through the snow and nearly sinking to her ankles. Other than grunting with effort as she plows across the clearing, she doesn't seem to notice the cold, trudging forward resolutely toward the cabin door on the far left, closer to the side of the mountain.

Even with the warm coat, I'm relieved to make it across the clearing and into the longhouse. Also, because it's easier for me to see inside the dimly lit space.

The inside space is long and rectangular, with a set of stairs at the far end. They lead up to a loft that sits around three sides, and it looks like there are multiple internal access points to the turrets I noticed on the roof.

Most importantly, there's a firepit in the center of the floor immediately ahead.

I hurry toward it. "Jonah? Fire, please?"

While Jonah sets about creating a warm blaze—which I force my eyes to tolerate, given its warmth—Orlan lowers the keeper onto the fur beside the hearth.

I kneel there, too, bundling up a second fur to place under Emil's head.

Orlan's voice is quiet as he steps back. "I'm sorry I can't

do anything about his wounds. I'm not a healer. My specialties are transportation and weaponry. But I know enough about injuries to say that those are self-sustaining. Even if I could heal him, his wounds would break apart again."

"I understand," I say. "Thank you for bringing him here."

With a nod, Orlan moves away to join the hellhound on the far side of the room.

My pack gathers around the hearth after finding more fur rugs rolled up on the far side of the room, which they then lay around the fireplace to sit on. Anarchy hands me two of the furs to wrap around the keeper.

I'm torn between trying to make him warm—despite the fact that it seems nothing will do so—and needing to keep an eye on his wounds.

Even so, I do what I can, tucking the two rugs around him up to his chin while telling myself I can check his injuries from time to time.

Halle, too, settles close, although she finds her own corner of a fur to sit on.

Once again, Jonah has taken up a position farthest away from Halle, leaning against the wall on the far side, where he's half-encased in shadows.

I expect my pack to demand information, but Halle gets in first. "What happened?" she asks. And in the next breath, she grumbles, "And why would you drag the keeper into Veritas instead of me?"

I cast a glance her way. "Because I actually believe that you will tell me the truth. *Without* needing that room. The keeper would not."

She unfolds her arms. "Well. That's…" She splutters a little. "That's nice to hear, but you could have made that clear earlier. I don't offer my help very often, and I was a little insulted that you threw it back in my face."

I arch my eyebrows at her. "You would have thought it was strange if I trusted you too easily."

She gives that a moment's thought and then shrugs. "True."

I return my attention to the keeper and now my shoulders slump.

"I don't know what to do," I say.

I look up at my pack.

Anarchy prompts me. "Maybe if you tell us what happened?"

I sift through the information I gleaned while I was in Veritas and decide it's best if I recount it in a few simple statements, even if they're baffling. "He didn't tether my mother's magic. He did rip out her heart, but she was already dying. He can't achieve his own vengeance because those responsible for his pain are already dead, although their magic lives on. His name was taken from him. He is my enemy because his purpose is to constrain a power that my mother passed on to me. And he is..."

Now I stumble over the most baffling thing of all.

"Veritas insisted that he is light, not darkness."

Everyone around me wears creased foreheads, casting confused glances at each other.

Except for Halle.

And maybe Jonah, who has stepped back into the shadows at the side of the room.

"I believe I can fill in some gaps for you," Halle says. "If you're willing to answer some questions along the way?"

I don't see how I have a choice at this point.

I came to the Underworld because the keeper brought me here. My father is out there, no doubt looking for me, and now the keeper is barely alive.

"I am willing," I say. "Please tell me what you know."

CHAPTER TWENTY-NINE

*H*alle folds her hands in her lap.

"You told me that you only recently learned about your mother's mechanical heart," she says. "What do you know about it?"

"The dragon master, Ryuji, told me—"

Her eyes fly wide. "Ryuji? You spoke with the dragon master?"

"He gave us permission to stay on his island."

"Well. Then that rumor is true," she muses. "How on earth did you wrangle that? Dragon masters kill first and ask questions later."

"Well, they did try the whole killing thing," I say. "And it was all a bit awkward, but I convinced Ryuji to help us."

"Okay," she says, her eyes still wide. "So he told you about Galeia's heart."

"He wanted to find out more about my claws, since I cut up his scales with them." I grimace at the memory, but it was what saved my life. "He searched through the ancient texts and found that, in the history of our world, there have only been two other recorded cases of supernatural creatures who had claws like mine."

Halle nods. "The first would have been the Vandawolf."

"Yes, the Vandawolf, who was human. Until he was turned into a beast by supernaturals, who controlled an arcane power that nearly destroyed the world. At least, that's what Mother told me."

"I'm assuming, then, that the second recorded case Ryuji's texts spoke of was your mother," Halle says.

"That's correct," I reply. "He told me that the same arcane magic was used to create my mother's heart. But he also said there was no familial relationship between her and the Vandawolf. They were separate beings impacted by that magic at separate times."

Halle purses her lips. "Hmm."

I'm surprised when she doesn't sound convinced, but she continues before I can question her.

"How much do you know about that arcane magic?" she asks.

"I know it was infused into metal," I say. "I also know that it was considered so dangerous that every piece of it was destroyed after those beings were defeated. Except for my mother's heart."

"What else do you know?" Halle asks, peering as hard at me as I'm now peering at her.

"That's it," I reply.

She stares at me for a moment longer before she asks, "What about those arcane beings themselves? What do you know of them?"

I shake my head. "Only what I've told you already. They nearly ruined the world. The Vandawolf brought them down. Their metal was destroyed. Their magic no longer exists."

"Oh, child." She exhales so heavily that it's impossible for me to take offense at her tone, especially when she chews her lip sharply enough to break the skin and reveal the ashen flesh beneath.

She refolds her hands in her lap. Twice. "First, you should know that those arcane beings were called 'Blacksmiths'. They were so named because of their affinity with metal. I'm telling you that simply because it will make our conversation go easier if we call them what they were."

Again, she refolds her hands, a seemingly restless movement that tells me she's thinking hard before she speaks. "But you're missing a very important piece of information."

"Which is?"

"Not every Blacksmith was capable of the kind of destruction that warranted their annihilation. Oh, they became a cruel people, that's for certain, but not all of them could render the kind of power that belongs in nightmares. No. The Blacksmiths who had that sort of power were extremely rare."

I should be leaning away, preparing for the worst, but instead, I crane forward, thirsty for knowledge and answers, no matter what they are.

All around me, my pack—the dark elves, my brother, even Orlan and the hellhound—is doing the same, as if they're hearing things for the first time, too.

Once again, only Jonah remains in the shadows.

"You must understand, Veda," Halle says. "That even knowing about this power is dangerous. Very dangerous."

As she speaks, her pixie façade peels away and her death goddess appearance rises. One half of her face and body appears blackened and charred. Her eye on that side gleams red. Her clothing splits down the middle so that she's wearing black leather on her un-living side, although her other side remains alive.

But it, too, changes, becoming wizened.

Soon enough, her living half takes the form of a woman with

gray hair and slightly stooped shoulders. A much older version of herself than she's ever shown me.

"Many humans and supernaturals would kill to attain knowledge about the Blacksmiths." Halle presses her wrinkled, living hand to her charred heart. "Your mother knew this. I believe it's why she never told you these things. She wouldn't have been able to risk speaking of them once she was captured, in case she was overhead. Dark saints, if those *angels* had found out about the power she carried in her chest..."

Halle spits the word 'angels' as if there were no darker beings than those creatures of the light.

"I also believe," she continues, "that when the books of magic were created, part of their purpose was to drain all knowledge about Blacksmiths from the pages of every other book. Much like the keepers were created to drain and tether the magic of the dead. To keep it from falling into the wrong hands.

"Even my own family—my older brother, the wolf—was obsessed with attaining the books of magic and discovering the secrets they contained. As for how even a small piece of this information got into one of Ryuji's texts... well, I can only guess the books allowed it for some mysterious reason."

She peers at me meaningfully and I assume she's trying to silently tell me that *I* was that reason. As if the books had predicted I would be on that island, asking questions of a dragon master, at that point in time.

I shudder at the power that could have identified those events so accurately.

Halle takes a breath, swallowing visibly. "But you, dearest Veda, you have forced this knowledge to resurface. You have forced it to be spoken of once more by those of us who still remember it." She glances around at the others—my pack, her people, and finally, Jonah.

"I could ask everyone to leave," she says. "I could continue protecting this knowledge. Just as the keeper has continued protecting it, speaking in riddles, tell untruths to conceal all of the terrible knowledge from coming out." She rubs her face. "But what am I to do, dearest Veda? Dark saints, what should I do?"

When she looks up at me again, I say simply, "I am more of a danger without this knowledge than I am with it."

I take a deep, shaking breath as I voice the things I've learned about myself, even if I don't understand the *why* or the *how*. "My father told me I'm very difficult to kill, even if there was a vision in *The Book of Dark Magic* that showed my end. And even then, it was one supernatural who ended me. *One.* After I kill thousands."

Even the crimson wolves in Portland—powerful creatures of old magic—said I was dangerous. Dangerous and *wounded*. But they also said, despite their instinct to end me, that I should live.

"Then I went and killed a book of magic without understanding how or even knowing that I *could*. What else could I do without knowing the consequences? So, I say again, I am more dangerous without knowledge than with it. And here is what I also know..."

I cast my gaze across my pack, to Anarchy, Riot, Rumble, and Strife, these gorgeous dark elves with their luminous, blue eyes and lilac hair and dark-as-fuck souls. And then to my brother with all his strength, even if he was told his whole life until now he was weak.

"These beautiful, loyal, strong beings who have chosen to stand beside me... they need to know how to stop me, if it comes to it."

I pin Halle with my gaze. "So fucking spill it, Goddess."

Halle seems to manage a smile, although it quickly fades. "Very well. Then you should know this: The most powerful Blacksmiths were from two separate families. That is, separate Houses: House Ironmeld and House Silverspun. One tore the world apart. The other bent the fabric of reality to save it. Both at a terrible cost."

A shiver runs down my spine, my palm chilled where it rests near the keeper's face.

"One of those Blacksmiths was responsible for creating your mother's heart, but she never knew which," Halle says, pausing for a moment to let her meaning sink in. "She was a baby when it happened. She never knew if she carried pure malice or pure hope in her heart. She never knew if she'd been kept alive because of hatred or love."

The fear in Halle's eyes strikes me hard as she says, "And now, the question that plagues me is this: whose power have you absorbed?"

CHAPTER THIRTY

I'm frozen where I sit. "You think I absorbed..."

"Blacksmith magic." Halle nods. "From your mother's heart. From one of the most powerful Blacksmiths to ever walk this Earth."

I squeeze my eyes closed, remembering what the echo said in Veritas.

"The magic in your mother's heart should have died with her. Instead, she passed it on to you. It is a magic so terrible that wars were fought to defeat it. Hundreds died. The soil was turned to ash and the sky to blood..."

"It is a power that can transform any living thing," Halle continues. "Like a human man into a beast. An animal into a monster. Sky to blood. Earth to ash. Living flesh to stone. It is limited only to the imagination of its wielder." She shudders, her charred half becoming dull and gray.

"Do I control that arcane power?" I ask, seeking complete clarity.

Halle's expression is grim, her half-living, half-dead appearance remaining firmly in place. "You tore through *The*

Book of Dark Magic, which was created by Blacksmith magic. Your claws may be able to cut through many things, but only the strongest Blacksmith magic could destroy that book like you did."

Despite my need for answers and my determination to hear them, my hands start shaking.

There's a part of me that feels outside myself. It's a part that wants to run as far as I can away from everyone I care about.

Because... *dark saints*... I told a book of magic—one of *the* books of magic—to die. And it did.

What kind of terrible power is this?

No fucking wonder my mother wouldn't speak of it, and the keeper talked only in untruths and riddles.

If this is the sort of power that those Blacksmiths controlled, then I really am a danger to everyone around me. Just like Jonah warned.

I find myself looking to him now because he also said he had faith in my mother, and she wanted me to live.

And that's the only reason I stay right where I am.

Because she believed in me.

So now... I will believe that I am supposed to be here, sitting next to the keeper, my hand pressed to his heart, in an environment that seems to be calming him, even though I don't understand how.

I speak carefully because I need to face a hard truth.

"If I absorbed this power from my mother's heart... but she needed her heart to live..."

Halle doesn't respond, her unliving eye becoming dull while her living eye becomes shadowed.

"I was draining her life," I say, trying to breathe past the pain in my chest. "Her heart failed because I... because..."

Anarchy reaches for me, but it's Jonah who makes a move, stepping from the shadows. "Remember what I told you, Veda," he says. "Your mother wanted you to live. She had lived for thousands of years and she did it with purpose. You were very important to her. *You* were her purpose."

I swallow hard and breathe out the pain, refocusing myself with all my might, moving past the sadness to the questions that come with it.

Because I can't get lost in my sadness now. I need all of the answers. "If I absorbed this power from my mother, then why didn't she control it herself?"

"I have been asking myself the same question," Halle says, more quietly now. "She never exhibited any signs of Blacksmith magic. Until you tore apart the book, I would never have even considered the possibility that the power could be passed on, or that you might control it."

"You must have theories?"

"I have two. The first is most likely. Her mechanical heart was given to her as a baby. It transformed her the same way that the arcane magic transformed the Vandawolf. He didn't control Blacksmith magic, either."

"Whereas I was exposed to it from the moment of conception," I say.

She nods.

"Your second theory?"

"More complicated. You see, Blacksmiths couldn't access their power without specially forged tools. Those tools were a crucial conduit, without which they may as well have been human. Even the most powerful Blacksmiths couldn't access their power without their hammers."

"Hammer?"

She nods. "Black titanium hammers for House Ironmeld. Silver hammers for House Silverspun. Without their hammers, all Blacksmiths may as well have been completely powerless. If your mother did have the power, well... she didn't have a hammer. So her power may as well have not existed."

My forehead creases. "Then how did I access the power we

think I absorbed?" I ask. "Even if your first theory is correct—my mother never had the power because she hadn't been born with it—I would need a hammer. I don't have one."

"Well…" she says, peering at my hands. "You have your claws."

My forehead creases again. "My claws?"

Halle nods. "Metal is part of your body," she says. "But to really understand it, I have more questions for you, if that's okay?"

Before answering her, I lift my hands off the keeper, and, far more carefully than I ever have before, I extend the claws of both hands, studying them. "Okay."

"Only one hand is powered," Halle says. "Which hand did you use on *The Book of Dark Magic?*"

"My left."

"Then that is the hand with power."

It's also the hand I used to create the place with the cottage and orchard.

"When you struck *The Book of Dark Magic*, did you hit its core?" She hurries to explain. "Each book has a metallic core that would mimic the magic in a hammer."

My eyes widen. "When I broke through the book's surface, it felt like I was cutting iron. These two metallic forces—my claws and the book—they literally *shrieked* against each other."

I wince at the memory of the sound it made and the painful bolt of energy that traveled through my body and into my heart.

That was when I experienced the dark impulses for the first time. The impulses telling me to take control and mold the world to my wishes.

"Then the book's core could have acted like your hammer," Halle says. "A conduit for the first time."

It would explain how I've used my claws many times before without accessing this power. Like trying to break through the magic that was sealing my prison. Even fighting Halle's brother, then my father. All the fights when my claws behaved simply like claws. Even if they are powerful ones.

I relax a little. "So without a hammer, I'm not going to accidentally kill someone?"

She nods. "You won't."

I slump with relief, but my thoughts splinter in many directions. One train of thought is incredibly relieved because I don't have a hammer, so I don't have to be afraid of this power that enables me to kill or transform a living creature at a mere whim. The other is that I still have questions about my mother, and I certainly don't have answers about the keeper.

"What about my mother's parents?" I ask, glancing at Jonah. He urged me to ask Halle about them. "Everything you've said is based on the foundation that she wasn't a Blacksmith herself, but you said that without a hammer, you wouldn't know."

"You're asking if she was the daughter of a Blacksmith?" Halle asks, a little too smoothly. "I never considered it. First, because I assumed she was like the Vandawolf—affected by Blacksmith power without controlling it. And second, because of her hair."

I tilt my head, curious. "What about her hair?"

"All Blacksmiths had hair resembling fine strands of metal. Depending on their parentage, the color often matched their House. Your mother didn't have that hair. Neither do you. Which is to say, neither of you was *born* to a Blacksmith."

It doesn't escape me that if a Blacksmith were capable of causing such a transformation as turning a human man into a beast, then they could change the color of a Blacksmith child's hair.

But I guess for now, it doesn't matter. I have this power now either way.

My burning need for answers about the keeper pushes me on.

"What about the keeper?" I ask. "Do you have any knowledge about who he was?"

Halle is quiet. Pensive. She takes much longer to answer this time. "I didn't witness the creation of the keepers. I don't know who they were. But there are some clues."

My head lifts a little as a spark of hope lights within me.

"One thing was common knowledge at the time," she continues. "Each of the other keepers volunteered."

"Each of the *others*?"

"The old magic keeper, the elemental magic keeper, and the light magic keeper. They all volunteered."

"But what of the dark magic keeper?"

Now Halle shakes her head. "Nobody knew. There was no information about who he was or whether or not he had willingly given his life."

"How is that possible? How could nobody know?"

Halle contemplates the keeper for a moment before she continues. "Galeia spent years trying to find out who he was. She believed that the clues were in the absence of information." Halle appears to struggle to choose her next words. "That the silence around his identity was important."

That silence.

Always, it seems to come back to that awful silence.

I'm uncertain about why my mother would have been so intent on finding out his identity, but for now, the more important question is what she found out.

"Did she discover anything?" I ask, leaning forward.

Halle's lips purse. "Well, she had theories."

Damn. More theories. But I guess they'll be more than I had before.

"One was that a volunteer wasn't needed at all—that the arcane magic was so evil that the keeper sprang into existence from darkness itself," Halle says. "Another theory was that the dark creature who volunteered did so under strict secrecy. After all, a dark being choosing to do something so heroic? That might not go down so well with other dark creatures, and maybe they had a family to protect."

My forehead puckers, and without me saying anything, Halle nods.

"I agree. Neither of those rang true to Galeia or me. Which led Galeia to her final theory. A far worse one."

"What was it?"

"She believed that there could be no greater darkness than the corruption of pure goodness." Shadows grow in Halle's eyes, and, for a moment, her deathly side seems to spread across her living face. "How truly evil would it be to take an innocent being and force it into darkness against its will? Such a cruel act would create a force powerful enough to tether dark magic for millennia."

Suddenly, all I can hear is the echo that sounded in Veritas.

"My life was stolen."

"I paid the price for crimes that were not my own."

"What greater darkness could there be?"

"If you're right, then the keeper was—" The words stick so hard in my throat that I can barely utter them. "The keeper was a good person."

"A truly good, innocent being." Halle nods. "A being without malice or cruelty or spite. That was your mother's belief."

The shadows in Halle's eyes only deepen as she continues. "But there's more."

I'm struggling to process what I've just learned means, let alone that there could be more.

There is such a chaos of emotions within me now: disbelief, sadness, and, ultimately, rage.

Rage, because I am a dark creature who was also imprisoned for no crime at all.

The keeper wasn't even born into darkness, but he, too, was cast into it without reason or justification.

Oh, the vengeance I would demand if I were him.

A thousand times more furious than the vengeance I already want for myself.

Trying to control the fury in my voice, I ask, "What more could there be?"

CHAPTER THIRTY-ONE

Halle doesn't release me from her gaze as she says, "It was Galeia's belief that it should have been her."

My furious thoughts halt. "What do you mean?"

"Her heart was made from dark metal. Regardless of which Blacksmith had created it for her, and even if it had been created out of love, the metal from which it had been made wasn't pure. So the very thing that should have condemned her —that darkness—also saved her."

Sudden pain billows up within me and the pause in my fury ends.

Anger rushes back to me in a flood.

The echo that sounded within Veritas comes to my mind so clearly now, and its meaning is horribly transparent.

"I took her darkness so she could be free. I ripped out the malice so she could be at peace."

"I died so she could live."

"She lived while I died."

"It should have been her. Not me."

I double over with a groan and now Halle—and each member of my pack—edges toward me.

"Darkness?" Anarchy was already sitting closest to me, but she wraps an arm around my shoulders. She is always my protector, the one who worries about my emotions. "Are you okay?"

I can't answer her because it doesn't matter if I'm okay.

I force sound from my lips. "Halle, clarify this for me: Did any Blacksmiths have silver hair?"

"Yes," she whispers.

"Which House?"

There's a pause. "Silverspun. The House that created the keepers." But she hurries on. "That doesn't mean he was from that House."

I glare up at her, finding her as pale as she was when the keeper had first brought me to the Underworld, and she took a step back and asked him why he was wearing that face.

That green-eyed, silver-haired face that has always scared the fuck out of me.

"He could have chosen that face for many reasons," she says. "He could have meant it as a taunt. A rejection of the magic that created him. Hell, he could have even chosen it as a form of acceptance, because without their choices, the world we know would not exist."

She shudders and wraps her arms around herself. "I may not have witnessed the keepers' creation, but I saw the decay that stretched east. An entire fae city was wiped out. A Valkyrie village was infected, and all of its women became mortally ill. Animals were malformed... We hadn't seen a deer for years, let alone a natural wolf..."

Her focus becomes a little distant as she fixates on the wall—outside of which the two wolves may still be playing.

She shakes herself. "There are many reasons why the keeper could have chosen to show you that face."

Including because he was trying to send me a message about the power I control.

My fingers curl with frustration because only *he* can give me clarity.

"What about the face he's wearing now?" I consider his hair, how dark it is, but it isn't metallic and it never scared me.

To my surprise, it's Jonah who answers. "The face he wears now does not belong to a Blacksmith," he says. "Just as this longhouse would never have belonged to a Blacksmith."

I cast my gaze around the structure. "You said this was an En... En..." My forehead puckers as I stumble over the pronunciation. "How do you pronounce it?"

"Einherjar," he says, pronouncing it en-*hair*-yar with emphasis on the second syllable. "He has the same blue eyes as their greatest chieftain."

The form he takes when his mood is the darkest. He wasn't wearing it when he first met Jonah, and now I wonder if that was a deliberate choice on the keeper's part. Jonah would have recognized these eyes.

My hand brushes the keeper's cold cheek as I try to work through the threads of the weave of my mother's life and how it connects with the keeper's.

"Okay, then. Here is what I have: my mother's life was saved by a powerful Blacksmith whose identity is unknown," I say. "Whether or not it was given out of love or hate, the heart they gave her kept her alive until I came into existence and absorbed her power."

A lump forms in my throat. "In prison, her heart finally stopped altogether."

I breathe out. Then in. Pushing through the pain of those memories so I can continue. "Her heart started beating again when the keeper touched her. A final burst of life."

A final chance to speak with the keeper who'd taken her place in oblivion.

Oh, the gentle way she pressed her palm to his face...

I remember what the keeper said to me right after I read the book... When I'd screamed at him that my mother was alive and free and she could have come back for me.

He told me it wasn't that simple.

He never once told me that her heart had been failing because of me.

"The keeper did what he was supposed to do," I say, speaking around the tightness of my throat. "He took her heart so the metal it was made of couldn't be misused. He had no choice. That metal was infused with Blacksmith magic. It had to be contained. Just like Ryuji said. All of it gathered up and—"

"Take the crown."

It's such a sudden impulse coming from outside of me that I freeze.

Then, very slowly, I draw back the fur covering the keeper's chest, exposing his left hand where it rests against his heart.

That oh-so-small ring he wears on his finger.

It gleams at me, drawing me in as it always does.

My voice is cold with fear now. "Ryuji said that all of the dark metal, except for my mother's heart, was destroyed. He was talking about the hammers of the most powerful Blacksmiths, wasn't he?"

I pin Halle with a stare, but she doesn't answer me.

Her form flickers between dead and living, her face rippling between fully charred and that of a woman who has unwanted wisdom.

"Metal like that..." I continue. "Metal of the kind that was used to create my mother's heart. How could it ever be destroyed? All you could do is contain it. Put it somewhere nobody can reach it."

What better place to hide dark metal than on the head of the keeper in a realm from which he should never have been able to escape?

"Then I came along," I say. "I gave the keeper the power in my heart in exchange for vengeance, unwittingly bringing that metal out into the world. Unwittingly bringing into the world the power I absorbed, and now…"

Friction grows in the air around me.

My pack is suddenly tense. Halle is like a stone. Jonah has taken a step closer.

"Temptation," I say, repeating what the keeper said to me. *"Take the crown."*

I reach for the keeper's hand, slowly extending the claws of my left hand at the same time.

Take the crown that isn't a crown.

All of its power calls to me, all of the vengeance that the keeper promised me, right at the tip of my fingers.

A hammer waiting to be claimed.

CHAPTER THIRTY-TWO

*H*ow badly I want to take it.

How badly I was drawn to this crown when I first saw it on the keeper's head in that black-marbled place that he said belonged in a throne room.

But...

I didn't.

I didn't *take*.

When I met the keeper for the first time, instead of wresting the power from him, I *gave*.

I gave my heart instead.

I recognized that he'd been caged, just like I had been. I yearned for family and belonging, just as he must have.

And after that, just like he said, no matter what he put in front of me, I chose hope.

Because my mother taught me to believe that even dark creatures are worthy of love.

She may not have been able to tell me about her history, but she gave me what I needed.

If I take this crown, the keeper will die.

If I claim this terrible power, he will cease to exist. He will never have his vengeance. And my own will be empty.

There will be an empty space in my life because he is not filling it.

He... with all his complexity and lies and betrayal... he fills a place in my dark heart that I need filled.

So I retract my claws and withdraw my hand and fuss a little around his blanket, taking a moment to check his wounds.

He has stopped bleeding. The wounds are still open. But there are hints of healing.

Oh, my heart. The damage it can do to him.

Unless I can heal it fully...

There must be a way to mend the breaks.

Now that I have the answers I sought—or at the least the most pressing ones—I will find a way.

I have to believe that by mending my own heart, I can fix this.

Resolutely, I pull the fur blanket back up across his hand, covering the ring and pressing the material firmly over it.

I put away my fears and doubts because I realize what else my mother might have wanted me to know.

I speak aloud, a declaration I want my pack to hear. "There's a difference between darkness and evil."

I want Halle and her people to hear it, too, because it means everything.

I exhale every frightening thought I've had since I opened the door into this snowy place. No, even before that, the fears I carried when I stepped into Veritas, when I tore through the apple orchard, and even earlier, when I ripped apart *The Book of Dark Magic*.

All of my confusion vanishes.

With it, the friction around me vanishes, as if my pack had been reflecting my agitation and can now reflect my calmness.

Anarchy nudges my arm with hers. Across the fire, Lucian

gives me a nod. The three dark elf brothers give me varying smiles. A serious smile from Riot, a mischievous grin from Strife, and a chin tip from Rumble.

To Halle, I say, with a certainty I feel at the heart of my very being, "I left my cage seeking vengeance, and that is what I will have. Vengeance for all of us."

I cast my gaze around my pack, these dark beings who have chosen to stand at my side, and then I focus on the keeper, whose motivations are far more complex than I could ever have imagined.

I will have vengeance for my brother against the gargoyles. Vengeance for me against my father. And for the keeper…

Somehow… *Somehow*, I will have vengeance for him, too.

With that resolve, and maybe it is only wishful thinking on my part, I sense the rhythm of the keeper's heart becoming stronger.

"First, I need to rest," I say. "I need food—"

My stomach chooses that moment to make its unhappiness known with a low growl.

"And I need sleep," I continue, accepting my exhaustion, both emotional and physical.

"And then?" Halle asks.

"Then I'm going to see your brother," I say.

She stares at me in surprise. Then her eyes narrow. "To ask for information or to kill him?"

"Not to kill him," I say.

"A shame." She huffs before she glares daggers at Jonah. "Well. Good luck finding him."

Ignoring the jotunn, who is eyeing me cautiously, I give Halle a smug smile. "I already know where he is. He's with Elijah's mother."

Halle's eyes widen, her dead iris flaring with amber light. "On Mount Greylock? No, surely not. He would never be so foolish as to venture there."

I resist the urge to glance at Jonah, maintaining a deadpan expression as I return Halle's shocked gaze. I don't know exactly where Mount Greylock is located, but I'm sure my pack will help me.

"*You* certainly can't go there," Halle says, staring back at me. "That's a very bad idea."

I'm not sure why she's suddenly so worried until Anarchy leans in toward me. "Mount Greylock is a dangerous place to visit."

"As dangerous as Saber Lane," Lucian says, his golden eyes filled with a worry I can't ignore.

"Saber Lane?" I ask.

"Assassin territory," Lucian replies. "Mount Greylock is under the protection of the Assassin's Legion."

Hmm. That isn't happy news. Mom warned me about the Assassin's Legion. Their base is hidden in Boston and she told me to do everything I could to avoid them.

Riot speaks up, his voice as serious as always, but there's a depth of concern in his tone that, like Lucian's worry, I can't ignore. "If the same women who controlled Mount Greylock before we were imprisoned do now, then they don't need protection."

"I saw one of those women when we took Elijah to safety," Anarchy says. "I'm glad we kept our distance. Even the keeper was on edge around her."

"Who are they?" I ask, intensely curious now.

The four dark elves speak in unison. "Furies."

Oh. Fuck.

Riot elaborates. "We don't know much about the current state of affairs because of how long we were caged. But Mount Greylock has been their stronghold for millennia. You don't go there unless you have a death wish."

If the women who control Mount Greylock are furies, then

he isn't exaggerating. My mother was clear about them: Furies are vengeance incarnate.

But in some ways, that only feels more fitting to me.

It's their nature to see inside a supernatural's soul and identify every awful thing that supernatural has ever done—and then deliver terrible retribution for it.

I quickly recall what my mother told me about their abilities. They're self-healing, they have the power to inflict pain and disease, they carry whips that can flay the flesh from my bones even more effectively than light magic, and they wear multiple poisonous snakes around their bodies.

They usually live in threes, which triples the danger.

Anarchy chews her lip, revealing the sharp fangs she can use to immobilize prey. "You're strong, Darkness. But furies are built to take down any supernatural, no matter their strength. They are unique in that way."

"Judge, jury, and executioner," Lucian says. "They're a contradiction—dark creatures who kill dark creatures."

I consider my pack one at a time. Each of their concerned faces.

Oh, if only creatures of the light could see the extent that dark creatures can *feel*. Just how much we worry and care.

"You can't come with me," I say to them. "Not to a furies' nest. Even if you could, I would ask you to stay here and watch over the keeper."

"No, Darkness," Anarchy whispers. "There must be another path. If you need information about your father's operations, there must be another way to get it."

"There isn't. My mother had a wealth of knowledge, but that information is over twenty years old. Taiven didn't share the inner workings of his empire with anyone but his generals—correct, Lucian?"

My brother nods, although it's a reluctant movement.

"And Halle's knowledge is as dated as my mother's," I say, which leaves only her brother.

"What about Jonah?" Anarchy persists, turning to the jotunn.

He shakes his head. "Veda is right. Only James can predict what Taiven will do next."

"But the furies—"

I reach for Anarchy's hand before she can continue. "They will only harm me if I deserve harm." I pin her with a determined look. "If that means they say I deserve death, then I fucking deserve death."

CHAPTER THIRTY-THREE

My pack doesn't argue with me much longer before they capitulate to my wishes.

There's a part of me that thinks they only let the subject go because of how tired I must look. I guess it's hard to argue with someone whose eyes are closing and who can't stop yawning.

I can't remember the last time I slept. If I count the hours since coming to the Underworld, it could be as many as thirty-six, although the passage of time here is very difficult to measure.

Halle ushers Orlan and the hellhound out with a promise to bring food, since hunting in this place seems fraught. Not to mention, wildlife seems scarce. A fact I quickly ascertain with a brief expansion of my senses.

She promises that Orlan will come back, since he will have to transport me to Mount Greylock, but it seems my pack doesn't quite trust her because the three dark elf brothers casually declare that they're going with Halle and Orlan "to help with the food."

The fire is warm and the rug beside the keeper is soft. I barely keep my eyes open while Anarchy relocates herself to sit next to Lucian on the other side of the fire, and Jonah announces that he'll find water.

An hour later, I've eaten, hydrated with as much water as I could drink, and settled down on the fur with my pack standing guard.

Five hours after that, I wake to a quiet I wasn't expecting, finding myself alone inside the longhouse.

I'm tucked in next to the keeper, a fur around both of us.

With a start, I listen for his breathing, my hand darting out beneath the fur to press against his chest.

I exhale my relief when I register his steady breathing.

Thank the dark saints.

The gash above his eye looks like it might be healing. The cut on his cheek has faded. But when I check his chest, the wounds there are still disappointingly deep, even if the blood has stopped flowing.

I make out Anarchy's quiet voice outside the longhouse, along with Lucian's and Jonah's. They're talking about a time long past. Or, rather, Anarchy and Jonah are. Lucian seems to be mostly listening.

I don't want to leave the keeper, but I force myself to rise, reaching under my coat—which I somehow slept in—to tear a strip off the hem of the gauzy dress.

I will need to protect my eyes if it's daytime on Mount Greylock. It will also help with the brightness of the snow immediately outside the longhouse.

Pausing at the door, I consider the wall of weapons that sits on the left of it.

There are blades of all kinds, each one appearing sharp and well-maintained, along with multiple bows and several quivers of arrows.

But above them all is a war hammer with a block-shaped head carved with runes.

My eyes widen at the sight of it.

Its wooden handle is broken in half, badly splintered at the break point but clinging by a single strand of wood in the middle.

I find myself reaching for it, wondering if the metal part carries magic, but even when my fingertips brush it, nothing happens.

It's ordinary metal.

Still, I'm intrigued that it rests in pride of place above the other weapons.

As if there is value in a broken thing.

I can't stop myself from turning back to the keeper. "Who are you?"

Who *was* he?

He has worn so many faces. It feels like they mean something, but then, some may not. To read into all of them…

I shake myself.

What matters is that I keep him alive, and keeping him alive hinges on the thread between him and me.

I have to heal his heart.

I tug the fur coat more closely around me as I step out into the snowy landscape, finding Anarchy, Lucian, and Jonah watching the wolves play.

The beasts don't flicker out of view as quickly as they did before.

"We've been watching to see whom they run to greet," Anarchy says quietly and without turning toward me, her panther senses no doubt telling her I was awake and coming her way. "But so far, the image doesn't last that long."

"Family," I say. "It has to be. He misses them."

Lucian regards me with his golden eyes. "No longer your enemy, then."

"Oh, he's my enemy." I blow out an exhale. "But enemies can be allies, too."

Lucian nods. "Like gargoyles and shadow panthers."

Anarchy gives him a dark smile. "All it takes is a little bloodshed."

I stifle a laugh that quickly fades when the door opens across the clearing, and Halle bustles back in. She's still sporting her half-dead, half-wise-woman appearance, but she's wearing sensible boots this time.

"Do not endanger yourself," she says to Orlan, who stops inside the door. "Take Veda only as close to the nest as is safe. And keep an eye out for Taiven's followers. If he's had any kind of inkling about my brother's whereabouts, he will have scouts around."

Orlan doesn't appear fazed. "To avoid them, I should take Veda closer to the furies' nest. After all, a safe distance for me is a safe distance for Taiven's followers."

Halle huffs. "Well, it depends which foe you would prefer to face: Taiven's followers or the furies."

"The furies won't tell Taiven where Veda is," Orlan points out. "His followers will."

"Curse your logic," Halle says, and I'm surprised to see that she looks genuinely worried, her hands clasped hard and a growing tension around her eyes.

It occurs to me now that maybe… just maybe… beneath her cold façade and dead exterior, there's the heart of an alpha who cares about her people.

Orlan gives her a smile. "You know I'm a thinker."

"Even thinkers can die," she snaps.

I hurry toward them. "But Orlan has me. I'll keep him safe until he can transport himself out of there." My forehead puckers. "Actually, I don't expect you to stick around, Orlan, so how will I let you know when I need to come back?"

"I can give you a temporary rune," he says. "Best to put it behind your ear, where it can't immediately be seen by your adversaries. Press the rune like a call button, and I'll come back."

I don't know what a 'call button' is, but the intent is clear enough. I'm not sure how I feel about him placing a rune on me, though.

Halle exhales heavily. "Fine. But go before I change my mind and make you both stay. You're a darn sight safer here than out there."

Orlan steps back toward the open door, his quick steps telling me that Halle really might be in danger of stopping us.

I give Anarchy a quick hug and my brother a nod. Lucian learned to distrust hugs, but my pack is working on that.

Soon enough, I exit the cold landscape and take a last look back at the place the keeper created before the door closes behind me.

CHAPTER THIRTY-FOUR

I arrive on Mount Greylock in a crouch, Orlan's hand resting on my shoulder.

I'm immediately aware of the crunch of fallen leaves beneath my boots and the shadow of trees around me.

I blink against the influx of light, judging that it must be early morning out here.

I'm glad I thought to cover my eyes as I assess my surroundings: the trees and the steep slope ahead.

Rising to my feet, I listen for the sounds of anyone nearby.

Orlan remains beside me, also rapidly surveilling our surroundings, both of his hands raised, ready, no doubt, to call his magic if needed.

Everything is quiet.

The tension remains in Orlan's shoulders as he continues scanning the trees. "Continue toward the summit, heading east, and you'll find their cabin." Then he points in the other direction. "There are hiking trails and skiing facilities that way, and you don't want to encounter any humans who holiday there. There's also a War Memorial tower near the summit, but again, stay east of that."

I understand hiking, and I can picture what a memorial tower might look like, but I'm not sure about skiing. I don't waste time asking.

Now that we're away from the Underworld, where there could be many listening ears, I ask Orlan the question that could influence his ability to help me. "Halle seemed a little more concerned about your welfare than I was expecting. What are you to her?"

One corner of his mouth twitches up and he casts me a quick glance. "Just another orphan who needed a home."

He focuses on the side of my neck before I can ask him more. "Ready for the rune?"

I sweep my unruly hair to the side to expose the left side of my neck, suddenly aware of how clumped the strands have become. I lived for years with matted tresses. My hair was never so well-kept as it became over the last month of living on Ryuji's island.

Now it's messy again.

Wild-Haired Woman. That's what the keeper smugly suggested naming me. It might not be such an inaccurate descriptor, after all.

Orlan quietly presses his palms together, slowly pulling them apart to reveal a single, glowing symbol floating between them. It's about the size of my thumb.

Still moving carefully, he taps the side of the rune with a forefinger to gather it up and then presses it to my skin beneath my left ear.

Meanwhile, I remain alert to our surroundings, but we're still very much alone.

From the corner of my eye, I catch Orlan peering at the spot beneath my ear, a crease growing on his forehead.

"What is it?" I ask.

"The rune is starting to fade already. Your body must be rejecting my magic."

As annoying as that is in this instance, I'm not sorry my body is taking care of the external magic placed on it. "How long has it got?"

"Maybe an hour at most. If it's still there, you'll feel three little bumps. The bumps will disappear as the rune's power fades."

"Then I'll have to be quick."

He scratches his chin as he scans the trees again. "If you don't summon me, I could come back at a predetermined time—"

"And walk straight into danger if I'm already dead? Not a good idea."

"We'll see," he says.

As grateful as I am that he would consider it, it isn't a good idea. But I can tell I'm not going to influence his decision. After all, I'm not his alpha. "If you choose to come back without being summoned, please return to this spot, where it's safe enough."

He nods, presses his palms together, and then, with a flash of light, disappears again.

The air tingles with his magic, and then that, too, fades.

It hits me then that I'm alone. Without my pack. It's one of the few times they, or the keeper, haven't been at my side. In fact, it could be the first time since I stepped through the broken wall of my cell that I'm completely alone in a fight.

I tell myself this situation doesn't scare me.

I survived many years on my own.

But it makes me realize how badly I want to make it back to them. I have family now and I won't squander that gift.

Keeping my eyes and ears peeled, I proceed up the slope, staying to the east, as Orlan suggested, and remaining within the shadows beneath the trees as much as I can to spare my eyes.

I've left the gauzy dress hitched up around my thighs to

ensure the material doesn't hinder me and I keep my claws at the ready.

Up ahead, I finally make out a small log cabin.

It has a shallow porch at the front and appears to be made out of roughly hewn logs. It looks rustic. Old. Definitely drafty.

I slow my pace because the furies must be either within the hut or the nearby trees, but still, I don't sense anyone.

I certainly don't sense James's presence, and he's the reason I'm here.

Pausing at the edge of the clearing, I force myself to relax.

I don't have a lot of time before the rune fades, but I can't rush this. So I lean back against the nearest tree trunk, clasp my hands in front of myself, and prepare to wait.

They won't tolerate my presence for long. I'm certain of it.

Unless Orlan brought me to the wrong place…

I banish my doubts. I'm here now and I can summon him back soon if this is all for naught.

A few moments later, the scent of wildflowers fills the air around me.

It's a new aroma, slightly reminiscent of the overly floral fragrance that radiated from one of the angels I encountered after I escaped my cell.

My nose wrinkles.

The scent is incredibly irritating.

"Poison?" I ask quietly while I stay exactly where I am and resolve to avoid any sudden movements.

"Compulsion," replies a serene voice in a pitch that is distinctly female. A curious tone enters her voice. "Which normally works."

I locate the sound of her voice behind me and to my left, but much higher than I was expecting. Certainly not at ground level.

I didn't think furies had wings. I can't hear the wings

beating, and it'll require a significant shift in my posture to turn and look.

For the moment, I remain exactly where I am, although I succumb to the urge to shrug my shoulders. "What were you trying to compel me to do?"

"Submit to my will."

"Huh." I purse my lips. "Well, I'm not inclined to do that."

"I suspected as much," she says. "Which sadly means *I'm* more inclined to kill you."

The calm breaks, the air shrieking with the sound of a whip's deadly tips coming straight at me.

CHAPTER THIRTY-FIVE

I dart away from the tree just as three metal-tipped lashes smash across the wooden trunk.

They hit the wood right where I was standing and flay it as effectively as my claws would have.

Wooden shards fly around me as I come to a stop farther inside the clearing, my ears ringing with the shrieking whip's movement as it recoils only inches from my face.

Fuck!

I force myself to stay where I am, crouched and ready to fight.

A lone woman levitates above the ground only five feet away from me.

She retracts her whip with an expertise that tells me it may as well be another limb to her. Completely under her control.

Some aspects of her appearance align with what I imagined a fury would look like. She has lush, golden hair and is dressed in a skin-tight, black, leather bodice and long pants.

Her black whip consists of a shorter central rope that splits into three long, metal-tipped lashes. I don't know the technical names of the parts of a whip, but I know I need to avoid all of them. Even the handle can be used as a bludgeon.

Surprisingly, it appears that only a single snake slithers around her body, and, while it hisses as it slides across her torso, it stays close to her skin instead of baring its fangs at me. It, too, is golden like her hair.

I was certain that furies had more than one snake. I also check for the other two furies since they always move in threes, and I'm concerned when I don't see or sense them.

The woman doesn't waste time with words.

She moves fast.

Her whip was already in motion, and now, with a flick of her wrist, it changes direction, once against whistling toward my head.

I dart left, ducking and rolling and judging a safe distance by a matter of inches. My right hand snaps out, claws extended, aimed perfectly to cut right through the whip's nearest lash before it reaches me.

To my shock, my claws rake across the side of the lash but don't slice through it.

What the...?

The force of my push causes the lash's tip to recoil right toward my face. At the same moment, a zap of energy rushes back through my arm, a nasty sting.

I throw myself backward, retracting my claws and backflipping through the air, landing clear.

Or so I thought.

Pain spreads through my cheekbone, and a quick touch tells me I'm bleeding, black blood dripping down to my chin.

My healing power kicks in quickly, and, judging by the look on the woman's face, she isn't happy that the wound is closing so quickly.

As I regain my balance, the lashes recoil and the woman raises her arm, spinning her whip around above her head.

The lashes *whoosh* as they pass through the air.

I watch them carefully, visually following their path around and around, judging my ability to either evade them or get in close to her before she lets them loose again.

She snarls at me, her eyes glittering and golden—even more golden than my own eyes. "I am a necessary evil where all other justice fails. My whip is retribution. It can't be evaded. Not by any power on this Earth."

Well, damn.

Just as she extends her arm and the whip shrieks toward me again, I leap forward, my feet leaving the ground as I jump the distance to reach her in the air.

My right claws strike toward her neck.

At the same time, my left hand wraps around the handle of her whip—just above where she holds it. In that heartbeat, I sense the leather beneath my palm, the anger in the material, and the anchor point of the three lashes. If I can just get my claws between the lashes to the anchor point and slash them apart, maybe I can snap the binding holding the whip together...

My eyes widen in the heartbeat that it takes her to tip her body sharply left to evade the oncoming claws of my right hand. In the same move, she wrenches her right hand at my face, wresting the handle out of my grip and knocking the butt of it into my left cheekbone.

Her strength is immense, and it's like being hit by a rock.

I sense the skin across my left cheek splitting, and then, worse, the bone beneath it breaks.

Pain explodes across my face as I crash to my right under the force of her punch, dropping wildly toward the ground.

But, by fuck, now I'm mad.

And I'm just as fast as she is.

I leap right back at her even as the whip's lashes rake painfully across my chest. My leg muscles bunch at the same time my left hand closes around one of the lashes. I may not be able to cut it, but I can use it against her.

I leap upward, once again aiming for her neck, but not to slice through it.

Whirling the dangerous lash back through the air, I crash into her, whipping my arm left and wrapping the lash around her throat.

The impact of my leap sends us spinning through the air, a wild rotation in the direction opposite that in which I wound the lash. The briefest smile touches my lips until I become aware that she's using those split seconds to return the favor.

The cold leather of a second lash wraps around my neck.

And then we hit the ground.

Fear floods me as I brace not only for impact, but for the possibility that my neck will snap and there's nothing I can do about it.

CHAPTER THIRTY-SIX

A second before we hit the ground, her fist collides with my side, forcing me into a tight spiral.

Oomph!

Somehow, we land on our sides, now back to back, our shoulders gouging the ground.

I try to shove myself upright at the same as she does, both of us headed in the same direction. The movement wrenches my head back so sharply that the backs of our heads knock into each other at the same time.

Crack!

My vision swims. Her groan of pain is louder than mine.

The whip's handle has ended up pressed between what must be her shoulder blades and my shoulder blades, which is anchoring us both right where we are, and it's not as if either of us is going to let go of the lash we've wrapped around the other's neck any time soon.

There we sit, back to back, lashes around each other's necks.

All I can do is tug at the lash, unable to cut through it, keeping my free hand between it and my throat to give me space to breathe.

I'm satisfied that at least she's gasping for breath as hard as I am.

But damn. What now?

Something cold moves against my lower spine, and I squeeze my eyes closed at the possibility that it's the snake. I expect to feel its bite any moment now...

I'm surprised when I don't.

For a long minute, we remain sitting like that, the backs of our heads pressed painfully against each other's, neither one of us loosening our grip.

Her rasped question breaks the strained silence between us. "Why didn't you... use your wings just now?"

I rasp back. "How do you know... I have wings?"

She makes a sound that could be a snort. "I'm a fury."

I consider my response. My muscles are straining. Sweat drips down my brow. But if I let go of the lash around her neck, I have no guarantee she won't break my neck immediately.

"My wings are useless."

She's quiet for another moment, her breaths rasping audibly, and then she says, "I think you've become so good at getting back up after you fall that you've learned to survive without the ability to fly."

My eyes widen.

I've fallen many times. Failed many times. Been beaten so many times.

She whispers, "My name is... Rebella."

One who rebels.

I struggle to reply, partly because I'm still processing what she said and partly because it's becoming increasingly difficult to speak and breathe at the same time. "That's quite... a name."

"I was one of three furies, but not any longer," she says.

"Oh?" It hasn't escaped me that the other two furies I expected to encounter haven't made an appearance.

I fully anticipated that they might emerge from the cabin

because I have a sense that it's well lived in. Maybe it's the various scents in the air around it or the homey appearance of the place, despite its rugged aspects.

"I lost my sisters long ago," she gasps. "In the fight against the primordial deity, Typhon. That fight left me in a cage. I believe you understand what that feels like."

I shudder despite myself. If her story is true, then she is yet another powerful woman put in a cage.

Still, I'm surprised at how candid she's being. "Why are you telling me this?"

"Because I don't like being indebted to a dark creature, and I would much rather kill you, but... *Damn it...*"

The lash around my neck loosens.

I'm shocked to realize she must have let go of her end of it. Which means I'm free. But *she* isn't.

I could use her choice against her, but I didn't come here to kill her.

Letting go of the lash I was holding, I roll away from her, coming up in a crouch, now facing her.

I drag air into my chest as fast as I can while I wait for my lacerated vocal cords to heal. "Indebted to me? How, exactly?"

Her chest is heaving. The golden snake slithers up and around her neck, slowly gliding in a loose circle that appears protective of the bruises I left on her.

Bruises that are rapidly fading.

"You protected my son and ensured he was escorted to safety."

"Your son is Elijah," I say. And then I add cautiously, "He's a good kid."

Her eyes glisten for a moment. "Elijah is one of a kind." She presses her lips together, taking a deep breath. "He's safer with the supernaturals of St. Michael Cemetery than he could be out here with me. They understand what it's like to be.... unusual."

Well, the way she describes the supernaturals of St. Michael

Cemetery makes me want to meet them. From what I know, one of them is also a fury and they're all extremely powerful, but I have no other information about them.

Rebella takes another shuddering breath, blinking hard at the tears in her eyes before she tips her chin at me. "What do I call you?"

I arch an eyebrow at her. "You're a fury. How do you not know my name?"

"I know you currently call yourself *Veda*."

I narrow my eyes. "That's right."

She peers at me. "Is that really your name?"

What a question.

But I guess it's valid coming from a being who can see into my soul.

"What would *you* call me?" I ask, genuinely curious.

She arches an eyebrow at me. "What else do you call a riddle except a *riddle?*"

Ha, that's what I'd call the keeper. "Then call me '*Riddle.*'"

She snorts, but her eyes become piercing, the golden hue increasing in intensity. "Perhaps I would rather call you '*Vulture.*'"

My brow furrows. "If I'm correct in my understanding of the animal world, vultures pick over carcasses. I think I'm offended."

"Oh, but vultures have a crucial role to play in an ecosystem," she says, her gaze so sharp now that it feels like she's flaying my skin from my body with her eyes instead of her whip. "They clean the bones that other predators are too lazy to clean. They consume diseased flesh to ensure the rot does not spread, enabling the good health and survival of others."

She inches closer to me. "Vultures can tear at the rotten soul of an ecosystem with an efficiency that's breathtaking."

I allow myself to grin because I guess a vulture doesn't sound so insulting, after all.

"Of course," she continues, "they are not loved for it."

I exhale my sigh.

But it seems she has decided to persist. "You seek to excise your father's evil, do you not?"

I can't help the challenge that rises to my lips. "What makes you think I'm not equally evil? I'm a dark creature, too."

"There's a difference between darkness and evil," she says.

It was only a few hours ago that I came to the same conclusion.

But then... she *is* seeing into my soul.

She may be deliberately reinforcing my own conclusions.

But for what purpose?

She let me live. She's chosen to give me more information about herself than I expected, and now I need to know why.

CHAPTER THIRTY-SEVEN

"What do you want from me, Rebella?" I ask.

She gives me a look that's suddenly so bleak, it cuts into my heart. "I want you to end your father's reign so that my son can come home." Her voice becomes a snarl. "I want you to do what even the assassins haven't been able to do: tear at the rotten soul of that ecosystem until it's clean again."

My chest squeezes. But of course, I should have guessed that her wishes would align with mine.

Even so, I'm cautious. "In your version of a clean ecosystem, what happens to dark creatures?"

"Balance," she says. "Darkness is needed. Just as light is needed. The Nostra Empire used to respect this, but your father has been tipping the scales in the wrong direction for the last two decades, influencing other dark creatures to make choices they would not otherwise have made. He must be stopped."

She takes a shaky breath. "Come with me. I will take you to Jormungandr now."

That's James's true name. Jormungandr, the World Serpent.

She turns toward the far corner of the cabin and sweeps past it, pausing only to check that I'm following her.

I consider what she said as I follow her around the side of the cabin, processing the heart of her message.

Dark creatures need balance.

We need our darkness. But we also need the light.

I follow Rebella through another layer of trees before we exit into a wide clearing.

A bench is located on the far side, but otherwise, the clearing is empty.

A moment after we step into the clearing, James appears abruptly between the trees, taking quick strides toward us. I eye the air around him, taking note of the glimmer in the air when he appears.

He hurries straight toward me. But it's clear he's speaking to Rebella when he says, "Good. You didn't kill her."

Rebella gives him a smile as she saunters up to him, draws him to a stop, and plants a kiss on his lips. "I tried. But she's as resourceful as you said she is."

James returns Rebella's embrace, his arm remaining around her as he returns his attention to me.

I'm surprised—but also not surprised—to see the affection between them. The fact that a fury like Rebella could love this old god, who must have accumulated layer upon layer of blood on his hands, is stunning to me.

At the same time, I knew Elijah came from somewhere.

I'm also a little uncertain of the changes in James's appearance.

He's a tall, lean man with dark-brown hair that falls across his brown eyes. His previously short and neatly sculpted beard is longer and scruffier, and the scar that runs down the left side of his forehead and cheekbone seems more pronounced.

The last time I saw James, he was dressed in a tailored suit. Now, he's in jeans and a flannel shirt that looks as roughed-up as his beard. The only really consistent aspect of his appearance is the katana sword resting in a scabbard at his back, its braided handle visible over his right shoulder.

I eye him warily, thrown by the drastic change in his appearance and conscious of the weapon at his back.

Not that he needs it.

He wears living snakes across his torso that masquerade as tattoos and come to life when he needs them. They can immobilize their prey with a single injection of poison.

Come to think of it, it makes him a little like Rebella in that aspect.

He greets me formally. "Veda Nostra, Daughter of the Nostra Empire. Welcome."

Well, it certainly beats *Daughter of Assholes*, the title I adopted when I was on Ryuji's island.

Given how formally he greeted me, I return his salutation in kind. "Jormungandr. Old god." I arch an eyebrow at his beard. "Looking your age."

Without responding to my verbal jab, he gestures to the bench. "I'm sure you've come for information. I'm happy to give it. But I'm also certain that being out here in the open is as bad for your health as it is for mine. If you will sit, Rebella will guard our location, and I will answer your questions as promptly as possible. Then we can both disappear again."

I'm not entirely sure where he intends to disappear *to*. Or where he might have come from just now. I guess I assumed he would be hiding out in the cabin, but instead, he's gesturing me toward a bench in an open space that feels unnecessarily open and exposed.

But he's offering answers, and for the first time in a long time, I don't doubt I'll get the truth.

Possibly, it's something to do with the fury casting her daunting gaze over us.

Furies hate lies.

I try to hide my smile as I picture her setting upon James at the first hint of an untruth.

I take a seat and don't mince words. "How do I destroy my father?"

James gives me a sudden smile. "You already are. Destroying him."

I scowl. "I thought you were going to give me prompt answers."

His hands rise, a placating gesture. "I'm not evading your question. But I want you to know that you're playing a far cleverer game with your father's fate than I ever anticipated you might."

I lean back a little, contemplating the old god. "You expected me to be reckless."

"I truly thought that if Galeia's child were ever to escape the prison we searched desperately to find for years... well, I thought you would be blinded by hate. How could you not be? I anticipated that you would strike with swift and violent retribution." He tips his head as he studies me. "Which would have gotten you killed."

I grit my teeth. "Ending Taiven Nostra is certainly on my mind."

James gives me a soft smile. "Ah, but your mother was an extremely intelligent person. I'm certain she foresaw that if she told you the truth—that your father was the monster who forced you into darkness—you would have gone straight for his throat.

"Instead, you slipped into his life without warning. You went to him with an impossible love in your heart. And, when you discovered that your love was misplaced, you struck with increasing impact." James's smile turns dark. "It is the careful knife that is the most effective."

I suppose I didn't see it like that, but it feels more real as James continues.

"You have systematically stripped away the outer layers of your father's armor," he says. "First, you gave me my freedom, which in turn gave Jonah his freedom. Then you stole your father's most valuable possessions: not only *The Book of Dark Magic*, but also his only heir."

My eyes widen. "You mean Lucian?"

James nods. "Lucian may have suffered at Taiven's hands, but without him, Taiven can't promise his followers that the Nostra Empire will continue beyond his own death. He can't promise them stability. You've thrown it all into disarray."

I chew over this. I'm certain that Lucian was never encouraged to understand how crucial he might be to our father's hold on power.

James gives a sudden snort. "Then you went and made friends with the crimson wolves. Of all the fierce creatures you could have made peace with. *And* allied yourself with the dragon masters. A nearly impossible feat, even for other dragon shifters. Between the wolves and the dragons, you have secured powerful allies who not only walk in the light, but also have significant influence over the actions of other supernaturals."

James eyes me. "Most importantly, and perhaps most astonishingly, you haven't killed a single supernatural in the process."

As I chew on what he said, he continues to study me.

"You may have even paved the way for a reconciliation between me and my sister," he says.

"Ha!" I scoff at that. "Halle would rather char your bones."

He sighs softly. "I would have thought so, too, but here I am, out in the open, and she hasn't come to kill me yet."

He looks dramatically around at our surroundings, as if he expects the goddess to appear at any moment.

I hate to burst his bubble by telling him that might have something to do with the fierce woman guarding us.

His tone becomes disgruntled as he continues. "Actually, I thought I might be higher on Halle's list of priorities."

I consider him carefully, refocusing the conversation with a certainty I can't deny. "I can't wield a careful knife any longer."

A hint of wariness enters his eyes. "Can you tell me why not?"

"The keeper is dying," I say. "I don't know how to save him, but I know that the time for patience is over."

James's expression grows immediately grim, and, across the way, Rebella startles, glancing back at us.

"This is very bad news," James says.

A silent communication occurs between him and Rebella, at the end of which she gives him another bleak look.

When he speaks, James sounds unexpectedly hesitant. "Before I give you my advice, Veda, may I ask you a question?"

"Okay."

"Did the keeper offer you his crown?"

"I refused it. Taking it will kill him."

"Damn." James stares at me for a long moment. I stare right back at him, unflinching even as his eyes take on a slightly crimson hue, an alarmingly powerful color.

Then, his gaze flicks once more to Rebella. She tilts her head, a knowing expression on her face. What she thinks she knows, I can't possibly discern.

James returns his attention to me, his voice unexpectedly hard now. "So you have chosen to forgo limitless power—power that would allow you to claim the Nostra Empire without a fight—because it would mean the death of your..." He falters. "What is the keeper to you?"

Friend. Enemy. Lover. Confidant.

Wild, dark presence in my life.

A good person caged for the survival of others.

My own personal monster.

I breathe out. Then in. The same way I saw the crimson wolf do in the forest of Portland.

But no matter how hard I try to calm my response, all I can do is snarl. "That's none of your fucking business."

"I see." James remains grim. "Then you're correct: the patient knife is no longer an option. You must cut Taiven off at the knees. Swiftly, decisively, and publicly."

"How do I do that?" I ask, mentally noting the distinction between killing my father and bringing him to his knees.

For a moment, darkness flashes within James's eyes, and I'm suddenly overwhelmed by the possibility that an entire world exists within his mind. The mind of the World Serpent is constrained within this living body.

"In a fight you must win on your own, Veda," he says. "You must fight without your pack. Without backup. Since you have chosen to forego the power we all fear, you must prove that you are just as formidable without it. No matter what, it must be a definitive kill."

"Who?" I push. "If not my father, who do I need to kill?"

James pauses before he says, "The gargoyle king."

I don't hesitate.

"Gladly," I snarl. "That's the clan that betrayed Lucian's mother."

James nods. "The very same. I didn't think you'd have a problem with it. Their leader calls himself a king, but he doesn't have a shred of royal blood in his body. It was Lucian's mother who carried that line, descended from the last gargoyle queen—Queen Incorruptible—herself. It was why Taiven wanted her."

Well, it's no fucking wonder Anarchy was so delighted to lick up Lucian's blood if it's royal.

I can't stop my teeth from sharpening. "Tell me about this false king."

"His name is Gregor Stonne. He has proven very difficult to

kill, primarily because of your father's protection. But he will be vulnerable for the first time tonight."

I jolt a little. It's sooner than I thought it'd be. "How so?" I ask. "If he's so hard to kill, suddenly making himself vulnerable seems out of character."

"It is." James nods emphatically. "But you disappeared for two weeks, and your father's search has turned up empty—"

"*Two weeks?*" I stare at James in confusion, trying to make sense of that timeframe. I was gone for a month on the island and it's only been two days at most since I stole the book. "It's only been two days."

James blinks at me. "You stole the book two weeks ago." The crease in his forehead clears. "Oh. But of course. You've been in the Underworld."

I nod.

"Time passes more slowly there," he explains. "A day in there is a week out here. It's a quirk of hell. The price for visiting is time."

Damn. Well, what's done is done, so I quickly gather my thoughts. "Okay, so the longer I evade my father, the weaker he appears."

"And the more flustered he becomes. He has demanded a meeting of the heads of the most powerful dark families. Human and supernatural alike. He is desperate to crush the rumors of your growing strength and shore up his control of the Nostra Empire." James pauses to smile at me. "You pushed him to this."

"Me and my careful knife," I murmur.

"You must go to this meeting. Announce your claim to the empire in front of the other families."

"But rather than assassinate my father, I will challenge the gargoyle king instead?"

"You must kill him on the spot. Only then will you convince

the other families of your strength and force your father to bow to you."

I scoff. "Taiven will never bow. He will fight to the death."

"Of course. At which point, you must kill him," James says. "But only after you give him a chance to yield."

"Why?" I ask.

James considers me quietly for a moment. "You are not your father, Veda. You must show the other leaders that you have the power to end your enemies. But you must also show them that you are completely in control. *You* choose when you will or will not strike. You are above them. Always. Only then will you control the empire."

Control is everything.

My mother drummed that into me. Damn, she was smart about what she taught me.

But in the last two days—or two weeks, as it turns out—I've learned how much control I *don't* have. Wresting it back is going to take a lot of conviction.

"Where is this meeting taking place?" I ask.

"At the White Wing Tavern. 8 P.M. tonight."

My eyebrows arch in surprise. "But I know that place. It's more public than other places my father could meet with the leaders. Why would he choose such an exposed position?"

The White Wing Tavern is where I met James and Jonah for the first time. The front of the building is a regular restaurant. Behind and beneath it is a maze of underground corridors and tunnels.

I'd gained access to one of its hidden rooms through a green door that Mom had told me about, which was situated at the back of the restaurant. As it turned out, Halle had placed a spell on that door and the corridor beyond it with the intent to kill anyone who stepped inside it. Her target had been James, since it was their own special entrance.

I'd waltzed through the door and the corridor without a

scratch or even any awareness of the danger that place had posed to me.

"He *knows* you know about the White Wing," James replies. "After Jonah and I met you there, we told him about you."

"Ah." I purse my lips. "So he wants me to come for him."

"You've evaded him for two weeks, Veda. If he can't find you, he'll lure you in."

"He's confident he can beat me."

"Like you, he needs his victory to be seen by the other leaders."

I breathe out carefully as I consider my options. Not many. Or rather, none. "I'll walk into a trap."

James grimaces. "Effectively, yes."

Is it still a trap if I know about it?

Maybe. Maybe not.

I suddenly narrow my eyes at James. "You've been out of his inner circle for weeks now. How do you know about this?"

"I have a contact in the gargoyle clan," he says. "Someone who isn't so happy with her clan's leadership—"

He doesn't have time to say more because across the clearing, Rebella suddenly startles.

"Incoming!" she cries.

"Ours or Taiven's?" James asks, his shoulders tense as he rises half out of the seat.

"Ours." Her eyes are wide. "But that's just as fraught. You know how protective they are. Veda's intentions have been very unknown. They will fear the worst and attack first. They will think only of protecting me."

My senses are prickling and my back is suddenly itching like mad. That unwanted crawling sensation floods me, as if my wings will release despite my efforts to control them.

My focus is drawn to the sky, but I can't see past the canopy of branches.

I find myself bracing for the ear-splitting sound I would hear each time the air dragons visited the island, because the power currently screaming in our direction is as immense as that of the dragon masters.

My claws snap out and I'm on my feet in an instant. "Who are they?"

James grimaces. "Assassins."

CHAPTER THIRTY-EIGHT

The branches above me billow violently as two figures drop into the clearing only ten paces away.

I get a split-second glimpse of what must be wings, although it's difficult to tell the color because of the glow around them both. An electric-blue energy that swirls powerfully in the air between them, a connection that takes my breath away.

One is a woman, the other a man. Both are taller than me. Their muscles are clearly defined by black, skin-tight clothing that conforms to their bodies and extends from the tops of their boots to the bottoms of their chins.

The woman has mahogany-brown hair pulled back in braids and bright green eyes that speak to an intelligence of mind. Judging by the smoothness of her skin, she might be only a few years older than me, but it's hard to tell with supernaturals. Even Anarchy looks twenty-five despite being thousands of years old.

The man has dark brown hair with a wave in it. It frames his unforgiving features: a strong jaw, a slight cleft in his chin, and eyes with silver streaks in them.

They're both focused entirely on me.

It looks as if Rebella is about to jump in front of them, but they're already storming toward me and I don't blame her for staying out of the way.

Judging by their intense focus on me, she should not get between them and me.

My mother would have told me to run from this fight. They aren't holding any visible weapons, but that doesn't mean anything. Assassins can kill just as effectively with their bare hands.

It isn't cowardice to understand when an opponent is stronger than I am. And I have far more important battles ahead of me today.

So, in the heartbeat that I have left before they reach me, I touch the rune behind my ear, seeking the three little bumps Orlan mentioned.

They're gone.

So is my easy way out of here.

While Rebella has lurched back, James is also on his feet, urgently holding out his hand to me. "Come with me!"

It doesn't matter if I would have accepted his help.

The assassins move unbelievably fast.

They're already on me, and they work in a unison that snatches the air from my chest.

The woman's hand flies toward me, palm flat, while the man circles to the side. If their intention is to contain me, then I can see how they're trying to make it happen. She will knock me off-balance. He will pin me from the side.

I have a heartbeat to react.

With a sharply indrawn breath, I focus on my left and the small space they left open.

Spinning out of the path of the woman's strike, I leap into the clearing.

It's better here without the bench at my back. More space to move.

I expect them to come right back at me and I'm surprised when they both seem to miss a beat.

Now behind the bench and closest to the man, James is still reaching out his hand for me. "Come with me, Veda!"

His gaze passes wildly around the clearing, and, despite the very short space between him and the male assassin, James doesn't focus on him.

It takes me a moment to wonder if…

He can't see them?

Both the man and the woman have straightened, an alarmed glance passing between them as I focus directly on them.

It seems to confirm my theory.

They don't stop.

The air around me bursts to life with streams of power, beating against me like the wind as they come at me once more. Both of them at the same time.

The man uses the bench as a launching pad, gaining air and coming down on me, preparing to hammer me with a fist from that height. The woman comes in beneath the arc of his trajectory, crouching and sweeping her legs as if to topple me from my feet.

I leap and dart left, narrowly avoiding both of them, but I'm not prepared to let them get away with it.

I kick out as I leap, my right foot hitting the man squarely on the shoulder as he comes down, giving me a platform that allows me to push myself farther away from both of them.

He's knocked off-balance, and her leg swishes harmlessly through the leafy forest floor.

I land at a crouch and quickly rise back to my feet as they exchange another alarmed glance.

So far, they haven't spoken a word—not to me, or to each other, or to James or Rebella, for that matter—but now the woman strides toward me on her own, her right fist aimed for my face.

Her voice is controlled even as she punches at me. "It's clear you can see us," she says. "Are you a fury?"

I'm too busy avoiding her fist to really consider her question. "Huh?"

"Are you a fury?" she asks again, her tone harder this time.

A glance at Rebella—who *is* a fury—tells me that Rebella is following our movements around the clearing, her posture clearly indicating that she wants to get between us. At the same time, James has backed away from the bench, his focus now on the ground, as if he's following the movement of the leafy debris we're kicking up with our feet. I guess that's one way to track what you can't see.

But if Rebella can see the assassins, that would explain why the woman asked me if I'm a fury.

I duck the woman's next fist and anticipate her follow-up kick, deftly evading her attacks while steering clear of the male assassin, who has moved toward the middle of the clearing and watches us intently.

"No," I say, speaking quickly as I anticipate the woman's next moves. "I'm not a fury."

Well, actually, I wouldn't know. Halle sidestepped, telling me about my mother's parents earlier. A move that I shouldn't have let her get away with, now that I think about it.

"Then what are you?" the woman demands to know as she keeps coming at me, her fists and feet moving increasingly fast. Every few seconds, she aims a hit at my face, but it's a plucking movement, as if she's trying to remove my blindfold.

I duck and dart and evade each of her attempts to make contact.

"I'm a Blacksmith," I snarl back at her.

Even though that isn't entirely accurate, I feel like it's splitting hairs right now to tell her I wouldn't have been born with this power except for my mother's heart and even though I might control this power, I can't access it.

But, hell, it feels nice to say it out loud.

For all of two seconds.

She misses a step, pulls her next punch, and tips her head at me. "A what?"

"A Blacksmi—" *Well, fuck.* Halle clearly wasn't lying about Blacksmiths being long forgotten.

Assassins study every creature they could possibly ever come across, so if anyone would know what a Blacksmith is, they would. *And...* they don't.

I shrug. "Never mind."

The rush of energy around her only increases as she resumes her attacks, and it's all I can do to avoid them. At some point, I'll have to stop evading and start attacking, but I'm not there yet.

"There are only three kinds of supernatural who can see through our invisibility," she says, her voice tighter than before, her fists and feet moving impossibly fast. "You can't be one of the other two kinds. So you must be a fury."

"If you say so," I snarl. And then, on pure impulse, I follow up with a dark grin. "Maybe I'm a vulture."

She stumbles. Given how agilely she was moving before I spoke, it's a sure sign that I've surprised her, although I'm not sure how.

Her misstep takes her closer to my evasive maneuver, and my claws scrape across her side.

I didn't mean for it to happen. Maybe I should have put away my claws, but I wanted to keep them ready.

A jolt of energy bursts through me at the contact, and it shocks me to my core.

The energy suddenly streaming from her body is lively, alert, questioning, and full of wonder.

An energy that speaks to a mind not yet fully grown.

"Fuck!" I retract my claws as fast as I can and leap away from her.

Her cry of pain meets my ears before she, too, jumps

backward. The man has already thrown himself toward her, his arms wrapping around her before he pulls her away from me.

"I'm okay!" she cries to him. "I'm okay."

But I'm not.

I could have really fucking hurt her.

"Do not fight me!" I shout at her, retracting my claws fully and extending both of my arms, palms out. "It wasn't my intention to hurt you. Or your child."

The woman has stayed where she is while the man's arms are wrapped protectively around her. Her clothing is slashed from where my claws ripped through it.

She's bleeding from multiple cuts across her stomach. With a shot of fear, I can't see how deep they are.

Her clothing must have been designed to resist blades because I sensed the resistance in it when my claws cut through. The assassins must have thought there was no way I could slash it apart.

I force myself to keep speaking as I take careful steps away from them. "Your daughter is inquisitive. She wants to understand her world. I don't want her to learn that creatures like me are to be hated."

Mommy Assassin is staring at me wide-eyed, still clutching her side, her face pale with what is no doubt intense pain.

But I don't think Daddy Assassin is listening.

He seems fixated on the blood dripping from her wounds.

"My claws can cut through anything," I say, shaking my head firmly. "It wasn't my intention to—*Oh, fuck!*"

With a snarl, Daddy Assassin launches himself at me with all the fury of a protective beast.

I've learned a lot about combat from Anarchy, but I realize just how softly the woman was approaching me when Daddy Assassin strikes in a storm of movement.

The air moves around me as I leap and dart and duck and dart and leap and try to evade his every hit, and then—

Smack!

A fist that feels like a boulder collides with my face.

My jaw shatters.

Black blood sprays the ground.

The leafy forest floor rears up at me, and my chest fills with the scent of copper and soil.

I mentally scream at myself not to go down, but I'm already down, and now the world is threatening to go dark.

Fuck, fuck, fuck!

I can't even process the pain. I'm horribly aware of Mommy Assassin throwing herself toward Daddy Assassin. She's coming at us from one direction while Rebella rushes toward us from the other.

"Stop!" Rebella screams.

Daddy Assassin doesn't seem to be paying attention to either of them.

He drops to a crouch beside me while I desperately try to figure out which way is up and how the fuck am I still conscious?

Rebella's voice screams, as if from a far distance. "Do not kill her!"

But his fist is already crashing down.

CHAPTER THIRTY-NINE

The air rushes out of my chest as the male assassin smacks my spine right between my shoulder blades.

It isn't a terribly hard hit.

My bones don't break this time.

And I'm surprised when he jumps away from me so fast that I've barely registered the contact of his hand before he's several paces away from me again.

A second later, pain rips across my shoulders, and then I'm screaming. Even the pain of my jaw shattering didn't hurt this much.

My wings shoot out far faster than I can tolerate, extending the full five paces to each side of me, every long, jagged feather raking across the ground, some of them *ramming* into it.

My scream of pain is a mangled sound.

My jawbone is healing, but not fast enough.

Oh, please.

I struggle to push myself up to my knees, all the while trying to retract my wings because they're even heavier lying flat on the ground than they are when I'm standing up.

I spent the last month trying to increase the strength of the muscles in my back to be able to hold them up—let alone use them, but I've never had to try to stand with them fully extended.

Tears of pain fall down my cheeks and I can only imagine how they're mixing with my blood right now. So much of it dripping to the ground as I heave my arms and legs, groaning with effort.

I'm beyond vulnerable lying on the ground like this.

Heave, Veda! Fucking get up!

At the edges of my vision, I'm aware of everyone else in this clearing having come to an abrupt halt, but I'm certain it's only a matter of time before they'll burst into action once more.

I remind myself of what Rebella said to me.

I've gotten so good at getting back up after I fall, I've learned to survive without the ability to fly.

Well, now I need to get up again.

With that, I finally manage to push myself up onto my knees, blood dripping down my chin and neck while my heavy wings drag at my sides, their nightmarish feathers all clumped together.

I find myself the subject of stares.

Of course, James has never seen my wings. Rebella certainly sensed them because she asked me why I didn't use them when I fought her.

But the two assassins appear shell-shocked, their eyes wide and their faces pale.

"The other kind," Mommy Assassin whispers.

She mentioned three kinds of supernatural that can see through her invisibility and it seems I am 'the other', whatever that is.

Again, I remind myself that this quiet won't last.

I have to make decisions now about whether or not I'm going to continue defending or start attacking—assuming I can even get up.

But, damn, no wonder my mother told me to avoid these assassins.

There is a part of me that understands and respects Daddy Assassin's reaction. Hell, if only my own father were so protective.

But there is another part of me that's angry.

I didn't start this fight. I didn't even throw a hit. Mommy Assassin stumbled into my claws while I was trying to avoid her.

I zero in on her wounds. They've sealed up again. No more bleeding. She's healed.

Baby Assassin will be just fine. I guess that's something.

Even so, I square my shoulders as best I can and stare the assassins down as if I'm *not* crumpled on the ground and weighed down by heavy wings.

"If you want me dead, come at me," I say, convincing myself that every word I'm speaking will be true. "But do it now—because I won't give you another chance."

Mommy Assassin turns paler than I was expecting her to. "Your wings, they're—"

She doesn't have the chance to finish whatever she was going to say.

Out of nowhere, a freezing rush of misty air blasts into me, catching my feathers and nearly knocking me backward.

So much for the illusion of strength.

My eyes widen when the keeper appears in front of me, positioned between me and the assassins.

"Keeper," I gasp.

He's standing side-on to me, no doubt so he can keep both me and them in his sights, but it also allows me to see how deathly pale he is.

He's still wearing his angry face with the Einherjar eyes. So much angrier than he looked in the Underworld.

His lips draw back from his teeth in a snarl while a glisten of dragon scales appears across his skin.

"You can't have her," he rasps at the assassins. "She does not belong to you."

Both of the assassins are now pale, but the look they give each other...

I don't understand what it means, the way they appear so stricken as they stare at the keeper, the way they focus on his eyes, then the way they look at me and my wings...

As if something has shaken their foundations.

I don't have the chance to understand it because in the next moment, another blast of mist sweeps around me, a tumult of power, before the keeper throws himself toward me, hoisting me up into his arms.

Then the mist envelops me, the keeper's power compresses my chest so hard, I can't breathe, and I'm spiraling sickeningly through space.

CHAPTER FORTY

The whirlwind of transportation magic stops abruptly. The keeper's arms remain around me as my knees hit a floor I recognize.

I'm back in the apartment where we first stayed in New York. I catch a glimpse of the lounge room around us, the little kitchen on my far right, and the bedroom behind me.

Then my wings crash through the plush seat at my back, cutting through the stuffing and exploding fluffy bits of material into the air around us.

I can't turn to assess the damage because my head is spinning from the bumpy ride, and my stomach is billowing with nausea.

Being rescued in this fashion isn't doing me any favors.

I discover that I'm leaning to my left, my hand planted on the carpet while the keeper's arms remain around my waist. Somehow, he's gripping me beneath my wings and keeping me pressed to his chest while he, too, is on his knees.

I gasp for breath and squeeze my eyes shut to try to stop the world from spinning.

My voice is a dry rasp, but at least my jaw has healed. "How are you here?" My confusion at his appearance is replaced with intense concern. "You were unconscious when I left."

He scoops up my other arm—the one I planted on the floor —before he crushes me to his chest.

His voice is a broken rumble in my ears. "I woke up and you were gone."

"Oh. Okay," I whisper against his shoulder, and then I jolt again with concern. "My pack?"

"Safe," he says. "I convinced them to remain behind and give us space."

The hour that they will probably wait in the Underworld could equate to half a day here. I don't even attempt to do the math on that, but I picture Anarchy pacing the entire time.

"You put yourself in danger." The keeper snarls, demanding my attention.

I groan, still unable to fully open my eyes. "Isn't that what you wanted?"

"No." His chest deflates. Then he repeats himself. "No."

I crack open my eyes, taking deep breaths as the spinning sensation I was experiencing eases and I can move my head again.

Ascertaining that the light around me isn't going to upset my vision, I shimmy my hand up between us so I can tug my blindfold off.

I find myself staring up into his eyes, surprised by the face he's wearing now.

No more blue-eyed angry persona.

No more black dragon.

No more silver hair.

This is a new face and...

It doesn't scare me or feed my darkness or make me wonder what he's thinking behind the mask he's wearing.

I bite my lip, peering at him, shimmying my right hand

farther up between us to trace the line of his jaw and marvel at his new appearance.

His eyes are predominantly blue with flecks of gray, and his hair is the color of a wolf's fur. A gray wolf. Similar to the one that raced across the snow back in the wintery landscape of the Underworld.

He makes me feel impossibly calm, recklessly at peace. As if there were nothing to worry about.

We are a beautiful darkness, and that's all there is.

"What is this face?" I whisper, my breath catching. "Who are you now?"

His eyes crinkle at the corners and a hesitant smile touches his lips. "I think this is what I might have looked like." He gives a small shake of his head. "But I don't know. It's just a feeling."

I press my fingertips once again to his jaw, not quite daring to close the gap between our lips, even though everything within me wants to kiss this face that is so undeniably open to me.

There are no lies in this face.

Even so, he was badly injured and a fearful part of me understands that he is still mortally wounded. Somehow, he woke up and came to me, but these moments might not last long.

I need to speak while I can.

"I understand your anger," I say, refusing to look away. "I feel it, and I respect it."

He gives a small nod. "As I understand yours."

I hope he hears me as I continue. "You are entitled to your vengeance."

Again, he nods. "As you are to yours."

My other hand presses to his chest and I flex my fingers to his skin, registering the clothing he's wearing. A simple, gray tunic and pants. No more opulent silk or dark cloaks.

Simple, humble clothing.

I press my forehead to the edge of his jaw before moving upward to nudge my cheek to his. "Why do I feel so safe with you right now?"

It might not be the most important question.

Or maybe it is.

His lips move against my ear, and there isn't a hint of a threat in his voice, despite what he says. "You probably shouldn't."

Still, his arms stroke my lower back, easing the tense muscles, his fingers brushing up along my aching spine before stopping where the bulk of my wings prevent him from reaching further.

The way he presses my muscles on either side of my spine relieves some of my pain—the pain of releasing and carrying my wings—and I relax against him.

Finally, the clamped muscles ease enough that I can retract my wings.

The heinous, black feathers fold inward and disappear from view, and I slump against him with relief. His hands work their way up to my shoulder blades while I nestle my head in the crook of his neck and he rests his cheek against my forehead.

And now I need to face what I know is still true.

"You're dying," I whisper, hoping that, by some dark miracle, he will tell me he no longer is.

"I am."

I don't fight the catch in my voice. "You're hiding your wounds from me again."

"Yes."

"Is being awake now... Is it harming you?"

He's slower to answer and I read the worst into his silence.

"Then stop it!" I snap. "Stop being awake!"

He strokes my hair, strokes my back. "You can't prevent my death, Caera. But there are things I need to tell you before I go."

"What could be so important that you'd hasten your death—"

He presses his lips to mine.

A soft kiss that steals the words from my mouth.

When he pulls back, but not far, he says, "I need you to know that despite all of the darkness in you, and despite all of the darkness in *me*, and despite your father's predictions and your need for retribution and the fact that you could rend the world to pieces if you chose to…" He stops to take a breath, the calm in his voice enfolding me. "Your heart gave me something I didn't have before and I never expected to feel."

"What could that possibly be?" I ask, my voice bleak.

"Faith," he says.

I continue to search his eyes, a new pain entering my chest, and once again, I feel all the little fissures in my heart, all the pieces, sliding apart. "It can't be worth it. For a heart that keeps breaking and won't heal…"

His lips rise in a soft smile. "It's worth it," he says. "Even now, the heart you gave me hammers in my chest with all its beautiful darkness. Your pain. Your fury. The protectiveness you feel for your pack. Your reason. Your logic. Your restraint. Your ability to reject what you could take in the present because you're determined to achieve a greater purpose." His thumb gently strokes my jaw, his gaze impossibly calm. "You proved to me that I still have a soul."

A light enters his eyes that wasn't there before. "You gave me a gift because if I have a soul, then I can find peace. I can join my ancestors where their magic is kept safe by the old magic keeper and—"

"No." I snarl, sliding forward, slipping my legs to either side of his hips, wrapping my legs around him, wrapping my arms across his broad back, holding on to him as hard as I can. "I won't allow it."

"Caera," he says. "You can't stop this. It's already done."

I shake my head rapidly, refusing to listen. "No."

"Caera." His voice rumbles again.

My forehead crinkles against his chest because he's used that word several times now, and I'm starting to wonder what it means. "What did you call me?"

"Caera," he says. "Beloved. My heart."

Hot tears spill down my cheeks. Since I stole the book, so many secrets and lies have been exposed. I've done things I never imagined that I could. Nearly all were by accident or instinct. I had no plan. I followed no set path. But somehow, it's all led me to this moment.

A moment when I need to decide what he is to me.

He was my enemy by birth. But now…

My mother's voice echoes back to me.

You were loved.

I am loved.

I have no name for the keeper now. What do I call a being who gives me a beautiful night sky and then tells me he can't share it with me?

"I won't let you die," I say. "I will heal my heart and you will heal with it."

"You can't stop this. What matters is what you do with the crown—"

"I don't want it."

"That's why you have to take it." His fingers brush my cheek, coaxing me to look at him. "It can't fall into the wrong hands."

"It shouldn't fall into *my* hands," I say, adamant, because even now, even with all the honesty in his eyes and the absence of subterfuge, I sense there's something he isn't telling me.

And then it hits me.

What he's been hiding from me.

"I gave you the power in my heart." I try to speak past the fear rising within me. "If you die, what happens to that power?"

His jaw clenches, and I know the answer.

"It will die with you," I whisper, a deep horror billowing within me. "I will become heartless. Alive but without feeling. And I will lose my reason. My protectiveness. My restraint. My *feeling*. All of the things that make me *me*. All of that will die with you."

I try to breathe. "When you die, I will become a monster."

CHAPTER FORTY-ONE

I recall the way Lucian described me in the vision he'd seen in *The Book of Dark Magic*.

"In the book, my eyes were dead," I say. "I had no heart. No soul."

I fight the sick, clawing feeling wrapping itself around my chest. A cold chill fills my bones.

I speak rapidly as an awful panic billows in waves through me. "This is how it happens, isn't it?" I ask. "You die, I lose my heart, and I take the crown without hesitation. Then, I wreak justice on every dark creature who was complicit in my mother's imprisonment. Everyone who profited from my father's regime while I was caged. The entire Nostra Empire. Human and supernatural. I raze it to the ground in cold-blooded murder."

I give a bleak laugh. "But why stop there? *The Book of Dark Magic* could only reveal the fates of dark magic creatures, yes? What's to say I don't tear through other beings too? After all, with that kind of power, I can kill anything. Dragons, angels, witches, shifters, old gods. Who would stop me?"

I'm gripping the keeper so hard that my claws must be biting his back and sides, but all I can hear is my father's question when he trapped me in his lair.

"Have you ever seen true darkness?"

"Who would stop me?" I ask again, my voice like stone. "Some red-winged creature who doesn't get to me until I've taken a thousand lives?"

The keeper has remained impossibly calm, letting me speak all of my fears, as if he knows I need to voice them.

But now, he says, "*You* will stop you." His gray-blue eyes are suddenly piercing. "Because before I die, you will take back your heart's power."

I jolt away from him, but he doesn't let me go. "But that will kill you instantly. Just like taking the crown will kill you." My voice is a snarl now. "Both of those acts *will kill you.*"

"Yes."

I bare my teeth at him in all my wolfish fury. "No."

He gives me a gentle smile. "You must, Caera. Just as you must take the crown. Keep your heart. Take the crown. You will do these things—"

"No!"

"You will do these things." His voice remains calm. "Because your heart tells you they are right."

"Not right for you."

One corner of his mouth hitches up in a crooked smile. "Even so." Then his smile fades. "I want you to see something."

I don't like that he's veering our conversation in another direction, but I can't deny the solemnity in his expression. "What is it?"

"Will you come to the mirror?"

I answer him by wrapping my arms and legs more firmly around him. "I like it here."

In response, he presses his cheek to my face again, the corner of his lips brushing the corner of mine for the briefest moment, before he gives a grunt, repositions his hands, and pushes himself to his feet while I cling to him.

"Then you can stay here," he says, ambling toward the bedroom.

He carries me through the door and into the large dressing room next to the bedroom, keeping me close as he approaches the floor-to-ceiling mirror that sits against the wall at the end of it.

From the corner of my eye, I make out the treasures I left on one of the nearby shelves: a row of makeshift blindfolds from various sources, including my mother's old shirt; the two feathers my father tore from my wings; and the jewelry box in which I deposited the page from *The Book of Dark Magic* that my mother left for me.

I wonder if the page has become blank or if, somehow, it survived the death I wreaked on the rest of the book.

I'm not sure it would be wise to check.

I slide my feet to the floor as the keeper turns me to face the mirror.

Now that he's standing behind me, I'm struck by how tall and muscular his new form is. More imposing than any other persona he has taken on before.

It's astonishing to me that I don't feel any sort of uncertainty or worry around him.

"Do you remember the first time you saw yourself?" he asks.

How could I forget?

"I thought I was looking at a stranger," I say. "No, actually, I thought my reflection was an attacker."

It was nearly impossible to recognize myself. Not only because I'd never seen my full body in a mirror before then, but because it didn't match the way I'd pictured myself.

My legs were longer than I'd thought they were in proportion to my torso, and my body was skinnier at the waist and curvier at the bust. At the time, I wasn't wearing much more than a ragged bra and underpants. Along with the black sash I took on impulse from the angels' stronghold and now sits on the shelf next to the jewelry box.

"You were fierce then," he says as he meets my eyes in the mirror. "Now you are even more so."

"I feel more broken," I say. "There are pieces I don't know how to pull together. Family, that isn't what I thought it would be. Adversaries, I didn't think I'd face."

"A pack who loves you," he murmurs. "A life to make your own." And then, he adds, "There is value in broken things."

Like the weapon in the longhouse.

"Except a broken heart," I say. "There is only devastation in that."

"Maybe." He tips his head. "Or maybe it can lead to new things. A new life."

I squeeze my eyes closed. "How long do you have? Before I have to choose?"

"I can hold on for another day. Maybe a little more."

I turn to face him, no longer able to contemplate that too soon, he won't be able to stand beside me in a mirror anymore. Not if I don't do something about it.

"How bad are your wounds now?" I ask. "The ones you aren't showing me."

He doesn't evade. "Not good."

"Then you need to rest."

I wrap my hand around his and tug him toward the bedroom. Those too-soft pillows and blankets aren't so repulsive to me anymore. Especially when I catch the way he stumbles just slightly as he follows me, along with the little hitch in his breathing.

Damn. I'm not sure how he's functioning at all.

With a jolt of fear, I remember the way my mother woke up before she died. That last burst of strength.

"You should have stayed resting," I scold him, pulling him toward the bed and lifting the covers with my free hand. "*In.*"

"I got tired of the cold." He gives me another crooked smile before he lowers himself to the edge of the bed.

"Well, you should have thought of that before you created a freezing landscape."

"I liked it," he mumbles as he slides into the bed, boots and all. "Did you see the wolves? They were some of the last…"

His voice fades as his head hits the pillow and, before I can answer, his eyes are closed, his breathing even.

I reach under the bedsheets to tug off his boots and straighten his tunic, only for his arms to wrap around me and pull me down to his chest.

"I think there might be a little bit of wolf in me," he murmurs as he slides his hands across the back of the sash that's keeping my dress tied together, and nuzzles the corner of my lips.

I scowl down at him, trying not to lie too heavily on his chest. "You should sleep."

"Fuck sleeping."

He pulls me closer, the desire in his eyes heating my body, as his hands stroke up my back to tangle in my hair.

I respond by dropping a kiss to his lips. It's a light touch, even though I want more.

"You're in control, Caera," he says, his voice husky when I break the contact. "As much or as little as you want."

He continues to stroke my back up to my neck, his fingertips grazing the skin beneath my earlobes.

I'm still nestled mostly beside him and now I slip my legs to either side of his hips, straddling him, a position that could mean power but doesn't feel that way.

I want him to survive. I want to give him vengeance—even though that vengeance is, at its heart, against me. I want his body. I want to let go of my fears, worries, and my control. Just once.

"I want everything," I say.

CHAPTER FORTY-TWO

He gives me a lazy smile. "Okay, then."

His fingertips stroke the side of my neck, the skin above my breasts, my shoulders, then my back, following the shape of my spine.

I lower my head to his, my lips exploring his jaw, his neck, his shoulders—as far as I can while he's dressed.

Both of us learning the shape of each other's bodies.

He wraps his arms around me so that he can sit up beneath me and I can slip his tunic off his head. When he rests back down, I undo the sash keeping my dress in place and let it fall to the sides, exposing the space between my breasts and my pelvis.

I'm not wearing a bra or underpants. I cut through them in the Underworld and this dress is all I took from the closet there.

His palm glides all the way up the center of my chest from my stomach to my jaw.

I notice the calluses on his palms. Hands that possibly worked hard before he became the keeper. Or maybe *would have* worked hard if he'd had the time he deserved.

I welcome their rough texture. Welcome the heat they bring

to my body as he explores the curve at my waist, tugging the material aside so that it cups my breasts, still not exposing them.

I trace the muscles of his chest, my fingers flexing against his skin as I memorize his form. *This form.* The one that might be truest to who he would have been.

Then I shrug off the dress.

He's seen me fully naked before, but his lips part as if he's seeing all of me for the first time, his gray-blue eyes drinking me in.

I drop my mouth to his, inhaling the scent of snow and apples, filling my head with a fragrance that might once have existed, but I'm certain it doesn't anymore.

We've proceeded slowly, almost cautiously, but the way I lean forward presses his hard cock against my clit, and I can't stop my moan.

He's still dressed in pants, a layer of unwanted material between us, but it doesn't stop the pleasure from striking through me.

Every feathery brush of his hands has built my anticipation, and I can't deny the rush of sensation now.

Neither, it seems, can he.

He rears up beneath me, once again into a sitting position, his hold on me becoming firm as he supports my back with one arm, encloses my right breast in his other hand, and closes his mouth around my other nipple.

I gasp at the sudden influx of pleasure, the hot rush of *need* as he strokes and licks my breasts while grinding upward against my core.

I nearly scream at him when he breaks contact.

He growls against my breast, his gray-blue eyes seeking mine. "Talk to me, Caera. I can't spare any magic to tell me what you want or when you're ready. You have to tell me."

I'm torn between wanting more of exactly what he was giving me and needing him fully naked beneath me.

"I want you naked," I say.

My declaration brings a new heat to his eyes and a smile to his lips. He quickly tips us to my right, rolling us over so that our positions are reversed. At which, he promptly slips to the side of the bed and stands to remove his pants, stepping out of them while facing away from me.

I'm not about to waste the opportunity to explore his body, sliding to the floor behind him, my palms pressing to his back, tracing the shape of the muscles across his shoulders and down his sides.

Every part of him speaks to a rough existence, the kind where wood is hewn by hand, and food is grown or hunted, an existence far simpler, but much harsher, than must exist in the glittering city outside these walls.

For an unwanted second, I see again the cuts and slashes across his body that are tearing him apart. The image of them is so clear that I can't stop the sob that rises to my lips.

He turns immediately, having made it out of his pants, catching me in his arms.

"Ignore the pain," he says, a firm command. "Focus only on these moments."

His lips crash against mine as he gathers me up against him. The way his lips fit mine, the way he claims every part of my mouth, drives my fears from me.

I drop back onto the bed, my legs dangling over the edge of it as I reach for him.

"Like this," I say. "With you standing."

Gravity will be easier on me like this. Far easier to take it slow if I need it slow this first time.

I meet the heat in his eyes, the way he takes all of me in with his gaze, before he gathers my legs up around his hips, leaning forward to kiss my breasts and take his time fitting his body to mine.

It's a slow thrust, drawn out as I brace against him, testing my body by pushing against him until he fills me completely.

Every sensation that spikes through me is intense, but all of it matches my needs. Deep pleasure, needier than I ever expected, radiates from my core, bringing a heady moan to my lips.

He could have been made for me.

I could have been made for him.

I move first, rocking against him, riding the waves of pleasure as he withdraws and thrusts again, slowly at first and then faster. And then again and again.

Intense need builds within me as the rhythm takes over. Power. Pleasure. A pure abandonment of control.

Every stroke takes me higher, but also deeper, like diving into the ocean again, submerging myself beneath the waves and experiencing nothing but an intense desire that drives me on.

Even as it builds, it's splintering me, cracking apart the already shattered pieces of me, and I know there's no coming back from this.

No returning to who I was. There is only the ferocity of my moans and the fury of his eyes.

I reach the pinnacle and anticipate the crash.

But I'm not prepared for what it does to me.

The orgasm strikes through me and with it comes a wrenching pain, a rush of sensation up through my back.

My eyes fly wide as my wings threaten to extend.

"Up!" I gasp. "Pick me up!"

His arms scoop around me just in time, lifting me off the bed and up into his arms.

My wings release from my back, as black as shadows and as heavy as iron.

I sense the strength in his arms, stomach, and back as he swings me toward the empty wall behind him and pushes me up against it.

My feathers gouge the wall on either side of me before my wings fold neatly at my sides, settling into constrained folds for what might be the first time ever.

All of this, I register, even as pure pleasure rides my body.

Somehow, we've stayed connected, and I fight not to extend my claws as my back arches, my breasts grazing his chest.

I'm not done and neither is he. The hardness of his cock inside me tells me that.

I bite my lip as the corners of his mouth rise.

He's holding me in place, and gravity has driven me further onto him.

"I need more," I gasp in case he had any doubt.

His mouth claims mine and he groans against my lips, answering me with a thrust that's far more savage than before, but I gasp with relief.

Pleasure reignites within my core, intensifying beyond anything I've ever experienced as he keeps me against the wall, every hard thrust, a claim on my body.

Heat and need send my body into overdrive. Pleasure thrums through me. I grip his shoulders and meet his furious movements, my breathing heavy, my mouth hungry against his.

I give as much as I'm taking, kissing him as he's kissing me, rocking against him.

Nothing else matters but this.

The crash tears through me with a ferocity that fills my mind with oblivion, a dark, night sky, the crash of lightning over a churning sea, the scream of tearing feathers and metal on metal.

Energy crashes through me, streams of it whirling within my mind and body until I can't place myself in space and time, can't orient myself.

We hit the bed, and I don't know how we got there.

I don't fucking care.

I'm shivering with pleasure, holding on to every remnant

second of being connected to his body. Somehow, I've ended up on top of him, straddling him, my wings still tucked neatly in at my sides, but they're so long that they're cutting through the mattress.

My chest is heaving. So is his.

I'm covered in sweat, and so is he.

He strokes every part of me he can reach, his hands finding my back, my stomach, my breasts, my arms, and my neck before gliding down to my clit again.

There's a question in his eyes and a surprising insistence in his callused thumb.

I gasp at the delicious fire his touch brings.

Then, I adjust my position a little. Test my body by sliding a short way along his length as he hardens within me again.

As he starts to move, slowly this time, I meet his eyes.

I can't stop my heated smile.

I will never get enough of him.

CHAPTER FORTY-THREE

*H*ours later, my body is aching in the best of ways.

I'm lying on the keeper's chest, my upper leg hooked over his hips, my fingers tracing his side.

Many times, I thought to stop, to conserve his energy, but each time, he pulled me back to him with a need I couldn't deny.

Now, his breathing is deep, his eyes half-closed.

I don't want to break the contact, don't want this quiet to end, but my body needs to be taken care of.

"I'm going to the bathroom," I whisper to him, pressing a kiss to his lips before I shimmy out of his arms.

"Okay."

The rush of liquid between my legs is a new experience for me. I've made good use of the sheets multiple times over the last few hours. Now, too, I tear a few strips off the edge of the top sheet and wipe my thighs before I head to the bathroom to wash and pee.

When I return, the keeper's eyes are barely open. He's lying half under the sheet, half on top of it, his tall, muscular frame taking up more of the bed than I realized when I was so close to him.

"I didn't want to close my eyes until you got back," he rumbles softly.

I adjust the sheet so I can slip under it with him, nestling against his side and resting my head on his shoulder. Some of the mattress was torn up by the edges of my feathers, but I ignore the ragged bits.

"It's okay," I whisper. "Sleep now."

By the time I've stopped speaking, his eyes are already closed. Within seconds, he seems to be fast asleep.

Of course, there have been times when I *thought* he was asleep and he wasn't, so I wait a few moments before I whisper, "Keeper?"

He doesn't reply. His breathing remains deep.

It's just as well.

He wouldn't let me do what I'm about to do. Not alone, anyway.

It's a good thing my pack isn't here yet. They wouldn't let me go alone, either. By the time they get here, I'll be long gone and they won't know to where.

They won't be able to find me, and that's how I need things to be.

James wasn't wrong.

If I fight my battles with the keeper at my side, or my pack backing me up, then my enemies—my real enemies—will think that I'm weak.

I can't be seen as a feeble leader with a strong army, because then my adversaries will believe I'm nothing without that army. They will seek to destroy that army. And if I reveal how much my pack means to me, they'll seek to hurt me by hurting my pack.

As true as all that is, I need to prove the opposite.

I protect my pack.

Not the other way around.

I watch the keeper sleep for another long moment, afraid that his wounds might reappear now.

I'm not frightened to see them. They have to be faced. But I'm worried they'll be worse than they were before.

Finally, I force myself to rise, move into the dressing room, and consider my clothing choices.

I opt for simple jeans and a snug, sleeveless shirt. Both black —not that there's really any other color choice. I find a new pair of boots, ankle-length, which are easy to walk in.

Then, I face the shelf containing my treasures. All my various blindfolds. My feathers. The jewelry box containing the torn-out page my mother left for me.

When I first looked on that page, it contained a picture of a family that never existed: my father, his black wings extended protectively around my mother, who was holding a baby in her arms.

They loved each other.

Now, I leave that memory locked up in the box because that's where it belongs, put away in the dark.

I reach for my mother's old shirt. It's so tattered and threadbare that it barely takes up any space.

I swore I wouldn't retrieve this material until I avenged my mother, but I need her with me now. I need the strength of my memories of her. Just as I will take with me the knowledge of her final moments.

I tie the old shirt around my eyes, tucking it in tightly around my head. It isn't the most elegant look, but the aged weave is still the perfect protection for my eyes while allowing me to use my strong eyesight to see clearly.

Then I reach for the thick, black sash I took from the angels' stronghold. A place called 'the Cathedral'. I use it like a belt, hooking it through the loops at the waistband of my jeans.

It feels fitting to take it with me, since there is certainly a part of me that is an angel, even though there is a larger part of me that is a wolf.

Finally, I take my two feathers, using the angel's sash to tie them securely at my waist.

My father can kill me with these feathers. It could be reckless to take them with me, but they'll also be a temptation I'm certain he won't be able to resist.

I can draw him in closer this way. Close enough to use my claws.

Satisfied that I'm ready, I check the time. Enough to arrive when I need to.

As quietly as I can, I creep past the keeper, pausing only at the bedroom door.

I close my eyes, unable to turn back now.

I tell myself I have time to save him. He said he could hold on for another day, and I've only used up a third of it.

Vengeance will heal my heart.

It *has* to.

With that thought, I continue on, reaching the outer door and slipping as quietly as I can through it, stopping in the corridor outside to listen in case the keeper woke up.

My senses tell me he's still sleeping deeply.

I turn and hurry away.

Vines and flowers cover the tavern's front wall, the scent sweet and cloying.

The vines reek of magic. Halle's magic, to be precise. I recognize it now from the slightly charred threads that extend along the length of each vine, along with the vaguely charcoal hue at the center of each flower. Marks of Halle's power.

She is a contradiction of death and life, and so are her vines.

I approach the tavern door cautiously, remaining aware of

the supernaturals I've already identified standing guard at points nearby. Mom taught me how to identify the energy around supernaturals to determine their species, even if they're in a completely humanoid form.

When I first emerged from my cage, I was putting my knowledge to the test, but now I make my assessments with confidence.

There are various species congregating in groups of twos and threes along the street and lurking in the shadowy corners, indicating the clans and packs my father has called here tonight: wolf shifters, bear shifters, vampires, demons, and dark witches, but surprisingly, nobody that could be a gargoyle yet.

Unless...

My eye is drawn upward to the top of the four-story building on the opposite side of the street. Two stone monoliths rest at each corner of that building's flat roof.

Stone gargoyles. They're resting in crouched positions, their wings spread and clawed hands gripping the ledge.

Well, hello there.

I pause for a moment in case any of them make a move, and when they don't, I proceed to the front door, making sure to stand clear of the humans I pass along the way.

The last time I came here, the keeper transported me. This time, I followed the mental map Mom gave me. I stuck to the shadows as much as I could to rest my eyes from the brightening streetlights as the night deepened around me. The lights reflect off so many surfaces: vehicles, buildings, windows —even the pavement.

When I first came out in public, I was worried about wearing a blindfold that might attract attention, but it turns out that humans are far less concerned with an odd-looking passerby than they are with the conversations they're having with metal boxes held to their ears—cell phones? I think that's what they're called—or rushing to wherever it is they're going.

The wash of noise around me isn't welcome, but I'm managing to tolerate it, along with all the smells.

The tavern appears completely calm inside. Patrons sit at neat tables and at the bar, and there's a quiet hum of conversation.

There's a sign on the door announcing that the tavern is closed for a private function.

All of the patrons are human. But I also make out the lumps and bumps in their jackets and bodices that speak to a multitude of concealed weapons.

I'm nearly certain that they will be from different families. Just because their leaders all follow the Ultima Nostra doesn't mean they're allied with each other.

The seemingly calm situation inside the front room could be an explosion waiting to happen—a suspicion on my part that's proven when I push the door open and conversations die, causing nearly every human in the room to reach for a concealed weapon.

Half are pointed at each other. The other half at me.

I consider the barrel of the pistol resting on the counter just inside the door.

The human whose hand rests on it stares hard at me, his focus on my blindfold. He's a different man from the one I encountered the first time I was here. That time, the keeper had used his compulsion power to ensure we made it to the green door on the far side of the room without being stopped.

Now, I'll have to rely on my words.

"I think you know who I am," I say before the man can voice whatever threat is no doubt on his tongue. "I also believe you must have some idea of the carnage I could cause if opposed."

I've never tested my body against bullets, but I do trust my rapid healing power.

And, while I'm not certain that the humans in this room are entirely informed about the supernatural nature of the Ultima

Nostra, I'm not against revealing my wings and finding out if their metallic nature will make them strong enough to shield me from projectiles.

"It is my preference to pass quietly through this room and into the next one," I say, projecting my voice so that there's no doubt the humans in the back can hear me.

"You are free to ignore me and continue about your..." I glance at the tables. Not a single meal. Most glasses are still full. It seems they're taking their duties seriously. "Business," I finish.

The man behind the counter twitches, but I suspect it's more of a nervous twitch now than anything else. His heart is hammering, and the sweat on his brow is glistening.

It makes me wonder if my father deliberately put a more fearful person in this spot, since a gunfight out here would certainly make things more difficult for me. It would be easier to capture me in the ensuing chaos. And I'd be forced to use up more energy in the meantime.

The man behind the counter isn't a coward. Far from it. He simply wants to live.

Before he can do something about his fear, I glide my hand across the weapon and slice neatly through it with my claws. I ensure I only extend them enough that even close up, it looks like I parted the weapon simply by touching it.

Sliced-up bullets roll across the counter and *clink* against the raised edges of the countertop.

I'm a little concerned the sound will trigger the other humans, but they don't react. Even if the tension in the room rises higher.

"There," I say softly. "Much better."

The man steps back, both hands palms up.

Turning calmly, I step into the room, swaying to the left to pass wide of the nearest table. "Excuse me." I smile at the men sitting at it. And then the next table. "Don't mind me."

I move on past the next table, which has a greater number of women sitting at it, to whom I tip my chin.

When I reach the final table, one of the men sitting at it stands up. He isn't exactly in my path, but I stop and consider him.

His heartbeat is steady and his brow is clear. His anxiety level is the opposite of that of the man at the counter. He's completely cold. Completely in control.

It doesn't escape me that he's positioned closest to the green door.

"You have a death wish," I say to him. And then, more of a guess, I add, "You need a purpose."

"My purpose is to stop you," he replies, at which the tension in the room rises again.

"Well," I say, taking a moment while I quietly prepare to draw my claws again, "what counts as stopping me?"

"Killing you."

"Do you think you can?"

"Yes."

I tilt my head. Then, speak slowly. "You believe you can kill me when my own father—the man who tells *your* boss what to do—has tried and failed. That's a little insulting to him, don't you think?" I purse my lips. "Does my father know you feel this way?"

A slight crease appears in the man's forehead.

"It's probably better if I don't tell him," I say.

As I speak, I take note of the painting of vines and flowers—an image of the same kind of greenery that grows on the front wall of this building. They seem to be moving, just like they seemed to follow my movements the last time I was here.

One of the vines is peeling off the wall, taking solid form and snaking silently through the air toward the man's back.

The man gives a snarl that doesn't bode well, and now I sense his blood pressure rising.

I narrow my eyes at him, even though he won't see it behind my blindfold.

Leaning toward him, I growl right back at him, my voice full of force now. "You can sit down. Or I can bloody you up, drag you in front of my father, and tell him you think so little of him. Just to be clear, it's only because I'd love to see the look on his face that I'll kill you *after* I present you to him. Now, which would you prefer? Sit or die?"

His blood pressure eases and he suddenly grins at me.

He doesn't sit down, but he does stand aside.

Hmm. I take a more careful look at him. Light-brown hair, unremarkable brown eyes, and a large physique, but without any defining features that make him stand out. He's definitely someone's top henchman. The disappear-into-the-background-until-he's-needed-to-dispose-of-the-bodies type. Likes a good threat. Appreciates a little blood. Wasn't going to let me pass unless I showed some mettle.

I keep him in my sights, conscious of the retracting vine, which settles innocently back against the wall.

I hiss at it as I push open the green door, mimicking the sound the shadow panthers make when they're unhappy. "I didn't need your help."

Quickly, I step into the short corridor beyond the green door.

When I first entered this hallway, I didn't realize that it was concealed from the room beyond it. I can see clearly into that room, but anyone in that room can't see me until I step completely out from the end of the corridor.

The first time I did it, it must have looked as if I'd been stepping through the wall itself.

Last time, the room ahead was filled with tables. Men were drinking and gambling, completely oblivious to our imminent arrival.

Not so now.

A near-*army* of men and women waits on the other side of the corridor. All of the men are tall and burly. All are sporting weapon belts carrying blades. In addition, I catch flashes of short, sharp claws on their hands. But it's the gray wings resembling rock that give them away. Each tip of their wings has a claw that looks as merciless as a dagger.

They're gargoyles.

The women among them are stunning. They're beautiful and far more petite than the men. They're also wearing harnesses filled with weaponry, which I have no doubt they know how to use.

This is a clan of mercenaries, and they're ready for my arrival.

I will only have a small element of surprise and I plan on making the most of it.

Stepping right up to the edge of the corridor, I extend my claws and take a few deep breaths. I focus myself while I plot a path through the room, taking note of the small gaps and tiny vulnerabilities. I imagine that being hit with a gargoyle fist will be similar to being hit by the male assassin, and I plan on avoiding both fists and blades.

With a final roll of my shoulders and a step back to give me speed, I prepare to enter the gargoyle's den.

move fast.

Leaping from the corridor and running at full speed, my arms pumping, I aim for the biggest guy on my right, using his body like a ramp and his shoulder like a springboard before the other gargoyles can even react to my presence.

They probably expected me to saunter out and challenge them without any respect for their strength.

I'm not so foolhardy.

My goal is to evade and get past them.

But they aren't about to make it easy for me.

As I leap from the first gargoyle's shoulders into the gap I plotted, the gargoyles are already reacting.

I don't know why they carry so many blades because their wing daggers are incredibly efficient, slicing through the air on my right and my left fast enough to cut across my back and gut me at the same time.

Evading them means dropping and rolling, and I really didn't want to be on the floor where they could easily kick me.

Although...

I ram my claws into the calf of the incoming gargoyle on my

left before I throw myself upward, twisting and dancing through the next space, then up another gargoyle's body before I somersault through the air, kicking hard off another's head and shoulders before landing and clawing another's arm. I meant the last as a defensive blow to stop his oncoming blade, but it happened too fast for me to fully retract my claws, so I slice across his forearm badly enough for him to roar with pain.

It's a sound that seems to shock the other gargoyles, freezing them for a second.

Fuck me.

Are they not accustomed to being hit and sliced up at all?

Possibly not.

The next man's wing shoots in front of himself—an attempt to use it as a shield—as I charge straight for him, taking advantage of the pause around me to gain as much ground as I can.

I have no doubt that his wings would normally be an effective shield, just as dragon scales are normally impervious to all blades.

My claws slice right through his wing, but I withdraw them before they can shred his wing into ribbons. I don't know if gargoyle wings can heal, and don't want to permanently maim anyone.

I'd rather not leave grudges in my wake.

I catch the widening of the gargoyle's brown eyes—maybe he's surprised I didn't go for the kill—before I spin into the gap behind him and charge through it.

Both of my hands shoot out, ready to raze across the chests of the gargoyles coming at me from each side.

They must not have missed what I did to their comrade's wing because they leap backward as fast as they can.

Suddenly, I'm at the far door.

Surprisingly, nobody's coming for me.

Behind me, both men and women crouch and slump, their

wings hanging low. Their bodies are so bloody that I replay my actions in my mind. Did I really whirl through them so hard?

Yes.

Yes, I did.

I consider them carefully, drawing myself upright when they remain where they are, not a single one coming at me.

They may be vicious mercenaries, but their heartbeats tell me they aren't all cold-blooded killers. In fact… the way they're already assessing each other's wounds tell me they have a close pack mentality. It's the kind of pack mentality that means their leadership determines their actions.

A toxic leader makes for a toxic pack.

Well, fuck that.

Taking a chance to pause for another moment, I snarl at them. "My father put you in front of me like animals to slaughter. I would never do the same."

With that, I ram my claws through the door's handle, shredding the wood and cutting through the lock before I hurry on through.

I stop.

Gad and Valki stand on the other side of the corridor I've entered. Gad's vampire fangs are extended and Valki's muscles gleam a little, even though she's furiously chewing gum, an action that seems to keep her berserker nature under control.

They both take a glance at the carnage I left behind before the broken door swings closed.

"Fuck it," Gad says, tugging at the collar of his shirt. He's wearing a business suit, and as usual, there's a drop of blood on his white collar.

He glances at Valki and she gives a nod, lowering the arm on which she wears a metal wire that she likes to use as a garrote to strangle people.

"Your father's this way," she says. And then, beneath her breath, she adds, "He can fight his own fucking battles."

If I peer closely at them both, I can make out what looks like a burn scar across Valki's bare shoulder, visible because of her short-sleeved shirt.

And a similar burn scar across Gad's temple.

Most likely from slaps of light magic.

I snarl. "I see my father's been making use of his new power."

Neither of them answers me, but they flinch a little, a confirmation of my guess.

Then Valki chews more furiously on her gum and mutters around it, "Fucking light magic. Should be fucking outlawed."

Gad throws her a warning look, and she snaps her mouth closed so fast that her teeth *clack*.

We turn the next corner and then another, finally stopping at a set of large, wooden doors.

They both shuffle on the spot.

It won't look good for them if they open the door for me.

I grin at them.

I've wanted to clobber them both and I can't say my dark heart won't enjoy it.

My fist shoots out, smacking Gad across the face so hard that he drops to a crouch as I spin and rake my claws lightly across Valki's arm, drawing enough blood to make a mess without causing any real damage.

As their shouts ring out, I shove on the door and step inside.

My entrance causes a stir, but that was to be expected.

All heads turn in my direction, and I take it all in within a few seconds.

The room is far larger and more grandiose than I was expecting.

It has a black marble floor that makes me think my father deliberately chose to mimic the dark keeper's realm—which he no doubt saw in *The Book of Dark Magic*.

A throne sits on a dais at the other end. The dais is cleverly situated at the far end of a long table so that it sits above and beyond the table, keeping the Ultima Nostra's throne above every other seat in the room.

I rapidly count thirty people sitting at the very large table, all of them spread out in a way that tells me they don't like each other very much.

They each have another person standing at their back, possibly a beta in the case of the shifters, or a second-in-command for the humans and the other supernaturals. They will be those leaders' generals and I won't underestimate them.

My eye is drawn to the bright spot near the throne where the keeper of light magic stands, her shoulders slumped.

She looks thin. Fragile. Her eyes are the same empty, golden orbs that they were when I first saw her.

At that time, her labored breathing had caused her to sway from side to side, but now I can barely hear her breaths because they're so shallow. Her clothing remains the same: golden armor from her feet to her chin. But it now hangs off her thin frame as if she's been sucked dry. The curved blade that rests in a harness at her back, the handle of which is visible at her left shoulder, seems to be dragging her down.

He must be draining her too much.

What's also clear is that there are no other supernaturals standing at my father's back. His generals are gone. I took them.

Still, my father doesn't deign to rise from his throne.

He languishes there, his feathery, black wings nestled at his sides and easily accommodated by the throne's width.

He is luminescent. His golden eyes gleam and his skin practically sparkles. He is a perfect, powerful dark angel.

"Daughter," he calls across the distance. "You're finally here."

As if I kept him waiting.

He waves at the end of the table nearest to me, where there's an empty seat. His gesture is relaxed, but his voice is a firm command. "Sit down."

I shun the empty seat and walk to the right of the table

instead, steering wide enough of the standing people that they can't reach out and strike me without leaving their posts. But close enough that it's clear I'm not afraid of them.

I flick blood off my claws as I go.

The tension rises around me. The leaders haven't made a move, but they're all watching me with a reassuring amount of wariness. I'm glad they won't underestimate me.

I assess each of them as I walk, identifying the energy around them and finally pinpointing the gargoyle king. He's sitting halfway along the table on the left side—opposite to the side I'm walking on. It puts him farther away from me, but it lets me see his entire face.

He's as burly as the gargoyles I fought minutes ago, with short, dark hair and thick eyebrows. Even thicker fingers are folded on the table in front of him as he leans slightly forward.

A blonde-haired woman stands at his back, her bare arms covered in tattoos, one of which depicts the same mountain scene Lucian wears.

Before I pass the gargoyle king's position, I remove my blindfold, ensuring he will see my golden eyes.

I don't need the blindfold's protection in this room where the light is dim. If I have to draw a little of my black blood to fully prove my heritage, I'll do that, too.

All in good time.

For now, I tuck my mother's shirt into the pocket of my jeans and focus back on my father.

Baring my teeth, I announce my intentions for all to hear. "I'm here for your throne."

CHAPTER FORTY-FIVE

As I continue to prowl toward my father, he smiles as if he couldn't be less concerned.

"Of course, you're here for my throne," he says. "I was just telling my people—"

"I killed your book."

His smile slips a little.

"Shredded," I say. "Stabbed. Dead. *The Book of Dark Magic* is no more."

A murmur rises from the group.

My father has stiffened. He was obsessed with that book. For decades, it claimed his mind and his heart and overcame his reason.

He gives a harsh laugh and another dismissive wave of his hand. "So you claim. But stories are only stories. There is no proof of it."

"If that is what you choose to believe," I say.

"Where is your keeper?" he asks, seeming to go on the attack now in this war of words we're having. "Where is your pack? Dead, perhaps?"

I can't hide my reaction fast enough.

"Or… *dying*," he says, his smile returning. He saw the way the keeper had been weakened in the catacombs. My father wanted my heart to break because then the keeper would break.

"Yes," I say, choosing not to hide the truth. "My keeper is dying. But so is yours."

It's a guess, but my father's expression becomes stony, a wiping clean of his emotions.

"You've taken without giving," I say. "And now you've taken too much."

I've reached the dais now, and he doesn't have a guard to stop me from stepping up onto it. Certainly, none of the leaders or their generals has moved to stop me.

Of course, I'm now at a very real risk of being attacked from behind.

I keep my ears peeled, listening for any hint of movement among the leaders, any jumping heart rates that could indicate ill intentions, as I veer away from my father and continue toward the light magic keeper instead.

I fear her magic, but as for the woman herself…

"Who was she?" I ask, keeping my voice raised, clear for the listeners, as I glance at my father. "Do you even know?"

He scowls at me, but he doesn't appear so comfortable on his throne. In his hubris, he's allowed me to get too close to him and he has no backup except this golden-eyed woman whose magic is waning.

James was right about the careful knife.

I remain wary of my father—the possibility that he might lash out at any second, since he's allowed me so close now—as I step right up to the light magic keeper.

He seems to relax again. "By all means, Daughter. Try to take her power from me. I will enjoy the scent of your burning flesh."

I don't know how he captured her or what mechanism he's using to control her.

I gave my keeper the gift of free will, but it's clear this

woman has none. *The Book of Dark Magic* must have shown him what to do, but the emptiness of her eyes...

It's as if she's here.

But she also isn't.

What strikes me most is that she made a choice once—a voluntary choice—to save her world and now she's paying a new price for it. A price she doesn't deserve to pay.

With a growl on my lips, I'm about to turn back to my father with a furious rebuke, but then—

Her energy vibrates. It's only the smallest tingle, but I realize that I extended the claws of my left hand and they must have come very close to brushing her form...

The hum of power around her increases in strength when I move my claws close to her again.

The magic that created her exists within me.

When I drove my claws through *The Book of Dark Magic* back at the catacombs, this keeper was present but standing behind me. I didn't see what impact it had on her. Maybe none. Or maybe it had a big impact that I didn't witness because my only thought at that moment had been of my own survival.

"Darling Father," I say quietly. "Did you consider that she might not like being used in this way?"

He gives a snarl, finally launching himself out of his chair. "Enough of your talk! I've let you breathe the air of this room longer than I should have."

I ignore him.

I came here to kill the gargoyle king and then my father, but *this* I need to do first.

With a scream of rage, I drive my left hand, claws extended, through the light magic keeper's form, bracing for agonizing pain.

Bracing for the fury of light magic to flay the flesh from my bones.

She is insubstantial. Nothing more than ghostly. A fact I didn't realize the first time I saw her.

My hand and arm move straight through her, still completely visible to me.

But her weapon—*oh, her weapon*—it scraped and scraped against the stone wall of those catacombs in a way that drove shivers down my spine.

Clang!

My claws meet the weapon's hilt, and a bolt of burning energy strikes through me.

A chiming sound rings through the air as if multiple strings had been plucked at once.

I'm aware of every dark creature in the room crying out and clutching their ears. My own ears are instantly bleeding.

But I'm also aware that everything is slowing down.

The chime continues in one long note, light magic as pure and strong as dragon's fire filling the air and taking control.

Everyone except the light magic keeper and me seems to pause and become frozen in time.

The keeper of light magic opens her eyes, looking at me with a clarity I wasn't expecting.

"Break this blade," she whispers, her voice muffled because of my burning eardrums.

Her voice sounds like that of an older woman, certainly older than her younger face implies.

"The walls of my Realm had become thin. Just like the wall of the dark keeper's Realm. Your father found my Realm. That dark book showed him how." Her upper lip curls with fury. "He couldn't command me, but he took my weapon. It pulled my power with it. You must break it, just as you broke that book."

I struggle to speak. "But this blade—"

"Is only a duplicate. It was needed to create me and now its purpose is spent. It is nowhere near as powerful as the blade it's modeled on," she says. "The original blade is safe where it can't hurt anyone. If you break this metal like you broke the book, you will free me."

The chime is already fading and I know I don't have long before everything speeds up around me again.

Despite the terrible, horrible pain of making contact with her light magic, I can't help but smile.

"Go back to your Realm, keeper," I command her, my claws digging slowly into the blade's metal, connecting with the metallic core that was used to create it. "Do what you were created to do. The walls of your Realm will be healed, and you will not be used against your will again."

My claws finally break through the metal.

Snap!

She vanishes instantly and so does her blade.

My father resumes his leap toward me, his roar sounding dull now that my ears are damaged.

I'm more aware of my burning palm than I am of his approach. The skin across my left hand is stripped off, and my left arm trembles uncontrollably.

Dark saints, the burning scent that fills the air around me turns my stomach.

I stumble, but it helps me because my jerky step takes me out of my father's path.

He's screaming at me, but bless my ears, I can't hear what he's saying.

I'm done with him.

I'm done with his games.

I'm done with the pain he caused.

The careful knife is no more.

I am a sharp weapon, and I will no longer be constrained.

CHAPTER FORTY-SIX

I leap away from my father, registering his confusion, before I bound onto the table and break into a run toward its central point.

"Gargoyle king!" I shout. "For your crimes against my brother and his mother, you will die first. Now choose: Fight or die!"

It seems he was prepared for the challenge. He's been throwing glares at me ever since I arrived. He will have heard that Lucian formed an alliance with me.

"You are the one who will die," he retorts, jumping to his feet so quickly that he knocks his chair backward.

While the supernaturals around him scatter, he extends his wings and rises into the air, a great brute of a man swooping toward me.

His skin flushes gray as he flies, a coating of stone that he will no doubt believe can repel my claws.

As he storms down on me, I leap up to meet him, the muscles in my legs bunching and pushing me higher while my right hand stretches out.

My claws slice from his neck to his crotch before I land neatly on the table, covered in blood.

His body hits the surface behind me, sliding partway across the table before coming to a stop at its edge.

His wings conceal most of the gore, but not the thick trail of blood he leaves across the table's surface.

I'm aware of a movement on my right—the female gargoyle was lurching toward me—and my right hand has shot out to meet her.

She stops. Right before my claws would have impaled her chest.

Pinpricks of blood form before the droplets slide down her bare clavicle to the top of her shirt.

There's a terrible silence around me and maybe it's only because my ears are so damaged, but the blonde-haired woman backs slowly away from me, removing herself from danger, her hands rising, palms out.

Her lips move, but try as I might, I can't hear what she says. Too hard to read her lips.

She eyes me warily while I rise to my feet with a snarl on my lips.

"Fight or die," I say.

I have no clue if I shouted or whispered my command, which is now directed at my father this time. "Or *bow*."

His head snaps up where he stands at the edge of the dais. His focus was on the dead gargoyle king, but now it's firmly on me.

"Bow?" he snaps, a word I make out from the movement of his lips. It's easy enough to read it because he enunciated it with clear disgust. "*Never*."

"Very well."

I stride toward him, deliberately stepping through the blood. It's not as if I can avoid it. It's dripping from my hair and my shoulders, sliding down my chest, covering my burned palm. Hopefully distracting from how badly my left arm is shaking.

The leaders and their generals all back away as I pass their locations, and when even one of them stays a little close, the female gargoyle shouts something at them. They snarl and glare at her but quickly step away.

As I walk, I watch my father, knowing that this is the last chance I'll have to say what I need to say to him.

"She died in my arms."

He was already pale, but now he blanches.

"She spent years trying to breathe the stale air and survive on crumbs. But before she died, she taught me everything I needed to know."

Not all the things I wanted to know.

But everything that has kept me alive and brought me here to this moment.

Where I will seize my vengeance or die trying.

"You put her there because of me," I say. "And in so doing, you created the thing you feared." I flick the blood off my claws again. "Behold, Father. A daughter covered in dark blood."

Taiven's golden eyes are full of hate. The animosity in them would have crushed me before, but now it makes my choice easier.

As I draw to the end of the table, I know what he's going to do.

He'll leap for one of the feathers I've tucked into the angel's sash at my waist.

It's the only way he can kill me—by using my own metal against me.

I jump from the table, landing at a crouch, not taking my eyes off him for an instant, rising once again to my full height.

"Choose," I say. Maybe a whisper. Maybe a roar.

He sweeps toward me in a flurry of wings, his right hand

outstretched. He's moving fast, a blur, as fast as a dark angel can move, using his wings for speed, but they're his undoing.

Oh, wings.

Always a fucking liability.

I sidestep his lunge and sweep my claws through his outstretched wing, cutting through the bone and sinew, sending feathers floating through the air around me before the lower half of his wing drops to the floor.

His eyes are wide as he whirls to face me. His mouth is moving, but again, bless my ears.

I ignore his mouth and watch his hands.

I leap up onto the dais as he rages at me again, this time with fists swinging.

When I first fought him, I didn't have the combat skills that I have now.

I duck his swing and step inward, my claws ramming upward beneath his ribs and tearing into his chest.

His eyes widen with shock and he gives a strangled gasp.

His legs give way, his weight suddenly dropping onto my hand, which only takes my claws deeper into his chest.

He falls to his knees in front of me.

Both of us are now kneeling, facing each other.

I can tell he's gasping for air, but even now, his focus flies to the feathers at my waist. He's close enough to grab one of them and ram it into my heart.

His right hand moves, but my left hand is quicker. Despite its trembling, my aim is accurate, my claws driving forward through the back of his wrist and pinning his hand to his chest.

At that moment, my ears clear and sounds rush in.

He's gasping for air, just like I thought, but he's also speaking.

"...tell you where *The Book of Old Magic* is. Let me live..."

I narrow my eyes at him. "Why would the location of that book matter to me?"

"It can save… your keeper…" Black blood bubbles between his teeth. "Let me live… I'll tell you… where it is…"

I exhale a quiet breath. "Like *The Book of Dark Magic* was supposed to save my mother? No, thank you."

With a terrible snarl, I rip my claws in opposite directions, cutting across my father's chest and arms, tearing his body open before I let him fall to the floor.

The life fades from his golden eyes, the light in them becoming dull until they turn a washed-out yellow color. No longer golden. No longer powerful.

Just like that. He's gone.

I rise to my feet, standing over him, conscious of the gore on my chest and arms and… well, it's pretty much all over me.

"Anyone else?" I ask.

The room is silent.

I turn to cast my gaze across each of them, taking note of their faces. Strange seeing these faces for the first time today, and yet they are the faces of my future. Supernaturals who form this empire I came to claim.

I wait another moment, but nobody moves.

"The Nostra Empire is mine," I say to them, my voice level and calm.

Still, nobody moves or speaks.

"I will not rule the empire like my father did. I have new rules." I pin each of them with my gaze. "You may not like my rules, but if you follow them, you will have my protection. If you contravene them, I will mete out punishment in the form of death."

I point at my father and then at the gargoyle king. They are my examples and I'm certain the images of them will be burned into the memories of these leaders for years to come.

"Do not challenge me. I will kill you," I continue. "Do not come for my pack or my family. I will kill you." I lift my chin and allow a smile to touch my lips. "Obey me and you will thrive."

I extend my claws and growl at them. "Now choose: Fight and die. Or bow and live."

The thick silence around me quietly breaks.

Whispered footfalls sound as the leaders and their generals step forward, forming lines on each side of the table.

In unison, they all take a knee.

The gargoyle woman raises her head first. "Ultima Nostra," she says, her voice clear and strong. "Long may you reign."

CHAPTER FORTY-SEVEN

The Nostra Empire is mine.

I should feel elated, but my chest feels empty.

Without my pack, the family I've found, and without the keeper, there is only the cold comfort of a power I've paid a heavy price to claim.

I need to get back to the keeper as quickly as I can, but I also can't rush this initial time with the leaders of the dark families, not when my reign is new.

No matter how much blood I shed to get to this point, I have to solidify my intentions and my control while the scent of death is heavy in the air to ensure there are no creeping doubts in their minds.

It takes an hour to give the leaders their orders and set my ground rules.

They don't like my rules, just as I anticipated. Telling dark creatures to curb the worst of their natures is no small thing. But they can also see the benefits. Reduced heat from the Assassin's Legion, for one.

The whole time, I shun the throne my father lounged on. I'll have the damn thing destroyed the first chance I get.

When Gad and Valki finally slink into the room, cautiously asking if I need anything, I tell them to bring towels.

Then, when the leaders finally disperse, each one bowing to me and restating their allegiance, Valki asks me if I want a shower.

She and Gad stand nervously, watching me as I consider her question.

I guess they're wondering if I'm going to kill them.

"A shower. Clean clothes. And the quickest passage southwest," I say before I give them a hard stare. "I have something to take care of and then I'll be back. When I return, you will be ready to show me every corner of this place and tell me everything you know about my empire. Even if you think I won't like to hear it. I want truth, not lies."

They glance at each other. "We can do that."

"Good." I don't trust them enough to tell them where I'm going—the location of the apartment. That sort of trust has to be earned—and right now, they're afraid of me, not loyal. I'll separate from them before I get anywhere near the apartment just to be safe.

I would be more worried about leaving these premises if the Nostra Empire revolved around its buildings or any particular territory, but it doesn't.

It revolves around its ruler.

Wherever I go, that's where the empire is.

Another hour later, I've washed, dressed in jeans and a T-shirt that fit me well enough, and left the underground pathways beneath the White Wing Tavern behind, along with Gad and Valki.

I make it back to the apartment just as the sun is rising, only to realize that I don't have a key.

Before I consider how to break in without damaging the door too badly, it flies open, and Anarchy stands within it.

"*Darkness!*" she scolds me. "Where have you—?"

She inhales deeply before her pupils dilate, and she quickly pulls me inside, leaning close to me.

"Any chance you were covered in gargoyle blood a short while ago?" she asks while her brothers gravitate toward me.

Shadow panthers crave gargoyle blood, so I shouldn't be surprised.

I catch sight of Lucian in the background. I'm certain that Orlan must have brought my pack here—a certainty that's confirmed when the bright-eyed warlock steps into view from the side of the lounge room.

"Keep your licking to yourselves," I grumble at the dark elves as they crowd me.

It can't help that I'm carrying my mother's shirt and the black sash in a plastic bag—both of which I quickly washed but haven't properly cleaned. The material was soaked in gargoyle blood.

Anarchy smacks her lips. "There's just a little drop you missed right here."

She swoops in and runs her tongue across my earlobe before darting back with a grin. "Got it."

Her smile quickly fades.

So does mine. "The Nostra Empire is mine."

My declaration feels hollow.

The dark elves give me quiet nods before Lucian steps toward me, reaching for my hand.

"The keeper isn't doing well," he says.

Vengeance wasn't enough.

As soon as I destroyed the light magic keeper's weapon, I knew it wouldn't be. My keeper was broken long before I met him.

I exhale slowly, trying to take control of my aching sadness. "I'm going to need your help," I say to my pack. "You, too, Orlan. There are things I need you to do, and you can't question them. Please trust that I'm making the only choices that I can."

I wait for them to acknowledge me.

"We're here," Anarchy says. "Say the word and it will be done."

My legs are wooden as I step between them and make my way to the bedroom.

When I round the corner and step inside, my hand flies to my mouth and my eyes fill with tears.

Gone is the man who held me in his arms only hours ago.

The keeper's face is past pale, a gray tinge now at the edges of his lips and extending across his hollow cheeks.

Once again, he lied to me—this time about how much time he had left. I wouldn't have gone to fight my father if I'd known the keeper had only had hours to live.

He's lying on his back, his chest bare, his arms crossed over his torso, his left hand covering his right.

The dark crown is fully visible on his left forefinger.

His breathing is shallow, a whisper in the silence.

I try to move past my pain.

I know what I have to do. I realized it when I drove my hand through the light magic keeper's insubstantial form and cut through her weapon to free her. To *command* and free her.

I squeeze my eyes closed, and when I open them, I draw on all my fury because without it, I won't be able to do this.

"Orlan," I say. "Come here. I need you to be close by and ready to use your transportation magic."

He ventures into the room, keeping near to the wall beside the door, his voice conveying his uncertainty. "Veda?"

"When I ask you, I need you to take the keeper away from me."

His forehead crinkles, but I continue before he can question me. "You will take him to St. Michael Cemetery."

Orlan startles. "What?"

"That's where Elijah is," I say.

Orlan widens his eyes at me. "That may be so, but there are

also other supernaturals there who won't take kindly to my arrival."

I turn to my brother. "Which is why you will go with Orlan."

Lucian shakes his head, his golden eyes filled with worry. "Veda, I don't understand this."

I take my brother's hands, holding them tightly. "You will understand. And I promise, no harm will come to you or Orlan. When the fury who lives there makes an appearance—which she will—tell her that the new Ultima Nostra sends you in the name of peace.

"Tell her that I am allied with Rebella, the fury of Mount Greylock, and now I seek an alliance with the supernaturals of St. Michael Cemetery. The fury will see the truth in your message, and she will not harm you."

"Sister…"

I give him a hard stare. "Can you do this for me?"

He nods. "I can."

I tremble with relief. It's only when I pull my hands away from his that I remember how badly burned my left palm still is.

I hide it quickly before he can see it.

To the dark elves, I say, "You will stay here with me. I will need you." I take another deep breath. "I will need all of the precious darkness in your souls and the power in your hearts. I will need you to be here with me and keep me steady. No matter what. Can you do that?"

They each give me solemn nods, and, even though they're resolute in their actions, I can hear the way their hearts jump and pound with uncertainty. They promised to do what I ask, but that doesn't mean they aren't anxious about it, an anxiety that I completely understand. But it can't sway me.

I turn to the keeper, approaching the right side of the bed and depositing the bag of soggy material and two metal feathers on the floor next to it.

Soon, those things may not mean as much to me as they do now.

I lower myself onto the bed, finding a spot that wasn't cut up by my wings so I can kneel on the keeper's left.

As my pack takes up position in a circle behind me—Orlan and Lucian to the right and the dark elves to the left—I reach for the keeper's left hand, wrapping my burned palm around his wrist.

My voice is strained as I whisper into the silence, speaking to him now as if he could answer me. "Do you remember when Ryuji and I spoke about a broken teapot?"

I wait a moment, listening to the keeper's heartbeat, waiting for it to respond to my voice, but it continues in its thready beats.

I force myself to continue, fighting to keep my voice steady. "I described that teapot as a thing of beauty created with care. But if I were to break it, I could use the pieces as weapons. And he said… that may be true, but with a steady hand and the right mix of lacquer and gold, even the smallest shards may once again form a thing of beauty."

I can't stop the hot tears from building behind my eyes, can't stop the ache in my chest as I rest my right hand over his failing heart.

Then I do what I swore I wouldn't do. I slip my left hand over the crown.

It's the first time I've willfully touched it.

Oh, he's run his hands over every part of my body while wearing this ring, but I've never reached for the crown. Never wrapped my left hand around it and called for its power.

Not like this.

I gasp as energy explodes through me, and my vision ignites with a dark flame that lights up my mind.

My dark hair gleams around my shoulders, the strands becoming luminous. Metallic.

The pain in my burning palm fades, and as fast as the agony recedes, those terrible, impossible impulses take its place.

Take control of the light and the dark.

Shape the world to match your needs.

Fight the old and find the new.

I push back against the impulses with all of my might as I slowly draw the ring along his finger without removing it completely.

There it rests, right at his fingertip, and there I will keep it.

Because when it leaves his hand, death will come for him.

I won't let that happen until my work is done.

Until this power has complied with my will.

"You helped give me the vengeance I sought. You kept your end of our bargain. So now, here I am, with a steady hand," I say to him, this man who stole my heart. "And I'm giving you lacquer and gold."

I fight against the fury and the malice. Fight against the cold darkness.

My voice builds in power as a whirlwind of energy grows around me.

"You will not be Emil anymore," I command him, this man who stood at my side. "You will not be *Enemy*."

I take another breath, shaking my head resolutely. "You will not be a demon or a dragon or a wolf or a draugr or any other supernatural creature whose form you've taken that did not belong to you. You will not be Diavolo and you will not be *Keeper*. Because if you are none of those things…"

Again, I force myself to breathe as my hands shake on the chest of this man who called me his beloved. "If you are not the keeper, then you won't die when I take this crown."

My right hand forms claws across his heart as the power from my left hand flows through my chest and down my right arm, and with that power, I pull and pull and pull…

I will take the malice so he can be free.

I will rip out the darkness so he can know peace.

The person I am will die so he can live.

My heart is pounding, flooding with feeling as I take back what I gave. Even after I gifted my heart's power, I formed bonds and found my family and made peace with my enemies.

And when my heart's power is fully mine again, I swear I will find balance. I will find a way through this cold malice.

I have to.

"I will take back the power of my heart because you won't need it anymore," I whisper, leaning over him as the clash of feeling and darkness becomes a storm within my mind.

A battle between my reason, my sense of justice, my intentions, and the cruelty that wants to claim me.

"You won't need my heart's power anymore because you will be new," I say, pressing a final kiss to his lips, taking a final breath of his scent.

There is value in broken things.

A broken heart can lead to a new life.

"You won't remember me," I say. "You will have a new life with a new name that you choose. You will have only the magic you were meant to have, and you will have all the goodness and light that was taken from you."

I sense the last threads of my heart's power pulling away from him and now I gather all of my intentions, everything I've spoken, and I prepare to let them loose through my left hand at exactly the right moment.

I will have a split second to save him.

A heartbeat between taking the crown and stopping his death.

Around me, streams of power have gathered, a beautiful darkness, a snowstorm of thought and feeling, all my commands ready to be unleashed.

I take a final breath and then I roar, "I will take this crown and you will live!"

As my command leaves my lips, I slip the crown from his finger and let my intentions loose.

You are not the keeper. You are new and whole. You are good.

You will not remember me.

Power spears through my left hand in a rush that forces a scream from my lips.

In that moment, I pray for his heart to start beating again, prepared for the terrible moment when it does.

Prepared for that moment because then he will live and I will lose him.

And there it is.

A steady beat.

Then I'm screaming and throwing myself backward, away from my pack, a snarl already growing on my lips. "Take him! Get him away from me! He must not be corrupted by this power. He must not remember what he was or he will break again."

Orlan and Lucian rush forward through the haze of energy, heaving and hauling my love's warm body off the bed.

All I can hear is his heartbeat, thudding strong and clear, and all I care about is the flush of new color to his cheeks and the way his hands are already moving and his eyes are already opening...

But looking at him will be my undoing, so I close my eyes.

I close my eyes and then he's gone.

I can't hear this heartbeat any longer. I can't inhale his scent, that crisp scent of wolves and snow and apples and *kindness*. All the goodness I returned to him that can't be a part of my life any longer.

A moment later, a wave of darkness passes through my mind.

It is forceful and demanding, a flood of power that wipes clean my thoughts, taking my anguish and my pain and dissolving them so fast that they are instantly forgotten.

Instantly inconsequential.

My gaze is drawn to my hands, where a flawless crown rests on my palms, ready to be placed on my head. Its sharp spokes rise up from its solid body, each one glinting and sparkling.

It is beautifully, perfectly dark.

And now it's mine.

CHAPTER FORTY-EIGHT

ONE YEAR LATER

There's a silence that falls whenever I enter a room.

At first, it didn't bother me. I needed the quiet to maintain my balance between my power and my reason.

Then it bothered me because it spoke to a fear that stilted communication, and it took a lot of work to encourage my people to step past that barrier.

Now, I'm accustomed to it.

Anarchy and her brothers are constant shadows at my back, dedicated to achieving everything I need. From the simplest things—a hot meal after I've traveled across the country—to the more complicated, like gleaning information about what's happening in the dark corners of my empire.

I haven't stopped to rest since I took the crown.

My father left decades of destruction in his wake. Broken packs. Families split apart. Dark spaces allowed to fester.

My rules are absolute. No subjugation or degradation of any member of any species, human or supernatural. No murder. Death happens only by sanction. And in those cases, I deliver it myself.

Right now, I step into the dark bowels of a nightclub owned

by a demon who will regret attracting my attention. He broke off from his leader—a demon who has himself struggled with my rules, but may the dark saints bless him, he tries.

The nightclub is hosting a rave tonight. A year ago, I wouldn't have known what to call this sort of event, but I know a lot of things now.

The dance floor is packed with people, strobe lights flash across the vast room, and the heavy thump of music fills my ears.

Neither lights nor sounds bother me like they used to.

And for once, it's too noisy and too busy for any of the supernaturals already present to take note of my arrival. I count both creatures of the light and of the dark, along with a few elementals, although the majority of the patrons are human.

I glide through the shadows, neatly sidestepping the dancers grinding their bodies together. I ignore the little packets being passed up ahead. It isn't drugs that bring me here tonight, although I have rules about those, too.

Anarchy is already here, dressed in black, sitting at the crowded bar on my far left, a thigh-high slit revealing one leg crossed over the other.

Her brothers are also positioned around the room, each of them in collared shirts open at the neck. Their pointed ears are concealed behind their hair, not that any humans would notice in the crush of bodies.

The elves are all breathtakingly beautiful, their blue eyes reflecting the flashing lights and their lilac hair appearing silvery in the haze.

For a moment, I'm reminded of the keeper, but I put him firmly from my mind.

He's out there. Somewhere.

After Lucian and Orlan transported him to St. Michael Cemetery, the supernaturals who live there took him in, and that was the last I knew of him.

After that, Lucian acquired control of the gargoyle clan. He and I debated about whether or not the previous general should take over. She was James's informant and a more than worthy leader, but she made it clear that new management was needed or some of the clan's learned behaviors wouldn't be stamped out.

While taking over the gargoyles was important for Lucian, it came with a price. It hurts him to be apart from Anarchy, but their bond is strong enough to withstand the distance, and I make sure to reunite them as often as I can.

Now, I move to the back of this establishment, toward the rooms that aren't open to the public. Shadowy places where dealings happen contrary to my rules.

I pass through a hallway that leads to a door marked as *Staff Only*. Mirrors line the wall as I pass.

Just as I barely recognized myself the first time I looked in a mirror, so too now, I don't know who the woman in the mirror is.

She is powerful. Her sleek, black hair is swept smoothly back, gray strands framing her face while the golden ends brush her shoulders. Not a knot in sight. Her body is lithe and strong and her muscles are honed, her body swathed in black pants and a black top.

She walks with purpose and self-assurance and is no longer wild-haired.

I dismiss my reflection as I push open the Staff Only door, which leads—as I knew it would because the dark elves conducted their reconnaissance well—into another corridor, at the end of which is another door.

I don't miss a step, ramming my claws through the deadbolt, keeping the second door locked before I push it open.

Large cages line the right-hand side of the dirty room beyond. Three of them contain a single occupant.

The demon I'm after is sitting with five other men, all bear shifters. They're drinking at a table in the center of the room.

Or, they were.

As I burst through the door, they fly up out of their seats, some reaching for blades, others for guns.

My wings sweep out around me, sliding neatly through slits in the back of my shirt to form a shield before a barrage of bullets flies at me.

I counted their guns before I spread my wings, and now I count their bullets, my sensitive hearing picking up each individual shot as the projectiles beat against my feathers.

They run out of bullets soon enough.

Silly of them not to carry more firepower.

With an outward sweep of my wings, I tuck them away again and charge forward.

I still can't fly. I probably never will. I've come to the conclusion that these wings weren't made for taking to the air, and I've resisted the urge to use my power to change their composition.

If I alter this part of me, where will I stop?

But I've certainly learned how to use them in a fight.

Within heartbeats, I've reached the men. The claws of my right hand slice through their blades—and their guns as they attempt to reload—while my left hand brushes their skin.

Death rushes across their faces and they crumple to the floor; all five bear shifters quickly downed, leaving only the demon standing.

Sometimes, I prefer to spill blood, but in this case, I would rather avoid any further trauma for the women in the cages.

The blood drains from the demon's face as he backpedals as fast as he can. "Ultima Nostra."

His finger continues squeezing the trigger of his revolver.

Click, click, click. As if bullets will magically appear in the empty cylinder.

"You know why I'm here," I say.

Words spew from his mouth as he attempts to use his power of compulsion on me. "Stay back. You don't want to hurt me. I haven't done anything wrong. I haven't—"

With a quick dart forward, my left hand closes around his throat.

His speech stops.

His life is instantly gone.

I lower him to the floor before I release him and flex my fingers.

My crown is wrapped neatly around my left palm, its impulses quieted by the death I've unleashed.

Ordinarily, I wear the crown like a bracelet around my left wrist, its spokes facing up toward my biceps. It adjusts its size according to my touch. If I want to, I can slip it all the way to my fingertips and then back onto one of my fingers like a ring.

It never leaves my body, and there isn't a blade in the world that can cut it off me.

At least so far. I know this because many have already tried.

I gave them swift deaths.

Before turning to the cages, I take control of my impulses. They are cold and unfeeling. But the darkness within my heart balances out their cruelty. As I came to understand, darkness is not the same as evil.

Anarchy and her brothers step quietly into the room behind me as I finally approach the women in the cages.

I don't let them out yet. Captives tend to run as fast as they can once freed—and why wouldn't they?—but it makes it much harder to get them back to their families.

"Answer my questions and you'll soon be free," I say to them. "Where are your homes located? Tell me, and my people will ensure you return safely to them."

Two of the women shrink away from me, as afraid of me as they should be. One of them glares.

I can respect that.

"You first," I say to her.

One by one, they tell me where they're from. I know that Anarchy and her brothers will be taking mental notes in the background, figuring out how to escort these women back to their homes as quickly as possible.

But I have one more thing to say. "Your freedom comes with one condition," I say. "Your captor is dead, and so are his accomplices. You will not seek vengeance against other dark creatures because of the wrong that was done to you. Others are not responsible for what happened here. You will accept that my justice is the end of it."

I don't wait for their agreement. I can't guarantee they'll give it, anyway.

I make way for the dark elves, then, stepping back toward the door.

Several men now stand in the hallway, their backs to me as they guard the door. One of them is the human who stood in my way at the White Wing Tavern.

He has proven very useful to me in the months since then.

He glances back, sees me coming, and makes space for me to pass.

I tip my chin at him. He knows what to do.

As soon as the women emerge, he and his crew will disappear inside the room. It will be completely clean in the space of an hour. Possibly cleaner than it's ever been.

I stride away into the thumping music, exhaling the scent of captivity and the memories that return to me. I push them away, as I've learned to do, and by the time I reach the dance floor, I've refocused myself.

Dealing with a demon is nothing compared to what I'll face tomorrow.

CHAPTER FORTY-NINE

My bare feet settle onto sand for the first time in over a year.

I stand at the edge of a pristine beach, the salty air making my hair clump in all its old ways as I take in the vast ocean I wasn't sure I'd see again.

Behind me is the long hut where Anarchy trained me and behind that is the vast jungle that makes up most of the island controlled by the dragon master, Ryuji.

The dark elves fan out around me on the beach, my constant shadows.

The warlock who brought us here departed immediately, just as I instructed him to do. I no longer need to rely on Orlan to transport me around. I have my own team of warlocks for that.

I debated long and hard about whom I should bring with me. I wanted Lucian to be here, too, but approaching this meeting with a larger-than-necessary entourage could be considered a threat.

I also debated coming alone, but Anarchy wouldn't allow it.

"Not against those beings," she said firmly. "You need us there."

"They have more to fear from me than I do from them," I pointed out.

She was quiet at that.

It's a hard truth that sets me apart, even from the ones I love.

Now, I wait at the edge of the beach for the arrival of the dragon masters and the other powerful beings they've invited to this island.

It's neutral territory. An act of pure trust for all involved.

Soon enough, a high-pitched shriek breaks the air. The dragon masters move so fast that it causes the air pressure to change and my ears to *pop*, but I'm prepared for it, quickly swallowing to alleviate my discomfort.

The wind billows around me as five air dragons come to an abrupt halt in the sky above the beach—an equal number to me and my four dark elves. Just as Ryuji and I discussed.

He is the first to drop to the beach.

He slows down as he approaches me, a little more wariness entering his approach the closer he gets.

He has jagged, black hair and fierce, dark-brown eyes while his skin is dusted in silver scales and his wings are so silvery bright that they reflect the afternoon sunlight.

He folds his wings away as the other dragons land.

I look for Ryuji's sister, Miku, who bonded with Riot. She lands to the far left of the group and stays well back. Her scales are pale teal while her wings are dark teal at the top, merging with ivory at the tips. Like Ryuji, her hair is inky black, but she has bright teal streaks running through it.

She scans our group and instantly spots Riot, who has taken a step forward. He stops himself, and it looks as if she's digging in her heels, too. It's clear to me that time and distance haven't broken the mate bond they formed, but they'll have to resist it for now.

I greet Ryuji formally, lowering my gaze when I bow to him in another gesture of trust. "Kaito Ryuji, son of Rin and Yuma, alpha of the Kaito Dragon Family. It's good to see you."

"Ultima Nostra," he says, returning my bow.

I wait for more, but that's all he says as he squints at me, studying my eyes and face.

"*Daughter of Assholes*," I whisper, arching an eyebrow at him. "Have I changed so much?"

He nods, and his focus falls to my wrist, where I wear my crown. "I'm afraid so."

I exhale a soft, resigned breath. "I suppose that's true."

Before I can say more, the sound of children's laughter startles me.

I swing toward the strip of beach behind me, surprised when a boy and a girl exit the trees a little farther along.

They're only fifty paces away and appear completely oblivious to our presence as they head toward the wet sand nearer to the water, each of them lugging a gauzy sack that appears to contain plastic buckets and little shovels.

I spin back to Ryuji.

"Sandcastles," he says with a smile. "My daughter loves making them."

I peer back at the children. I've never seen the girl before, but I'm surprised to realize that I recognize the boy.

He's grown much taller over the year since I last saw him, although he's still wearing sunglasses that are shaped to fit the contours of his face, and it looks like... if I harness my eyesight to its fullest extent... he's using less conspicuous earbuds than the headphones he was wearing when I first met him.

I gasp. "That's Elijah."

Ryuji nods. "His mother is here, but I hope you understand that she will need to keep her distance from you now."

"Of course."

There's a lot more blood on my hands since I first met Rebella, no matter how justified I've been in spilling it.

I consider the little girl. She would be about two years older than Elijah. She has straight, black hair cut short at her shoulders, a perfect rosebud mouth, and large, angular eyes. Her skin is light brown and her irises could be cinnamon brown, but I can't be certain in the light.

"You took my advice," I say to Ryuji, unable to stop my smile.

When I was last on this island, he told me that he had a daughter, six years old at the time, whom he'd never met. He'd bonded with her mother, but she'd had to return home to the United States when she'd become pregnant.

He hadn't seen her since. I told him to go to her already and tell her how much he loved her because, dammit, he was a light magic creature, and he had the freedom to love with his whole heart.

"I took your advice," he says, giving me a small smile. "Emika and her mother are part of my life now."

"Good." I clear my throat. "That's good."

Up ahead, the children settle onto the sand, Emika handing Elijah her 'favorite' spade to use.

Even as they play so innocently, I'm conscious of the power I sense within them.

Enough power to change the world…

My wariness only increases when another child appears at the edge of the trees.

Oh, I know this child, too.

He has raven-black hair and such crisp, green eyes that I can see them clearly across the distance. He would be about Emika's age, although he's taller. He's also as quiet as she and Elijah are. He carries himself with a quiet confidence that sends a shiver down my spine, just as it did the first time I saw him.

"That's Theo," I murmur.

"I believe you met the crimson wolves in Portland," Ryuji says, his tone careful now.

In some ways, I owe that boy my life. His mother was erring on the side of killing me, but he didn't want her to.

I look for her now, but like the other parents, she must be keeping to the shadows within the trees.

It's fair enough.

I deliberately chose to arrive out in the open. I need to give all of the powerful beings who are coming to this meeting the chance to see me. To see that I am not a monster.

Up ahead, Theo quietly approaches the other two children, his footsteps a little wobbly on the sand but no less indicative of his wolfish nature.

He stops at a distance, but Emika is quick to greet him. "Do you want to play?"

A smile breaks through Theo's serious countenance, and he gives a quick nod.

"Here," she says. "This is my second-favorite shovel. I'm sorry, but Elijah already has my favorite one."

"That's okay. Where should I dig?"

"Here," she says, pointing. "This spot is where I make the best castles."

Theo busies himself, filling a bucket while Emika tips out the one she already prepared.

"You're a dragon," he says to her.

"You're a wolf," she replies, smiling sweetly at him. "Elijah is sort-of a fury." Her brow crinkles. "Or maybe a god. His parents don't know yet."

Elijah gives a shrug as he focuses on patting the side of the mound Emika made.

"Hey, wanna see my wings?" Emika suddenly asks.

If she didn't have their attention before, she certainly has it now.

"Yes, please," Elijah says, sitting back on his heels.

After standing up, Emika shrugs her shoulders like Elijah did.

Her wings extend with a rush of power that floods the air so intensely it reaches me where I stand.

My eyes widen at the breadth of her wings.

The fierce, blood-red color of them.

They're so large that she topples backward, landing on her butt.

She's laughing hard. "They're too big for me."

Elijah breaks into a smile.

Theo has wide eyes. He shakes himself. "Wanna see my wolf?"

"Yes, please," Emika says, retracting her wings and leaning forward with Elijah, both in apparent anticipation.

A crimson wolf appears at Theo's side, an eerily powerful sight. It stands as tall as he is and its body appears insubstantial. I can see the beach behind it.

"Oh, I love him," Emika cries, reaching for the wolf's face.

Theo immediately steps back and the wolf jumps back with him, steering clear of her hand.

"Careful," Theo says. "His magic will bite you."

Emika retracts her hand. "Oh. That's sad."

Theo's shoulders start to slump, but Elijah interjects. "Wanna see my eyes?"

Emika breaks into a smile and Theo sits taller. "Yes!"

Elijah tugs at his sunglasses, removing them for a short moment.

I've never seen Elijah's eyes. He kept them covered during the whole time I was protecting him, but even across this distance, I feel the depth of his power.

For an unnerving moment, it seems as if he looks across the distance at me, his soul far older than the boy whose body it occupies.

And for another second, his focus also slips to Anarchy.

She protected him, too.

She tips her chin at him.

He returns his sunglasses to his face.

Across the distance, I hear Emika's whisper. "I love your eyes." And then to Theo, she says, "Your wolf might bite, but I love him, too."

My heart resumes beating a moment before Ryuji nudges me, forcing me to drag my attention away from the children. "It's time."

"Okay." But I pause, suddenly realizing something. "*Huh.*"

Ryuji arches his eyebrows at me. "What is it?"

My voice is soft. "Your daughter has red wings."

He gives me a look as if to say, 'what of it?' before a proud smile passes his lips. "Her wings are the same as those of one of the greatest dragons in our history."

"Right," I whisper.

As I turn away from the children, I meet Anarchy's eyes.

Red wings, indeed.

I shake it off as I follow Ryuji through the trees and into a small clearing that he must have prepared in advance. It doesn't take long for the influx of power within the trees to tell me that the other powerful beings he invited here have all arrived one way or another and are now approaching my location.

I step into the center of the clearing while the dark elves fan out a few steps behind me. Ryuji and the other dragon shifters fan out behind them. Again, this is what we discussed.

We're taking every precaution to make it clear that we're only here to talk.

The beings who are meeting me are all powerful creatures of light magic, elemental magic, and old magic. They're extremely strong, but I don't expect them to come close to me or even to reveal their faces to me. In fact, I fully expect them to use magic to conceal themselves.

I need them only to hear me because my people depend on

it. My people are dark creatures who never expect to experience love or support and want merely to survive.

Even if I want more for them.

I wait a moment, then glance at Ryuji, who gives me a nod. "They are all here now."

I lift my voice. "It is a mark of trust that you've brought your children with you. Please know that they're safe in my presence."

Far safer, actually, than they are without me. No dark creature would even dare to step foot on this island while I'm here. Except, of course, my dark elves.

"Even so, I sense your discomfort," I say. "So I will keep this brief. I am the Ultima Nostra. I stand above all other dark houses, clans, and packs. I make the rules by which they live, and I deliver judgment should they break my rules."

I cast my gaze around the clearing at all the shadowy faces.

"I believe you will have noticed the peace I have brought."

This is the moment when they could scoff at me. They could step forward and tell me that, yes, a greater peace may have occurred, but there are wars ahead of us.

To which I would reply: There will always be wars.

Their children will fight them. Those beautiful, innocent souls building sandcastles on the beach will face those battles.

But, by the dark saints, those wars will not happen for as long as I can stop them.

I wait for the creatures of the light to dismiss my statements, but...

They don't.

A tension I didn't realize I was feeling eases.

"I ask now that you acknowledge my purpose and respect my position," I say, knowing that what I say next will be much less palatable to them. "If there is a problem among dark creatures, I will deal with it."

I allow my teeth to sharpen and my claws to descend.

"If a dark creature steps outside the boundaries I have placed around them, *I* will mete out justice. As is my right and responsibility. You will stand aside. You will respect my ability to deal with my people."

Once more, I expect them to object.

Instead, I'm met with quiet.

I allow my teeth and my claws to retract. "I will take your silence as agreement." Then, I let a small smile touch my lips. "Of course, you don't have to worry. You won't be idle. My justice only extends to dark magic creatures. You will be busy enough managing your own kind."

And now I expect them to bristle.

But still, they don't.

So I finish with, "If you ever need my help, ask and I will give it."

Now, I'm met with a wash of surprise.

So that's what it takes to startle powerful beings.

Well, I'll take it.

I give Ryuji another nod. I'm done. My message was delivered. Only time will tell if they heard me.

With that, the dragon masters spread farther out around me, and the powerful beings in the trees must be dispersing because the heaviness in the air lifts.

Within minutes, a sense of peace descends again.

"I've said what I could," I murmur, flexing my fingers and rolling my shoulders to ease the tension in them.

I'm surprised when Miku speaks first. "You're welcome to stay for the night."

She glances at Riot, who hasn't taken his eyes off her, probably not even while he was supposed to be watching my back.

"Perhaps you might even enjoy a run through the jungle?" she asks.

"We would be honored to share a meal and stay until

morning," I reply, thinking quickly. "But I'm a little tired for running right now. With respect, I will stay here on the beach to rest."

Anarchy, Rumble, and Strife all suddenly appear very busy, muttering about helping me rest.

"A run would be good," Riot says to Miku.

She breaks into a smile and inclines her head toward the jungle.

They set off together and within seconds, they've disappeared into the wilderness.

For a moment, my heart feels lighter.

Perhaps more can come of this visit than I hoped.

I spend the hours before nightfall wandering the beach, making sure to keep myself far from the children, who soon disappear back into the jungle—no doubt back to their parents.

Ryuji tells me that I can't go wrong if I stay near the hut where I used to train, so that's what I do.

When the dragon masters bring us dinner, they sit down to eat with us, and I find myself relaxing again.

Miku and Riot haven't returned, but that's okay with me.

When the other dragons leave, only Ryuji stays, stopping to speak with Rumble and Strife while Anarchy and I head out onto the beach.

"I forgot how salty the air is here," I say, inhaling deeply.

She gives me a smile in the moonlight. "I didn't dream we'd come back here."

I pause, my feet kicking up sand. "You once said to the keeper..." I take a deep breath. "You said that the creatures of the dark had waited a long time for someone with the power to unite them."

"Yes," she says, contemplating me.

"Have I done it?" It's a question I've been asking myself for months now, the only question that gives me purpose. "Have I united them?"

"You have," she says. Then, more quietly, she says, "But you paid a price I didn't want you to pay."

She reaches across the gap between us.

It's rare for anyone to hug me now.

It's simply too dangerous.

She dares to press her palm to my heart. "He took a part of you with him." Her eyes fill with tears. "I miss that part."

She hurries away before I can speak.

What can I say?

I know there are parts of me that are missing. Parts of me that I've tried to find but can't.

I find myself wondering, and not for the first time, if *The Book of Dark Magic* hadn't shown me such a terrible vision of my future, would I have fought so hard for peace?

Would I have sacrificed so much?

I have brought myself to a place where a red-winged child will no longer face a future where she has to kill me. I have stopped what the book foreshadowed, and I no longer fear that I will become heartless.

How ironic that *that* book… the book that lied and served only itself… could set in motion the events that were needed to give dark creatures a place in the world.

Or, perhaps, that was its purpose all along.

The different paths I could have walked—or my mother or father could have walked—are too many for me to fathom. All the pain that led to the impossible: a truce between the light and the dark.

As Anarchy heads back to the hut, Ryuji passes her on his way to me, reaching me only moments later.

"I've come to say goodnight," he says. "I trust you have everything you need for now?"

"Thank you, yes."

He pauses. "You don't need my affirmation, but you spoke well today. They heard what you said."

I grimace. "I'm worried there weren't more objections."

He looks surprised. "Why would there be? You already proved your claims. If you had come to them a year ago with promises and no proof, then yes, they would have doubted you. But you spent the last year doing exactly what you said you would. They have felt the peace you've brought."

Once more, I have been a careful knife, excising the rot in my empire.

"*I* have felt the peace you've brought," he says. And then he speaks more hesitantly, which makes me narrow my eyes at him because he's normally forthright. "My sister…"

I wait for him to continue. "Yes?"

He clears his throat. "She hasn't been happy. I would like to change that. And luckily, what you said today has given her… *them*… a chance."

"If you're asking me if I approve of Riot and Miku's bond, then the answer's yes," I say. "Whatever it takes to keep them together, I'll make it happen."

"Even if, for them to be together, he must remain here with her?" Ryuji asks.

There's an instant pang in my heart, but I force it away. "Yes. Even then. If you will also allow it."

"I will."

"Good."

I fall silent, and so does the dragon master.

After a long moment, he breaks the silence again. "I remember when we stood on nearly this exact spot."

"On my last day on this island."

"You stood here and the keeper stood there." Ryuji points to a spot farther down the beach. "There he was, a being of incredible power, simply waiting for you to return to him."

I close my eyes against the heat of tears I refuse to shed.

My response is a whisper. "He is waiting no more."

Ryuji's hand is warm on my shoulder, a comforting squeeze, before his footfalls crunch softly on the sand, taking him away.

He doesn't have to walk so loudly, but I appreciate it because it's a distraction from my feelings.

Even so, it's a long time before I can open my eyes again.

The ocean spreads out in front of me, crashing waves I once immersed myself in. Hot sand I once lay on.

Heated hands and lips I once kissed.

I shake myself.

No more.

I turn back to the hut, only to freeze.

A man stands on the beach, fewer than seven paces away from me. He's a towering form, his shoulders impossibly broad. He stands fully in the moonlight, his silhouette shrouded in an ethereal light.

His eyes are a calm gray-green while his hair is the darkest gray like…

Wolf's fur.

My heart thuds.

I can't breathe. Can't move.

His voice is both gentle and powerful as he asks, "Did you really think I could forget you, Caera?"

CHAPTER FIFTY

I draw such a sharp breath that it hurts.

No. It can't be him. It looks like him. Somewhat like him. But it can't be him. "How are you—?"

How is he here?

"You can't be here." I stumble backward, desperately trying to remember that I can't go to him. I can't touch him. I need to keep him safe and alive, even if safe and alive means far away from me. "You can't come near this crown."

"I'm not afraid of it," he says, stepping toward me instead of away. "I'm not afraid of you, Caera."

I growl back at him with all my fury. "You may not be afraid, but *I* am. I lost you once. I can't lose you again."

He stops moving. "You won't lose me." The corners of his mouth hitch up. Hesitant. "I have power of my own. You gave it back to me. You can't hurt me."

"What… what power?"

Now, he smiles. "Come closer, and I'll tell you all about it."

I scowl at him, not quite believing him. Still, I take a very small step forward. "There. Now tell me."

He tilts his head. "That isn't close."

I glare at him. Then I take another step. Surely close enough now. "What power?"

He shakes his head, but his voice is gentle. "Not even remotely close enough."

To my dismay, he takes a step back. Away from me, and it's as if a thread between us stretches painfully. A thread I didn't know had formed between us so instantly.

Then he does it again, taking another step back.

My eyes widen. A louder snarl leaves my lips, this one filled with the fury of my power. "*Stop.*" My voice is a command. "Do not—" I draw a sharp breath, trying to constrain my fears and my needs. "Do not come back to me and then—"

He stops still, but only for a second.

His feet are moving again, but I can't let him go.

Only moments ago, I feared for him, but the power radiating out from him...

Oh, that power.

I don't know what it is, but it's even more intoxicating than the darkness I control.

Suddenly, I'm running toward him, throwing myself forward and into his arms. "Don't go."

He catches me, pulling me upward, enveloping me in arms that are full of strength.

My throat is so strangled with sadness and fear that I can hardly speak. "Don't go."

He cradles my head in his hands. "Caera, how could I ever leave my heart?"

He scoops me up and turns toward the trees, carrying me while I wrap my legs around his waist and hold on as tightly as I can.

With every step he takes, I push away my fears—so much terror that the crown will hurt him—but the light around him doesn't wane.

He doesn't falter or stumble.

Into the shadows we go and everywhere he steps, the light seems to grow, an impossible light that breaks through the darkness.

With it, comes calm.

More calm than I've experienced ever since I healed him and sent him away.

But at its edges is a tension I can't deny.

My cheek is pressed to his jaw and his eyes consume me. The touch of his hands consumes me. I don't know how far into the wilderness he's carried me by the time he stops. There are paths and huts scattered throughout this place, and we could be near one of them or far away from all of them. I don't even care.

A sense of desperation rises within me because this can't be real.

He can't be real.

"You're a dream," I say, my eyes burning with tears. "I've conjured you with my hopes and you aren't really here."

His reply is a brush of his lips to the corner of mine. "I'm here."

"No."

I'm suddenly struggling in his arms, pushing myself to the ground.

"Too cruel." I shake my head at him. "I don't get a happy ending. I'm a dark creature. Love does not belong to me. Happiness is not for me to claim."

Tears drip down my cheeks, and I can't stop them.

I back away so sharply that I bump into the tree at my back.

He reaches for me, one hand raised, his gaze suddenly filled with concern. "You made a mistake," he says.

I was sliding to the side of the tree and now I stop. "What?"

"When you made me whole, you made a mistake." His hand remains raised toward me. "It's how I'm here. It's how I remember you."

"What mistake?"

"You commanded that I have the magic I was *meant* to have."

Once again, he edges toward me, his form so tall, so imposing that he casts me into shadow.

"I don't understand."

His tone softens. "I was meant to have the magic of your darkness in my life, Caera."

I've paused for too long, and now he reaches for me again, his hand rising to my cheek, the softest touch. "There is no balance for pure light without pure darkness. You are my balance."

He lowers his head to mine. Brushes his cheek to mine. "I'm here. I'm not leaving. You are my other half. I need you in my life."

I press my face to his, letting my tears fall, listening as he continues.

"At first, you were only in my dreams," he says. "Night after night, I would wake up feeling as if I'd been ripped apart. I had no name for you. I didn't know who you were. I searched for you among the light magic creatures, hoping to find you. Searching all the faces. But I was looking in the wrong places. Asking the wrong questions. I should have been searching in the shadows."

He stops to draw breath. "Finally, I asked the right questions, and the supernaturals who were trying to help me... they couldn't deny me the answers."

He slips his arms around me, pulling me away from the tree.

"You are every bit as ferocious as you were in my dreams," he says. "I want all of you. *Need* all of you. I can't fall asleep another night without you."

I don't wait for more. I can't.

I push myself upward, needing his lips on mine. "Then don't."

With a groan, his mouth claims mine.

I give in to the heady rush of need, tearing at his clothes, trying not to scratch his skin with my claws, which, despite my best efforts, just don't want to stay retracted.

There are so many contradictory parts of me. Metallic angel wings. Wolf's claws. Blacksmith's power. And right now, they're all clashing within me.

"Don't hold back, Caera." He groans against my mouth. "I don't want a restrained version of you. I want all of you."

I can't get my clothes off fast enough.

He can't seem to lift me fast enough.

Our bodies crash against each other, fitting perfectly as he takes me against the tree, every wild thrust driving me higher until a perfect release washes over me.

Oh, but it will never be enough.

We drop to the ground, me on top of him, where I plant my hands on his chest, drop my mouth to his, and kiss him while my body rocks against his.

All the push and pull.

The light and dark.

I don't know what his power is now. All I know is that it balances mine. All that matters is the rhythm we beat out together.

A perfect connection that's all ours.

My back arches as we crash again, our bodies slick with sweat, our chests heaving, and I drown in his eyes. Drown in his body.

And now—finally—I can believe that I'm not going to lose him.

We end up beneath a patch of clear sky where the branches don't conceal the beautiful darkness above us.

I'm not certain what the future holds for us, but I know one thing: I will fight for it.

I will not give up the peace I've wrought, and I will not give up his love as long as he's willing to share it with me. Never again.

I nestle against his side, my upper leg resting over his hips while I wait for my breathing to settle enough to ask him what I need to know. "What name did you choose for yourself?"

His voice rumbles at my ear. "Ah, but to tell you that, I need to tell you a story that started a long time ago."

I lift my head from his chest, needing to see his expression. "How long ago?"

He gives me a mysterious smile. "Very long ago. And it's a story that doesn't start with me."

I narrow my eyes at him, a little bit of darkness making me impatient. "A story that starts with someone else? Well… does it have betrayal and death and darkness? If so, I will listen."

He pulls me upward to kiss me, a demanding kiss that heats my body. So much heat that I find myself wondering how much of his story I'll listen to before I distract him…

"Betrayal," he says. "A lot of betrayal."

His fingertips play across my back as I wait for him to continue.

His smile grows. "Once upon a—"

"Ugh!" I press my palms to his chest, my claws extending as I slip my legs to either side of his hips. "Start like that and I'll find other things to do."

He laughs. "Wait, you need to hear the next bit."

I give him a pointed stare. "Which is?"

His voice lowers to a dark rumble. "There was a sky filled with blood, a beast filled with rage, and a silver-haired woman gifted with more power than she realized."

When I continue to consider him, he asks, "Want to hear more?"

I can't help my smile as I flex my fingers against his muscled chest and lean down to kiss him, inhaling his new scent and welcoming all the promise in his eyes.

"Tell me," I say. "Tell me everything."

A sky filled with blood, a beast filled with rage, and a woman whose power would alter fate… and lead to the creation of the keepers…

If you want to know more, check out the Kingdom of Betrayal series, starting with **A Sky Like Blood.**

A SKY LIKE BLOOD
(KINGDOM OF BETRAYAL #1)

I belong to the Vandawolf.

My heart and my power are his to control.

I am a Blacksmith, a wielder of the arcane magic that once scorched our land and brought blood-storms to our skies. Now, I live at the mercy of the Vandawolf, the dark king whose power forced the Blacksmiths to their knees.

But the price for my life is high.

When his enemies scheme against him, I cut them down.

And when the storms rage, I'm sent to fight the monsters that rise from our damaged land.

To fail is to betray the Vandawolf, and my family will pay the price.

Then a breathtakingly beautiful man steps from the blood-rain, and I'm faced with a terrible choice.

Do I end him or save him?

Is he a man or a beast?

Betrayal is only a step away.

Content information: A Sky Like Blood is fantasy romance, the first in the Kingdom of Betrayal series.

Recommended reading age is 17+ for sex scenes, mature themes, violence, and language. Ends on a cliffhanger.

ASSASSIN'S MAGIC

I am a hunter. The last of my kind.

Love is a risk I cannot take.

I've stayed hidden in the shadows, never revealing my power, but I can't stay hidden any longer. To avenge my mother's death, I must infiltrate the Assassin's Legion.

It's easier said than done. The Legion is brutal, unforgiving, and they don't welcome women. Staying alive will take everything I've got. Distractions will get me killed.

Distractions like Slade Baines.

He is relentlessly fierce. Destructively handsome. Disarmingly loyal. He offers me an alliance and I have no choice but to accept.

But he's hiding his true strength and I don't know why.

The answer could destroy my heart.

Content information: Assassin's Magic is dark urban fantasy romance, the first in the Assassin's Magic series. Recommended reading age is 17+ for sex scenes, mature themes, and violence. Ends on a cliffhanger.

Tropes for the series include rivals to lovers, found family, close proximity, academy romance, rejected bonds, Norse and Greek mythology, enemies to lovers, and supernatural mafia.

THIS DARK WOLF

(SOUL BITTEN SHIFTER #1)

I am a wolf shifter born with a human soul.

Packless. Mateless. Unable to bond.

Cast out of my pack, I live in a supernatural safe house filled with broken women. Other women come and go, but I remain.

I'm waiting.

For him.

Tristan Masters—the ruthless alpha of the most vicious pack in the city.

He fought for my life when my pack wanted to kill me. He saved me. I should be able to trust him.

But I know better.

Tristan Masters wants my wolf; my killer soul. When he's ready, he will use me to destroy his enemies.

Tristan thinks he owns me. He thinks there are no consequences because I can't bond to him.

He's going to discover that I am nobody's to command.

This dark wolf will bite back.

Content information: This Dark Wolf is dark urban fantasy romance, the first in the Soul Bitten Shifter series. Recommended reading age is 17+ for sex scenes, mature themes, violence, and language.

ALSO BY EVERLY FROST

KINGDOM OF BETRAYAL

(Fantasy Romance)

1. A Sky Like Blood

2. A Sin Like Fire

3. A Storm Like Iron

4. A Soul Like Glass

BRIGHT WICKED - COMPLETE

(Fantasy Romance)

1. Bright Wicked

2. Radiant Fierce

3. Infernal Dark

STORM PRINCESS - COMPLETE

(Fantasy Romance)

1. Book 1

2. Book 2

3. Book 3

ASSASSIN'S MAGIC - COMPLETE

(Urban Fantasy Romance)

1. Assassin's Magic

2. Assassin's Mask

3. Assassin's Menace

4. Assassin's Maze

5. Rebels

6. Revenge

7. Rogue

8. Assassin's Match

SOUL BITTEN SHIFTER - COMPLETE

(Dark Urban Fantasy Romance)

1. This Dark Wolf

2. This Broken Wolf

3. This Caged Wolf

4. This Cruel Blood

SUPERNATURAL LEGACY - COMPLETE

(Angels and Dragon Shifters)

1. Hunt the Night

2. Chase the Shadows

3. Slay the Dawn

4. Claim the Light

DARK MAGIC SHIFTERS

(Dark Urban Fantasy Romance)

1. Wolf of Ashes

2. Bond of Flames

3. Crown of Fate

DEMON PACK - COMPLETE

(Dark Paranormal Romance)

1. Demon Pack

2. Demon Pack: Elimination

3. Demon Pack: Eternal

MORTALITY - COMPLETE

(Science-Fantasy Romance)

Mortality Complete Set: Books 1 to 4

1. Beyond the Ever Reach

2. Beneath the Guarding Stars

3. By the Icy Wild

4. Before the Raging Lion

<u>**Stand-alone fiction - dark romance**</u>

Corrupt Me: Immortal Vices and Virtues

ABOUT THE AUTHOR

Everly Frost is the USA Today Bestselling author of fantasy romance, urban fantasy and paranormal romance novels. She spent her childhood dreaming of other worlds and scribbling stories on the leftover blank pages at the back of school notebooks. She lives in Brisbane, Australia with her husband and two children.

amazon.com/author/everlyfrost
facebook.com/everlyfrost
instagram.com/everlyfrost
bookbub.com/authors/everly-frost
goodreads.com/everlyfrost

www.ingramcontent.com/pod-product-compliance
Lightning Source LLC
Chambersburg PA
CBHW021217220726
48287CB00015B/1576